Reluctant Heroes

"I'm not going up that hill, sir. I mean it, Lieutenant, I'm not going up that hill! I'll stay down here and help the corpsmen with the wounded."

He jerked his head to the right and left; he seemed unable to control himself. His large round face looked very young under the rim of his helmet. "Something's going to happen, Lieutenant, I can feel it . . . I can't do it anymore . . . It's been too much . . ."

The lieutenant tried to think of what to say, but the man moved away. He was out of sight.

The lieutenant started up the hill. Below him, amid the din of o.c. rifle- and gunfire and explosions, he could hear marines shouting at one another. The lieutenant hollered at his men to work faster. The shouts below turned to screams and then to shrieks of obscenities, hurled against the enemy. The lieutenant had never heard men sound like that before. He yelled even louder at his men. It got dark. The lieutenant kept wondering what he would do if the captain and his men were overrun.

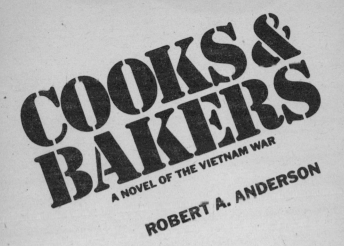

COOKS & BAKERS

A NOVEL OF THE VIETNAM WAR

ROBERT A. ANDERSON

AVON
PUBLISHERS OF BARD, CAMELOT, DISCUS AND FLARE BOOKS

COOKS AND BAKERS is an original publication of Avon Books. Th work has never before appeared in book form.

This is a work of fiction. Any resemblance between actual persons and characters in this work is purely coincidental.

Cover illustration by John Groth

AVON BOOKS
A division of
The Hearst Corporation
959 Eighth Avenue
New York, New York 10019

Copyright © 1982 by Robert A. Anderson
Published by arrangement with the author
Library of Congress Catalog Card Number: 81-66472
ISBN: 0-380-79590-6

First Avon Printing, March, 1982

AVON TRADEMARK REG. U. S. PAT. OFF. AND IN
OTHER COUNTRIES, MARCA REGISTRADA, HECHO EN
U. S. A.

Printed in the U. S. A.

WFH 10 9 8 7 6 5 4 3 2 1

To my parents

I wish to thank Joseph Spieler for his help with this book and the faith he had in it.

Table of Contents

1: A Day's Pay   11
2: The Ambush   29
3: Berk   37
4: The Operation   57
5: The Defectors   71
6: The Silver Star   85
7: The Captain   101
8. Con Thien   111
9: The NVA   131
10: Liberty   143
11: Cooks and Bakers   161

1: A Day's Pay

It started the evening before, when Wyatt Earp and his fellow agent rode out on a supply run from battalion. The tank and two amtracks came up through an opening in the barbed wire onto the sandy knoll where the company outpost was. It was finally a little cool, and a group of marines, some of them barefoot, stood waiting. It was an event. The amtracks brought the company's food, water, mail, and supplies, and usually a few marines either joining or rejoining the company. There was also the chance the tank would hit a mine.

The lieutenant watched the three vehicles come toward him. A week before, he had ridden out on a supply run like that himself. He remembered how he had sat on top of the amtrack among the young marines; the obscenities written on their helmets, the talk about how they hated Vietnam, how much time before they went home. The lieutenant had said nothing. He had smoked his cigarettes, wondering whether all the marines over here were like that. They had made it to the outpost without hitting any mines.

They didn't hit any mines this time either. The tank and amtracks came to a stop and the marines jumped off. Other marines began to unload supplies from inside the vehicles.

The two agents jumped down too. They were much shorter than the marines but dressed the same way—in jungle utilities—except that one wore a cowboy hat. They looked funny, the lieutenant thought, like children dressed as grown-ups. All the marines seemed to know them; they waved to the two and laughed, treated them like favorites. The younger one, who was wearing a pair of cheap plastic sunglasses and a floppy jungle hat, laughed and waved back, but the older one

11

with a cowboy hat didn't smile. They walked up to where the captain and the gunnery sergeant stood. The captain and the gunny were tall men and they looked twice as tall as the two Vietnamese. The captain and the gunny shook their hands, the captain first, and then he called the lieutenant over and introduced him.

"*Chao,* Wyatt," the lieutenant said to the older one. The gunny had already explained to the lieutenant that a marine had once given Wyatt his nickname; it had stuck.

Wyatt did look like some Vietnamese version of a wild-West gunslinger, the lieutenant thought. In addition to the cowboy hat, he wore a Western-style belt and holster with a .38 revolver low on his hip. His face was deeply tanned and wrinkled, and he looked and sounded solemn, as if he had been in a lot of gunfights.

The other's name was Tuyen and he seemed quite different from Wyatt. He acted in a friendly, animated way and seemed pleased that the lieutenant spoke Vietnamese; he shook his hand and laughed as if he had known the lieutenant a long time.

Wyatt gestured toward one of the amtracks. A marine was standing next to a third Vietnamese, a woman in her fifties wearing a faded black peasant's dress. Her hands were tied behind her back.

"Who's the *mama-san?*" the gunny said.

Wyatt spoke to the lieutenant.

"She's a prisoner," the lieutenant interpreted. "They're going to interrogate her tonight. She comes from one of the villages around here."

"That's great," the captain said. "That means we'll be getting something tomorrow."

The gunny said, "That's what makes Wyatt so valuable, Lieutenant. He comes from around here himself. He knows the people."

Later that evening the lieutenant walked across the knoll from his tent toward the company command post. Outside the captain's tent he saw someone walking away from a small tent to the left.

"Hello, Lieutenant." It was the gunny.

It was dark now, but the lieutenant could see the gunny's face looking down at him. The lieutenant was tall but the gunny was taller—a big man, with wide shoulders and a large stomach.

"You going with us tomorrow, Gunny?" the lieutenant said.

The gunny laughed dryly. "Wouldn't miss it."

"I thought you didn't go out any more. What have you got—two weeks to go?"

"I go out when Wyatt's here," the gunny said. "You'll see how he works. We're going to get something tomorrow, Lieutenant—you can count on that." He spoke in a gruff, theatrical way. The gunny had seen a lot of action, and the captain had told the lieutenant how the gunny liked to show off his knowledge of the war. The captain warned the lieutenant not to let the gunny boss him around.

"I figure this'll be my last time out," he was saying. He pulled on his mustache. "Something to remember this place by." He swore.

"Just who is Wyatt? I mean, who does he work for?"

"The Two-shop sends him out here," the gunny said, and explained that Battalion Intelligence paid Wyatt for each VC he helped the marines find. "Who knows what he does for the other side."

"Really?"

"I don't know, Lieutenant," the gunny said, but he said it in a knowing way. "Just guessing. Wyatt knows how to survive. He's been around quite awhile. He goes back to the French."

Then the gunny nodded his head to the side. "They're working on her now." There was a little smile on his big face.

"What do you mean?"

"What do you think I mean? They're *interrogating* her. Over there, in the tent."

The lieutenant looked at the tent.

"Water," the gunny said. "Wyatt always uses water. He's an expert with it. A couple of five-gallon water cans and he can make anybody talk."

The lieutenant realized it hadn't occurred to him what Wyatt meant by "interrogate."

"Why don't you go over and take a look, Lieutenant?"

The lieutenant looked at the gunny. The gunny stopped smiling.

"No, I don't think so," the lieutenant said.

The gunny shook his head as if to recover. "These people are brutal, Lieutenant," he said. "I've seen it. A lot. They can be awfully hard on each other. 'A people of fire'—that's what they call themselves." He paused. "What can you do? It's their country."

The lieutenant nodded his head and looked at the tent again. It was a small tent—shelter halves—with no light or sound coming from it. Compared to the captain's, it looked like a tent for midgets.

"Let's go in, Gunny," the lieutenant said. "About time for that meeting."

A half hour later Wyatt and Tuyen entered the captain's tent. Wyatt held up four fingers in front of his serious-looking face. Behind him Tuyen, in his sunglasses, grinned and chanted, "*Nuoc, nuoc.*"

"What does that mean?" the captain asked. "That she knows four tunnels?"

"No," the lieutenant said. "*Nuoc* means water."

But the captain was right: the woman had told them of four tunnels, Wyatt explained, in a village near the outpost.

"That's great," the captain said. "We've lost a lot of men to that vill, snipers and booby traps. It's about time we cleaned it up."

"Here, Lieutenant"—the gunny held out a couple of cigars—"tell Wyatt they're for him and Tuyen. That's what you've got to do, make them feel like they're the boss."

The lieutenant gave Wyatt the cigars and Wyatt solemnly thanked the gunny. Then the captain, the lieutenant, and Wyatt went over to the captain's map and planned the next day's operation. Wyatt wanted one platoon to leave early, while it was still dark, and encircle the village so no VC could escape. He would go with another platoon into the village. The captain decided the lieutenant's platoon would do the encircling.

"But I want you to go into the vill with us," the captain said to the lieutenant. "Your platoon sergeant can take over for the day. I need you as translator; plus I want you to see how these guys work. You'll see: it'll be different."

After the meeting the lieutenant started back to his tent. On the way, Tuyen came up and asked whether he could walk along with him; he said he wanted to talk.

As they started across the sand, Tuyen suddenly took the lieutenant's hand in his. The lieutenant had an impulse to pull it away, but he remembered that this was a custom. So they walked hand in hand.

Inside the lieutenant's tent they sat on cots opposite each other. Tuyen took off his hat and smiled. He had straight, shiny black hair, and a cheerful, good-natured smile. "I want to be your friend, *Thieu-uy,*" he said. "You're my first American friend." He asked the lieutenant how old he was.

"Twenty-two," the lieutenant replied.

Tuyen seemed pleased and announced that he was twenty-one. Then he asked the lieutenant how he had learned Vietnamese. The lieutenant told him about the language school he had gone to in the States. "Here, look," he said, and pulled one of his Vietnamese-English phrase books out of his pack and showed it to Tuyen.

Tuyen looked through it. "May I have it," he said, "as a present?"

Again the lieutenant was surprised. Then he remembered what he had learned about gift-giving in Vietnam; how it was an honor to be allowed the chance to give. He told Tuyen to take the book. Tuyen thanked the lieutenant. Now he could learn English, he said—"Make more money." And someday he wanted to go to America. "I don't like it here," he said.

He tore a sheet off the lieutenant's note pad and drew a map. He made an *X* with his pencil and said that that was where he lived, in the district capital across the street from the government compound. "I want you to visit me," he said, and handed the map to the lieutenant. Then Tuyen took his gift and went back to his tent.

The lieutenant had trouble falling asleep that night. He kept thinking about the next day, of what the captain and the gunny had said. This was going to be different, he thought, from the other time he had been out with the company, when they had swept a deserted village and found nothing. This time they were going to find something—some tunnels, at least. The lieutenant was excited. This was what he wanted to do: get to know and work with the Vietnamese.

It was cool. It was so cool that the lieutenant had rolled down his sleeves. The sun wasn't up yet, but it was light. The smell of mosquito repellent was strong around him.

The lieutenant, the gunny, and Wyatt and Tuyen stood quietly together, waiting their turn to pass through the wire. Wyatt wore his cowboy hat and pistol; Tuyen had on his plastic sunglasses, floppy hat, and carried a carbine. Both carried thin metal rods, like canes. The woman was with them too, squatting in her black dress. Her face was pale; she looked as though she had been crying all night. Then the marines ahead of them started to move. Wyatt poked the woman with his rod and the lieutenant's group started moving too.

They had to cross a rice paddy to get to the enemy village. They walked single file four or five meters apart on a narrow earth dike. The lieutenant was about halfway across when there were shots—three of them—then bursts of automatic fire. Who was shooting? The lieutenant saw a marine of him flop down into the rice paddy and he did too.

There was more firing, and the marines in front were running along the dike toward the village. The lieutenant got out of the water and shouted for Wyatt and the others behind him to follow. They ran, crouched low, the rest of the way to the village.

Marines were grouped on a trail and in an adjoining yard. "What happened, Gunny?"

The gunny looked down at the lieutenant and barked a laugh. "What happened to you, Lieutenant? Go swimming?"

The lieutenant looked at himself. He was wet all the way up to his chest.

"It's all right, Lieutenant," the gunny said, "only a sniper."

"A sniper? But what was all that firing?"

"That was us. Missing him, probably. Just like he missed us."

The platoon spread out and moved slowly through the cigar-shaped village, collecting the inhabitants as they went. Wyatt took charge of them, herding them along the main trail with his metal rod.

"What're we going to do with them?" the lieutenant asked the gunny.

"Just keeping them out of trouble," the gunny said. "This way they won't get hit by any crossfire. And they won't be able to warn anybody, either. Wyatt knows what he's doing."

Wyatt pointed to a particular house and told the lieutenant that this was where they should stop. Then he shouted orders to the villagers and they all sat down in the front yard, some of them spilling over onto the trail and the next yard. Wyatt told the lieutenant the marines should gather the rest of the villagers and bring them here. The lieutenant found the captain ahead on the trail and told him Wyatt's plan.

"Take one squad and stay with Wyatt," the captain said. "You're in charge there. I'm going to go on with the rest and look for that sniper." Then he said, "Remember—watch how these guys work. We won't always have them with us."

The lieutenant took the squad of marines and went back to the house.

"Spread 'em out around the hooch, Lieutenant," the gunny said.

The lieutenant watched Wyatt and Tuyen work. They started by the hedge at the rear of the back yard and sank their rods about three feet down into the soft, sandy earth.

Suddenly one of the marines shouted at Tuyen: "Look out! Look out! That thing might be booby-trapped!" Tuyen was near the hedge by the corner of the yard.

"What is it?" the gunny shouted.

"Jesus, it looks like a one-oh-five round and he's poking right around it with that goddamn stick." The marine moved away. Everyone was watching Tuyen now, but he seemed oblivious as he went on probing into the ground.

The lieutenant told Wyatt what the marine had said. Wyatt ran over, yanked Tuyen away from the hedge, and hit him with his rod. Tuyen bent over and put his hands over his head. Wyatt yelled, and continued hitting him.

The marines laughed, as though Wyatt and Tuyen were putting on a show for them. The gunny said, "That's Wyatt for you, Lieutenant. He knows how to train his men." He sounded approving.

Finally, Wyatt stopped. The shell turned out to be a dud mortar round, and it didn't look booby-trapped. Tuyen saw what it was and then he laughed good-naturedly. He said he hadn't seen it.

"We'd better blow it, Lieutenant," the gunny said.

One of the men set up a fuse and a stick of TNT and put it next to the mortar round, and the marines led the Vietnamese around to the front of the house while it blew. The explosion caused a sudden uproar of chattering from the villagers which almost as quickly died away.

Wyatt and Tuyen went back to work. Wyatt's rod struck something hard in the ground near the back wall of the house. A tunnel, Wyatt said. He probed in several places, a foot or so apart, to see in which direction it ran.

The gunny said, "Ask him if he thinks there's anyone in there."

The lieutenant asked and Wyatt said no, not in this one.

He kept probing until he found the entrance. It was covered by a piece of wood about a foot and a half square, camouflaged by dirt, sand, and dead leaves. Tuyen flipped the board aside with the tip of his rod.

The squad leader called for his tunnel rat. The tunnel rat went in with a flashlight and came out with some tobacco rolled up in a poncho, a diary, some socks full of rice tied at the end, and a couple of bottles filled with clear liquid.

"No weapons?" the gunny said.

"Nothing," the marine said. "I looked all over."

Wyatt and Tuyen split the tobacco and put the bottles inside the house.

The gunny said they had to blow the tunnel too. This time they used G-4. There was another uproar from the villagers when it blew, but this time the commotion was not as great as before.

The woman led them back down the trail the way they had come. With all the inhabitants rounded up, the village seemed deserted. The lieutenant had taken three marines, the gunny, Wyatt, and Tuyen. He had left the rest of the squad back at the house.

They went to a raised bank alongside the rice paddy at the edge of the village. Wyatt and Tuyen were acting more cautiously now and ten meters from the bank Wyatt told the lieutenant to stop. He sent the woman ahead; the three marines spread out, rifles ready.

The woman stopped and pointed to a spot on the ground ahead of her on the bank. Then she turned quickly and ran back. But Tuyen was there and he hit her in the face with the butt of his carbine and shouted. She turned around and walked forward again.

Wyatt reached out with his metal rod and flipped back the same kind of camouflaged wooden board that had covered the last tunnel entrance. Then he hand-signaled to the lieutenant, who started backing away.

"No," the gunny said, "he wants you to go up there. It means the opposite over here."

The lieutenant walked up to Wyatt. Wyatt whispered, "*Luu-dan.*"

"He wants a grenade, Gunny," the lieutenant said.

A marine went up and dropped a grenade into the hole and they all quickly backed off.

There was a muffled explosion and then they cautiously went back to the hole and looked in. It was half-filled with water.

"What does Wyatt think?" the gunny asked. "Is there anyone down there?"

The lieutenant asked and Wyatt said yes.

Suddenly Wyatt started shouting at the woman, and then Tuyen grabbed her and the two of them shoved her into the hole.

It was about three feet deep and she crouched with her head and shoulders above the ground. Wyatt yelled at her but she wouldn't move. Then she started crying; her gray and black hair was tangled and strands of it got wet on her face.

Wyatt spoke to Tuyen, who then went over to a bush, cut off two long branches, and brought them back. Then they started whipping her. She cried louder, and they whipped her more. Finally she put her head down into the hole, then looked back up and said something to Wyatt. Wyatt spoke to her and she did nothing. Wyatt and Tuyen whipped her again.

"What's going on, Lieutenant?" The gunny sounded impatient.

"She says there's a body in there, right in front of her," the lieutenant said. "That we killed him with the grenade. Wyatt keeps telling her to pull it out, but she won't."

"Why not?"

"She won't say. She's afraid of something."

Wyatt and Tuyen hit her some more. The gunny looked at his watch. "This isn't going to take all day, is it?" He sounded mildly irritated.

"I don't know," the lieutenant said. "What do you think? Should I tell them to stop?"

The gunny looked at the woman in the hole, then he turned

away. For a moment he seemed frustrated, confused. "No," he said, "it's their country. Better her than one of us. Tell them to try and hurry it up, that's all."

The lieutenant spoke with Wyatt again.

Finally they gave up. Wyatt held out his hand and helped the woman out of the hole, like a gentleman helping a lady. She squatted a few feet away and wept. Then Tuyen stripped down to his undershorts and lowered himself into the hole, facing the same way the woman had. He went in slowly, feeling around with his feet. One of the marines laughed at his bright red undershorts.

Suddenly Tuyen wasn't in the hole any more. He had leaped completely out of it, and now he was shouting excitedly and running for his carbine.

The gunny shouted too: "What is it?"

"He says the VC is alive," the lieutenant said.

Two marines rushed up and fired shots into the hole. Then Tuyen found the alternate entrance to the tunnel at the base of the embankment about ten feet away. A marine fired at it, too. Then another dropped a grenade in the first hole. There was a second muffled explosion. Then they all stood still and listened.

Suddenly there was a sound from inside the tunnel, like a loud gulp—so loud it seemed not to be human. There were three more gulps, right in a row. Then it was quiet.

Tuyen removed the cover from the alternate entrance. An arm lay in the mud. A marine pulled on it and the rest of the body came out. He was wearing a pair of black shorts; that was all. His body was pale and he looked young and strong.

"He's a big one," the gunny said. "They don't usually come that big." The other marines agreed. They said he was the biggest gook they had ever seen.

They turned him over and looked for wounds, but didn't see any. The gunny told one of the marines to strip him, but after he did they still didn't see any wounds.

"Drowned," the gunny said. "That's what we heard; that was him drowning. We never did hit him."

"Damn"—it was the marine who had done the shooting into the side entrance—"looks like I don't get another notch after all."

The gunny said, "Feel all right, Lieutenant?" There was half a smile under his mustache. "That's your first, isn't it?"

The lieutenant stared at the gunny's face. "I'm all right," he said quietly.

One of the marines volunteered to search in the tunnel for a weapon. If it wasn't an automatic, he said, he might get to keep it. He took off his clothes and made self-conscious jokes about how foul it was going to be in the hole. He took a deep breath and disappeared in the tunnel, then came up for air and went down again. When he came out his body was dripping mud and water.

"Nothing," he said. "Damn, I wanted one too."

The gunny swore. "Just a body," he said, "that's nothing. We need to get some weapons."

The marine shivered, dried himself off with his T-shirt, and dressed. At least, he said, he hadn't got any leeches.

The lieutenant and his group went back to the house; the captain was there with the rest of the platoon and the villagers. He said his group had failed to find the sniper. It was around noon, and the captain announced that they would eat now, but first he went off with a couple of marines to look at the body.

Close by, there was a shot. The lieutenant looked around but nobody seemed excited. Then he saw Tuyen walk in from the next yard, smiling, holding a dead chicken.

The lieutenant sat down against the front of the house and took off his helmet. It was hot, very hot. The sun was strong and his clothes had long dried; he felt drowsy. He smoked a cigarette and watched Wyatt, who was wandering in the front yard among the sitting and squatting villagers. He was talking to the children. The lieutenant was surprised that Wyatt would pay attention to kids. Then the lieutenant slept.

Tuyen woke him and said their meal was ready. The captain was back, eating C rations with the gunny, and Tuyen also offered them some of his food.

"Tell him no thanks," the gunny said. "I don't want to get the shits." The captain also declined.

The lieutenant sat with Wyatt and Tuyen; Wyatt handed him a bowl of chicken and a bowl of rice. The lieutenant ate with chopsticks, with the bowl close to his mouth, using the sticks like a shovel. Tuyen laughed and said the lieutenant ate like a Vietnamese. Then Tuyen handed him a cup and filled it from one of the bottles they had found in the first tunnel.

"Rice wine," Tuyen said, "it's good." At the end of the meal the lieutenant handed out cigarettes and they smoked together.

Wyatt spoke to the lieutenant in his low, solemn voice: "I have found two more tunnels."

The lieutenant looked in the direction that Wyatt motioned and saw one of the small boys Wyatt had been talking to. He was sitting alone by the side of the house, crying.

The lieutenant told the captain Wyatt's news.

"That's great," the captain said. "That makes four we can hit this afternoon."

The gunny said, "That's the way Wyatt is, Lieutenant. He's real good around kids. He's got a real knack for knowing which ones the VC are using."

The third tunnel was in the yard of another house just off the main trail. Wyatt stopped on the trail and whispered to the lieutenant to spread marines around the house, then he and the boy went to the edge of the yard. The boy pointed, and then Wyatt waved him away.

Wyatt walked slowly, reaching forward and tapping the ground in front of him with the tip of his rod. Tuyen was right behind him with his carbine. Behind Tuyen stood the captain, his pistol drawn and cocked. The lieutenant had his pistol out, too.

It happened fast. A part of the ground moved, there was a glimpse of an arm, shouts; then people rushing away. An object rolled toward the lieutenant's feet. Then the lieutenant was moving too, back, diving over a bush and onto the trail. There was firing. The lieutenant swiveled, keeping his body pressed to the ground.

A Vietnamese stood next to the hole with an automatic rifle at his hip. He was firing it in an arc. The lieutenant put his face in the dirt and pressed his body closer to the ground. Then that firing stopped. The lieutenant looked up and saw the VC running. The lieutenant aimed his pistol at the VC and fired. A marine to his right was on one knee, firing his rifle. The lieutenant couldn't see the VC any more. All the firing stopped.

Wyatt ran up to the hole, got on his knees, and spoke into it. Past him, in the direction the VC had run, a marine was pointing his rifle into the center of a clump of bushes. The gunny was next to him.

"He's in there, Gunny!" the marine was shouting. "He's in there! He's hit, but I think he's still alive! What should I do? He's got a weapon, Gunny—I think he's still alive!"

The gunny hesitated a second, maybe two. "Shoot him, goddamnit! Kill him!"

The marine pumped a dozen rounds into the bushes, one by one. Each bullet seemed to drain off some of his panic, until it was all gone. Then he reached into the bushes and pulled out a body; he and another marine dragged it over to the trail.

Back at the tunnel entrance, Wyatt was helping two Vietnamese climb out of the hole. Marines tied their hands behind their backs. One of them was a girl. Wyatt led them to the main trail where the three of them squatted. Twenty feet away, Tuyen bent over the dead VC's face. Suddenly he started yelling: "I know him! I know him!" Then he stuck the barrel of his carbine into the VC's mouth and squeezed off a few rounds.

The lieutenant looked at Wyatt talking to the prisoners. They were young—Tuyen's age, or maybe younger. Their faces were pale and their hair dark; they looked like brother and sister. The girl's hair was long and shiny and she had a full body. Their faces seemed shiny too. They looked strange, unnatural—as if they were so pale and shiny from living in the ground, or from suddenly being forced out of their hole. They seemed not to notice their dead and mutilated companion who had been with them only a few minutes before. They seemed to notice no one but Wyatt; he talked to them in low tones and held a cigarette to their lips for them to smoke. They answered him freely, in whispers, as if what they said had nothing to do with the big marines all around them.

The tunnel rat went down and brought up some grenades and medical supplies. The weapon the dead man had fired was an American-made automatic carbine. He had been a *dukich*—guerrilla fighter—according to Tuyen, who said he had once gone to school with him. The two prisoners were *can-bo*—political cadre. The first one, the one who had rolled a dud grenade between the lieutenant's legs and then got away, was a guerrilla too, Wyatt said.

"I'm going after him, Skipper," the gunny said. "Looks like he left a blood trail. I don't like the idea of him running around loose out there with a rifle." He took another marine with him.

They blew the hole and a marine took the prisoners back to the collection house. The rest, led by the little boy, went to another hooch. There were bricks on the ground by the side of it, like a patio, and the boy said there was a tunnel under the bricks, but he didn't know where the entrance was. Wyatt and Tuyen sank their rods into the ground between the bricks while the lieutenant and the captain stood in the yard watching. Tuyen's rod struck something hard.

The VC seemed to pop out of the side of the house, as though he had been part of the wall. Again the lieutenant was conscious of people rushing away. He ran, too, then ducked behind a tree. He turned and looked. The captain, still in the yard, faced the VC. The captain held a pistol, the VC a grenade. The captain fired, the VC threw, they both ran—in opposite directions. There was an explosion. Then another VC appeared; he too fired off a burst from his rifle and ran. Then there was firing all around. The whole thing had taken no more than nine or ten seconds.

After the shooting stopped, the lieutenant, the captain, Wyatt, and Tuyen went back to the side of the house. There they saw the alternate entrance to the tunnel from which the two VC had emerged.

The captain, angry, swore. "How could I have missed him? He was standing right there. How could we let them get away?—both of them! Damn it! We blew that one." He looked at his pistol. "This isn't going to look good," he said. "We had them surrounded. Something's wrong when they can get away like that."

Suddenly there were two short bursts of automatic fire; they sounded close by. For a moment they all stared in that direction.

"Take a couple of men," the captain said. "See what that is."

The lieutenant and two marines and Tuyen ran toward the back of the house, the way the VC had run, and then along a narrow trail. They came to a turning, rounded it, then stopped.

The gunny and another marine were standing on the trail, looking down at two dead VC. One had a big hole in his throat; the other was missing the side of his head.

"What happened?" the lieutenant said.

"He got them." The gunny nodded toward the marine standing next to him. His voice was a little shaky. "Damn, that was close. They turned the corner there, running full out, straight toward us. We were still poking around after that blood trail. It was them or us. I guess we were faster."

The marine showed them the captured rifle. It was an AK-47—a good catch.

It was late in the afternoon. Marines were tying up another prisoner, a girl Wyatt had talked into coming out of the tunnel they'd found under the bricks. She was a nurse, Wyatt said. There was also a cache of medical supplies in the tunnel.

Wyatt pulled the lieutenant aside and whispered: "What about the money?"

"What money?" the lieutenant said.

Wyatt told him that one of the dead VC had had a lot of money; Tuyen had seen the gunny take it.

The lieutenant asked the gunny about it.

"Yeah," the gunny said, "one of them had quite a roll. Looks like it might be a payroll." He pulled out a large wad of South Vietnamese notes. "What did Wyatt think—that I was going to keep it?" He laughed in a grim way. "Tell him we have to turn it in to battalion."

The lieutenant told Wyatt; he didn't say anything.

The captain said, "It's getting late. Let's get going to the next tunnel."

The lieutenant asked Wyatt where they should go now.

"*Khong*," Wyatt said, shaking his head. "Four tunnels today. That is all. Four tunnels."

The lieutenant translated for the captain.

"Bullshit," the captain said. "She still knows two more." He frowned and nodded toward the woman. "The kid showed us these two."

The lieutenant told Wyatt what the captain had said.

"It is time to go back," Wyatt said. "Four tunnels is all today." His face looked the same: wrinkled, solemn.

The lieutenant told the captain.

"But I *know* she knows two more. . . . Come on, Jim, you've been real good with him, can't you get him to do it?"

The lieutenant started to speak to Wyatt again, but the gunny interrupted: "That's the way it is with them, Skipper. They've done their day's work, now it's time to go back for chow. They could know a hundred more tunnels. But the war's not going to end today."

The captain flashed the gunny a look of annoyance. He looked at the lieutenant again.

"I'll try, Skipper, but I don't think it'll do any good."

There was silence. The captain looked from the lieutenant to Wyatt and then to the woman. Then he said, "Okay, forget it, let's get the hell out of here." He gave orders to his radiomen.

Just before they started to leave, the gunny pulled the lieutenant aside. He seemed embarrassed. "What is Wyatt going to do about that kid, Lieutenant?" he said. "He won't last a night in this vill after we pull out."

The lieutenant repeated the question for Wyatt. Wyatt pushed the boy away and told him to go home.

There was a celebration that night in the captain's tent. The last supply run had brought in beer, and now the captain, the gunny, and the lieutenant were drinking some of it, recounting the day's events. The gunny told how the VC in the second tunnel must have been behind the woman, not in front, holding her by the ass, ready to pull her down if she gave him away all the time that Wyatt and Tuyen had been beating her; how high in the air Tuyen had jumped—"ten feet, I'm not kidding, Skipper"—when the VC had grabbed him, how funny he looked in his bright red shorts. The captain claimed credit for wounding the VC who had left the blood trail, the one they never found; he talked again about how he should never have missed the other one, the one with a grenade. The lieutenant, smiling and laughing along with them, talked about how lucky he was that the grenade the VC had rolled between his legs had been a dud.

"Actually," the captain said, "we were all pretty lucky that none of us got hit. Next time we'll know better how to work it."

"Maybe you, Skipper," the gunny said, "but for me there is no next time."

Later Wyatt and Tuyen joined them, and the gunny handed out cigars. They all had more beers. Suddenly the captain said, "What the hell—tell Wyatt the money is his; he deserves it. That was the best day we've had in months. I'm not kidding—three prisoners, four KIA's, one probable—plus the weapons and supplies. I'll bet we get a message from division headquarters."

He went to his field desk, took the roll of notes and handed it to Wyatt. "But tell him to make sure he splits it with Tuyen," he said to the lieutenant. "It's for both of them."

The lieutenant told Wyatt what the captain had said. Wyatt quickly put the money in his pocket and told the lieutenant in a solemn way to thank the captain. He said he would be back, that he liked working with them more than with other companies because the captain let him run things his own way. Behind him Tuyen stood in his sunglasses and floppy hat.

A week later, in the evening, another supply run arrived. A group of marines stood waiting for the tank and two amtracks to pull up. The sun had gone down and it was a little cooler.

The gunny came up to the lieutenant. He had his helmet and flak jacket on and his backpack was full.

"I've said my goodbyes to the captain," the gunny said. "I guess I'll say them now to you."

"Good luck, Gunny," the lieutenant said. "We're going to miss you."

"Thanks," the gunny said, "but I don't think I'm going to miss you."

The lieutenant stopped smiling.

"Don't get me wrong, sir," the gunny said in a gruff way. "I just want to get out of here as soon as I can and never come back—never even think about this place again. I hate it." He swore.

"I understand, Gunny."

The gunny shook his head. "No disrespect intended, Lieutenant, but I don't think you do."

The gunny stared in front of him. His eyes had a hollow look. "That last time, with Wyatt in the vill, when those two gooks came running straight at me, something happened then. I knew I'd been here too long. I was lucky. If I'd been alone, they would have killed me." He looked at the tank and amtracks. Then he looked down at the lieutenant. "You had a good time that day, didn't you, Lieutenant?" There was half a smile under the gunny's mustache.

The lieutenant asked what he meant.

"I mean running around in the vill with those gooks, eating lunch with them. You worked with them pretty good—and it was your first time out. You didn't seem scared at all."

The lieutenant shrugged. He wasn't sure what to say.

"Just remember," the gunny said, "it's not going to be like that all the time. Someday you're going to think about going back, too. One way or another, you've got to go back."

The gunny stuck out his hand and said goodbye. He climbed up onto the amtrack and sat with the other returning marines. He looked like a hen, bigger than the rest. The tank swung around and went out through the wire, the amtracks following. The marines on the knoll watched the vehicles as long as they could see them.

2: The Ambush

It was just at the beginning of light. The patrol was passing a cluster of hooches—not enough for a vill, no name on the map. Suddenly the lieutenant realized that the marine in front of him had come to a halt. He turned around and saw that the others in the patrol—the ones he could see—had also stopped. They were all staring to their right.

The lieutenant looked and saw a figure squatting in the middle of a yard, fifteen meters away. Did he have a weapon? The lieutenant tried to tell, but the barely lit air between them seemed thick, like a haze, and he felt frustrated trying to see. The lieutenant knew that if it were night the marines would have shot him—if they had seen him. Anything in the dark was assumed to be enemy. If it were lighter they could have seen who he was. But now they all merely stood and watched.

The lieutenant knew he had to do something. He was the patrol leader and he could have given an order, but for some reason he didn't; he wanted to find out for himself. He walked toward the figure, his rifle at his hip. He knew his men were ready to fire too.

He went up to and stood over what turned out to be an old man with thin white hair and a stringy beard. The old man's pants were pulled down around his ankles and his bare white thighs seemed to glow, faintly, in the semidarkness. He looked up and smiled. The lieutenant smiled back. Then he returned to his position and signaled with his arm for the patrol to move on, still remaining silent.

They reached their first ambush site and half the patrol—

29

eight marines—dropped off in a clump of bushes next to a plowed field, fifty meters from a house. The rest of the patrol, including the lieutenant, moved on to the second ambush site a hundred meters farther, a small bushy knob at the edge of open, sandy terrain. It seemed like a good place to catch someone moving across. There were seven marines at the second site, and they split up into groups of three, two, and two, and took up positions on the little knob and began their lookout.

Five minutes later there were two short bursts of automatic rifle fire. It sounded far away to the lieutenant, as though it had nothing to do with them, but his radioman quickly called the other group and asked what had happened.

"Have report for you on one Victor Charlie," the voice on the radio said, "Kilo India Alpha. Over."

"Way to go!" the radioman said. "Are there any more Victor Charlie in the area and which way are they headed? Two Bravo, over."

"That's a negative, Two Bravo, he was all alone. Two Alpha, over."

The lieutenant, who had been listening to the transmission, said to his radioman, "Ask about weapons."

The answer came back: "Affirmative. One cartridge belt with two Mike-twenty-six hand grenades. That is all. Two Alpha, over."

They had got one—and with weapons! The lieutenant had heard how futile these ambushes usually were, how time after time the marines came back without seeing anything. But here, on his very first one, they had already got a kill.

The lieutenant got on the radio himself and congratulated the squad leader. He spoke the same way he had heard the captain speak with his platoon leaders. Then the radioman sent in the report to company headquarters. The lieutenant imagined the captain hearing the news, pictured the smile on his face.

Chapel, the radioman, said, "Sir, can we go over and take a look?"

The lieutenant considered the request, the way Chapel, who had been in Vietnam several months, had said it, as if going over to take a look was the normal thing to do. Then he said yes.

They stood around the body. It lay across some furrows in

the field near the house. It was lighter now, and the red on the dead VC's chest looked almost bright. He wore black shorts and sandals, no hat. An expression of grotesque surprise was on his face. The marine who had shot him told the lieutenant how it had happened: he had seen the gook coming, running straight toward him, had waited until he was only thirty feet away, then opened fire, aiming at his chest, then fired again. The lieutenant was impressed by this tall, wide-shouldered marine, and the competent, enthusiastic way he spoke.

"Probably a cadre," the lieutenant said. "I heard they only carry grenades." Going to or from a political meeting. This, the early morning, was supposed to be their favorite time for movement.

The cartridge belt wasn't really a cartridge belt, it was a regular marine web belt with two hand grenades tied to it with string. The squad leader pointed to a dark spot on the belt and said that it looked like an old bloodstain and that the belt had probably come off a dead marine.

The lieutenant's group went back to their little hill and resumed their positions. The lieutenant watched closely in the direction the VC had been coming from. He knew that the shots and their movements back and forth had compromised their position, but he had hopes of getting another, now that he had seen how easy it was. It was still before sunrise, and besides, they had to stay there anyway: like all the company's patrols, this one had been planned to last a specific amount of time. There were over three hours to go.

The lieutenant shifted position so his legs would feel more comfortable. The patrol had passed through a marshy pond on the way to the ambush site, and in the darkness the water had gone almost up to his crotch, making his legs feel cold. His utility trousers were still soaking wet.

Soon he felt hungry. Before they had left he had had only a biscuit and coffee in his tent. He whispered to Chapel and they decided to have something to eat. The lieutenant opened a C ration can and ate vanilla sandwich cookies with chocolate-cream filling; they made his mouth sticky and he washed water from his canteen around and drank until he felt full. From where he sat he could see the other pair, and they were eating too.

He was getting drowsy but fought it off. He got up and moved to where the three marines were. One was lying on his

back, eyes closed; another was reading a paperback book; the
third was sitting, looking out. The lieutenant glanced at the
book cover and saw that it was a mystery novel. He thought
for a moment of telling them all to look out, of showing he
demanded discipline. But it appeared that they were doing
what they always did on ambushes. He went back to his
position.

The sun was up now and it was hot; the lieutenant's
trousers had dried. There were people visible in the distance,
farmers at work in the rice paddies. It occurred to the
lieutenant that he was visible to them too. The sight of the
small moving figures at their daily tasks, indifferent to
the lieutenant and his men, the brightness of the day—so
unlike the darkness and cool of early morning—made the
lieutenant realize, with slight embarrassment, that their am-
bushing that day was over. They left an hour early. The
lieutenant's group went over to the first group in the bushes.

The squad leader said, "I think he may have been coming
from that hooch over there, Lieutenant. Maybe we should
check it out."

The lieutenant agreed. At least it was a chance to waste
some time so they wouldn't get back too early.

An old couple was sitting in the small dirt courtyard,
drinking tea out of dented metal cups. The lieutenant introduced himself and they greeted him with smiles and offered
him tea. They seemed relaxed, like retired people. The
lieutenant took a sip of the tea; it was lukewarm and weak.
He told his men to search in and around the house while he
questioned the old couple.

He asked about the man they had killed.

They shook their heads and said they didn't know what he
was talking about.

The lieutenant asked again, explained about the ambush,
pointed toward where the body lay, even acted out the
shooting.

They said they had heard no shots.

"But you must have heard the shots!"

They shook their heads. "*Khong biet,*" they knew nothing.
How could they know nothing? The lieutenant felt an urge to
take them and show them the sprawled body lying in the field.

Before he could question them further, they started talking

—so rapidly that the lieutenant had trouble understanding. But he could tell it had nothing to do with the dead man. It had to do with soldiers going through their fields, trampling their crops; how bad the war was and how they didn't want to have anything to do with it. Then they seemed finished. The lieutenant told them that his men would be careful.

Suddenly the squad leader called out, "Hey, Lieutenant, look at this!"

The lieutenant went into the house and the squad leader showed him two small cardboard boxes. They were bright red and yellow with Chinese characters. They looked out of place in the drab brown of the hooch.

"Could be VC supplies," the squad leader said.

The lieutenant picked up the boxes. They reminded him of packages of fireworks he had once had as a boy. He opened one and pulled out a small bottle full of clear liquid.

"What is it?" the lieutenant asked the old man, who had now come into the house.

The old man spoke, but the lieutenant couldn't understand. Then the Vietnamese opened his mouth and pointed to his teeth. The lieutenant told the corpsman to look.

"He could be right, Lieutenant," the corpsman said. "A lot of these villagers have some kind of mouth disease. This could be his medicine."

The old villager smiled at the lieutenant, as though proud of what he had shown him.

"Or it could be VC medicine," the squad leader said. "We've found a lot of it stored in these hooches."

The lieutenant looked at the squad leader's young, expectant face. Then he looked at the smiling old man. Suddenly he was sorry they had entered the house, annoyed with the squad leader's enthusiasm, disappointed with the brightly colored boxes. What would they do with the old couple, anyway?

"Let's go," he said. "Leave the boxes here. I'll report them when we get back."

The lieutenant went into the captain's sandbagged tent to make his report.

"Congratulations, Lieutenant!"

The captain was beaming. In his clean T-shirt and utility trousers he looked fresh and athletic, like a coach. His hair was closely cut and his face well tanned. It was a lean face and now it wore a comic grin under his pushed-in nose.

"Thanks, Skipper." The lieutenant smiled back. He liked it when the captain looked like that.

The lieutenant took off his helmet and sat down. He lit a cigarette and drank the rest of the water from his canteen. He was wet with sweat after the long hump back. His legs were tired and his back ached, but the pain felt good.

He told the captain about the ambush. They went to the captain's plastic-covered map and talked about other sites in the area that might be successful. The lieutenant had an idea for a two-man drop-off on the way back to the outpost; he said it might fool the VC.

A marine brought in the cartridge belt they had taken off the dead VC. The captain looked at it, and his expression changed.

"Shit," he said.

"What is it, Skipper?"

"We radioed to battalion that it was a real cartridge belt. When they see this they'll think we put it together ourselves after we killed some villager."

This had not occurred to the lieutenant. "No, Skipper," he said, "it wasn't like that, he really was a VC."

The captain looked skeptical. "Did you actually see him wearing it?"

The lieutenant hesitated. "No, but . . . ." He thought of the body, the excitement, the way the marine had described the shooting. "But I'm sure he was VC, Skipper; I'm sure he was wearing it." He showed the captain the bloodstain on the belt and told him that the VC had probably got it off a dead marine. He even told the captain about the old man they had seen taking a crap and how they hadn't shot him.

The captain's tone softened somewhat. "I believe you," he said. "It's just that I know what they'll think at battalion." He still sounded skeptical.

The lieutenant finished his report, put on his helmet and left. He walked toward his own tent over the sandy knoll. It was hot now. Very hot. In spite of the water he had drunk he was still thirsty. He looked at the olive-green water bag hanging in his platoon area. The water would be hot and taste of chemicals. He thought of what he had to do: clean his weapon, then hold an inspection to make sure the other men in the patrol had cleaned theirs. He would have to tell any marine with dirt on his rifle to clean it again. Afterward he had to supervise the digging of some new positions on the platoon lines. He wondered when he'd get a chance to wash some clothes; all of his were dirty, and there was nothing to wash them with. His legs were tired and his back ached.

3: Berk

The lieutenant had heard, when he first took over his platoon, that he was going to have problems. For one thing, the platoon was supposed to have sixty men, including attachments; when the lieutenant took it over, it had twenty-two.

"It's going to be a challenge," the captain had said the day the lieutenant joined the company. The captain had been standing in his tent looking down at the lieutenant with his thin, tanned face; he had a narrow black mustache that looked half grown. "It used to be a good platoon, but now there's a problem with leadership. The platoon hasn't had a lieutenant for a long time, and frankly, the squad leaders are weak. There's a lot of short-timers, too, and that's bad for morale—all that talk about how soon they're going home. You're going to have your work cut out for you."

The lieutenant, wearing his new jungle utilities and boots, had said, "I understand, sir. I'll do my best." He felt overweight and pale compared to the captain.

The captain had nodded. "Good. That's the attitude I like."

The next morning the lieutenant had to load his platoon for the first time. They were to sweep a deserted village five kilometers north of the outpost and search for VC. The captain was going too. "I like to break people in early," he had told the lieutenant.

The lieutenant got up at four, drank C ration coffee, ate a biscuit, then went over the plan with his platoon sergeant. The lieutenant was excited: this was to be his first time out in the field. He put on mosquito repellent, then went outside and assembled his men in the darkness near one of the openings in the barbed wire. He inspected the marines' equipment as he had learned to do in training.

At one minute after five the captain called on the radio.

"Charlie Two Actual, why the hell aren't you moving your platoon out? I told you we were starting at zero-five-hundred and I meant it, goddamnit!"

The lieutenant found the lead squad leader.

"Corporal Shields, why the hell aren't you moving your squad out? I told you we started at zero-five-hundred and I meant it!"

"But, sir, I'm missing a man."

"You're what?"

"It's Berk, sir, he—"

"I don't care *who* it is. We've got to go!"

"That's what I told him, sir. But he said he had to go, too."

"What?"

"He's taking a crap, sir."

The lieutenant swore. "Go *get* him!"

The platoon moved out and hiked six kilometers north and started the sweep. The sun came out and the day became hot. The village looked as if it had been deserted for a long time. Most of the thatch-roofed houses were falling apart; some didn't have any roofs at all. There were artillery and bomb craters all around.

The captain kept yelling at the lieutenant to make sure his men searched each house thoroughly. "Control your platoon, Lieutenant, control your platoon!" But the marines in the lieutenant's platoon acted as if they were on a training exercise they weren't very interested in. The platoon sergeant, Jackson, told the lieutenant that they had been there before and had never found anything. The lieutenant, constantly checking his map and compass in the heat and bright sunlight, sweating, yelled at his squad leaders.

They found no VC in the village, and after starting back to the outpost, the company stopped for a rest at the edge of a rice paddy, facing a tree line. Part of the sky had clouded over and it was drizzling now, cooling the marines off. There was an odor in the air the lieutenant had noticed before; it seemed to be everywhere, a mixture of burning firewood, cheap tobacco, animal dung, and dust.

Two old villagers, a man and a woman, approached the

lieutenant's platoon carrying a crude wooden stretcher. The man and woman were walking rapidly on a raised path next to the paddy, the stretcher between them. Their faces and legs were tanned and wrinkled, and they wore pieces of dirty cloth tied around their heads.

One of the marines stepped in front of them and ordered them to stop—"*Dung lai!*" He lifted the cover off the stretcher with the end of his rifle and stared down.

"Looks like one less gook," he said, and turned and grinned at the men near him, including the lieutenant. He was tall and wide-shouldered, with a big, red, young-looking face.

The villagers, who looked about half the marine's size, seemed not to be intimidated. They spoke rapidly, harshly, pointing at the body and gesturing with their hands. The lieutenant walked up to them.

"I think they're saying he was killed by our arty, Lieutenant," the marine said. "Looks like it's their son."

The lieutenant, ignoring the marine, questioned the villagers in Vietnamese. The couple answered so fast and excitedly that the lieutenant could barely comprehend them. He did understand the old man to say they were taking the body for burial.

The big marine mimicked the villagers' high-pitched voices: "You VC? Your son VC? Serves him right—serves all you gooks right. You stop helping VC—"

"All right, let them go," the lieutenant said.

"Yes, sir." The marine stepped aside and the two villagers trotted off quickly. "*Di-di, di-di!*" the marine shouted. "Go suck on betel nuts!" A few of the men laughed. The big marine followed the lieutenant and sat down next to him.

"Cigarette, sir?"

The lieutenant hesitated, then took one.

"You can never be sure," the marine said. "They could've been carrying VC supplies or something on that stretcher. You've always got to check these gooks out. You try to be nice to them and you get in trouble."

The lieutenant cupped his cigarette against the drizzle.

"I've seen so many dead gooks," the marine went on, "I don't even think about it any more. Been here two years now and plan on extending again. I'm gonna finish this thing. You just got over here, right, sir?"

The lieutenant nodded.

"Wait'll you go on an operation—you'll see some action. I've been on twelve major ops, myself—there aren't many grunts who can say that. You hear about Neptune? They flew us into this vill in the middle of the night, right in the middle of some big VC convention or something. Total confusion— screaming, yelling, grenades going off all over. You couldn't tell who the hell you were shooting at. The lieutenant that was with us then got hit the first minute, just about. I must've killed twenty gooks that night, at least. Of course, I never got any credit for it. Should've had a Silver Star."

The lieutenant looked to his right, at his men sitting on the trail.

"That was when ol' Charlie Two really knew how to kick ass. It didn't used to be like this, sir. It used to be the best platoon in the company. Everyone said that. Now it's just unlucky."

The lieutenant drew on his cigarette.

The marine said, "Where'd you go to college, sir? Is that where you learned all that gook talk?"

The lieutenant waited a moment, then told him.

"Did you like it there, sir?"

The lieutenant shrugged. The marine grinned. "Never went to college myself, sir. Always thought it was for sissies. I'll bet you'll find it's a lot different over here, sir."

The lieutenant turned and stared at the marine. His face looked too young for his body. It was full of freckles; his nose was wide and round. "What's your name, marine?" the lieutenant said.

The marine grinned again. "Berk, sir," he said. "Private Berk. The only buck private in the whole platoon." He seemed glad the lieutenant had asked.

The next day the lieutenant scheduled his first rifle inspection. He was nervous. He told Sergeant Jackson, his platoon sergeant, that he didn't know the M-16 well—he had trained with the M-14. Before inspection they both took apart a rifle.

At Jackson's suggestion the lieutenant inspected the squads one at a time so the men wouldn't have to stand long in the sun. The marines from the first squad, seven of them, stood outside the platoon tent, some of them in shorts and T-shirts.

They looked more like boy scouts than marines, the lieutenant thought. Shields, the squad leader, called them to attention as though they were on a drill field, but the lieutenant told him to let the men stand at ease. The marines were silent as the lieutenant inspected their rifles.

As he took Berk's and looked in the chamber, he realized he hoped it would be clean.

"There's some dirt in there, Berk." He showed it to him.

"No, sir, that's not dirt," Berk said, "that's oil. You've got to leave a little oil in there. This isn't like back in the States, sir."

The lieutenant turned to Shields. Shields had the same dumb look he always seemed to have. He said, "Shut up, Berk," in a forced, uncomfortable voice.

"But he asked me about my rifle, Larry," Berk said. "Didn't you, sir?"

"Shut up, Berk." It was Sergeant Jackson.

"But it isn't dirt, Jack," Berk said. He turned to Shields. "Tell him, Larry, tell him I'm right."

Shields looked at the rifle in the lieutenant's hands. "I think he's right, sir," he said. "I don't think that's dirt. That's oil."

The lieutenant looked at Jackson. He nodded slowly.

"All right," the lieutenant said, not very loudly, and handed the weapon back to Berk. His hands were trembling slightly.

Later the lieutenant told the captain he wanted to replace Shields as squad leader. "He just doesn't have any authority."

"I know," the captain said. "He's kind of a sad case. His father was a big marine hero in World War Two and practically forced him to join the Corps." He shook his head in disbelief. "But you really don't have anyone to replace him with."

The lieutenant nodded. "I'd like to make Berk the squad leader, sir."

The captain frowned. "Negative," he said. "Berk doesn't have the rank. And he won't get it either, because he screws up too much when he's not in the field. He's already been busted twice—once for being drunk on post."

"Maybe the responsibility will change him."

"Berk doesn't care about responsibility. I know your

problem—but you'll get some new squad leaders soon." The captain smiled. "I don't blame you, though—Berk's damn good in the field. I like him; he's gutsy. Won a couple of Bronze Stars."

The first sergeant, a short, roly-poly, middle-aged marine who had fought in Korea, didn't like Berk. "Watch out for him, sir," he had told the lieutenant when he joined the company. "Berk's disruptive, a bad influence. I don't care what he's done in the field, he's not a good marine. He only cares about himself."

Berk had a cry that sounded like a hog call. He'd shout it, high-pitched, in the platoon area whenever he felt like it. Other marines would shout it back; it was like the platoon slogan. Once the lieutenant was holding a map-and-compass-reading class in his tent for his squad leaders when suddenly, from right outside, came the cry: "*OOOOUUUUEEEE!*"

The lieutenant went outside and told Berk to shut up.

Berk grinned. "Gee, I'm sorry, Lieutenant. I'd never of done it if I knew you were in there." Inside the tent there was laughter.

The lieutenant planned a two-man drop-off as part of his next patrol. The company outpost had been taking sniper fire from a nearby village, especially right after the return of patrols, and the lieutenant's idea was to pass through the village at the end of the patrol and leave two men behind, lying in ambush. If the VC weren't watching carefully, they'd think all the marines had gone back.

"Great idea," the captain said when the lieutenant told him. "That's the kind of initiative I like. It's about time we caught those turds."

"Thank you, sir," the lieutenant said. "I'm going to be one of the two."

The captain frowned. "I'm not sure that's a good idea. I appreciate your enthusiasm, but I don't want to lose another lieutenant."

"I'll be all right, sir," the lieutenant said. "It's not that far away, just a couple of hundred meters, and I'll have the mortars on call."

The captain looked down at the map. "I don't know. . . . Who's going to be with you?"

"Berk." The lieutenant said it proudly. "I figure if I do it with anyone I'd better do it with Berk."

The patrol left early the next morning. The marines passed through rice paddies, villages, open fields. It was hot and they sweated heavily. They got back to the village near the outpost around noon.

Suddenly the point man sank down, slightly. Then he jumped back.

"*Punji* pit," he said, and pointed to the trail in front of him. To the lieutenant the trail looked no different there from the way it did anywhere else. The point man took out his bayonet and started to dig. Other marines helped him pull away a piece of bamboo matting covered with earth. Beneath was a six-foot pit filled with sharpened poles standing straight up.

"Freshly dug," Berk said, standing over the pit. "Charlie's around here somewhere." The other marines nodded and looked left and right. "Stupid shits," Berk said. He laughed. "They built the cover too strong."

The lieutenant smiled. It was the first time he had seen one of these pits that he had heard so much about in training. The sticks looked harmless, he thought—like children's toys. He ordered the marines to blow it with explosives and then they continued.

When they reached the other end of the village, the lieutenant and Berk silently stepped out of the column. They lay down next to each other by the side of the trail behind some bushes. Berk had a radio on his back and held his M-16. The lieutenant had a shotgun.

The lieutenant checked his watch. They had been there twenty minutes. Over an hour to go—unless they made contact. It was hot and the lieutenant felt himself getting drowsy. He had been up since four in the morning and he was tired. He wanted to get up and walk around a bit, but he knew he shouldn't. He looked at Berk. Berk's eyes were wide open, staring down the trail. He seemed completely awake and alert, no different from when they had first taken up their position.

The lieutenant shook his head slightly. Then he felt sleepy again. Could this really be happening? He remembered how he had sometimes become drowsy in training—had even nodded off—but had told himself that that would never happen in war. How could he be so drowsy now? Even as he felt himself get sleepier he marveled that it could be happening.

He heard a buzzing. Gnats. He remembered: he hadn't put repellent inside his ears. Maybe that was good, he thought; maybe the gnats would keep him awake. He looked at Berk again. The same. How could Berk do it? He hadn't moved at all—not once! Now the lieutenant wasn't watching the trail; out of the corner of his eye he watched Berk. If Berk could do it, he thought, so could he.

Suddenly Berk raised his rifle and fired a burst on fully automatic. The sound hurt the lieutenant's ears. Then Berk stood and fired again.

"Shoot, sir!" he shouted, and the lieutenant, now fully awake, fired his shotgun, pumped, and fired twice more.

"What is it? What is it?" The lieutenant looked down the trail for fallen VC, but it was empty. To the side, near him, some bushes fluttered slightly. The lieutenant realized he had just been half asleep. For a moment he had a vague memory of a dream about gnats.

"Four of 'em," Berk said.

"Who? What?"

"VC," he said, "with rifles."

"Really?"

"Yeah, they were coming right down the trail—saw me at the last second, turned and beat it. Couldn't have been more than fifteen meters away. We'd better get out of here, sir. They might be coming back with more."

The lieutenant checked the time; they had been there almost an hour. The plan had called for half an hour more. He looked back at Berk.

"Really, sir," Berk said. "Didn't you see them? If I'd had the shotgun I would've got them." He sounded eager, innocent. The lieutenant looked around at the hedgerows, hooches; there was no one in sight. Why was it so quiet? Where were all the villagers? The lieutenant pictured VC coming at them from all sides.

"All right," he said. "Let's go. Radio the CP and let them know we're coming in."

They went back to the outpost. The lieutenant made his report to the captain and then walked toward his own tent. From the platoon tent he could hear the sound of Berk's laughing voice. Then other voices were laughing too. Suddenly there was a loud, piercing cry: "*OOOOUUUUEEEE!*" The lieutenant felt his face redden.

Three weeks after the lieutenant joined the company, word came down that it was moving, along with the rest of battalion and regiment. They were going up north—to Quang Tri Province, the northernmost section of South Vietnam. The Army was to take over the area they were in, south of Da Nang in Quang Nam.

"It's a different war up there," the captain said. The lieutenant agreed. He had heard and read about the big marine outposts near the DMZ and the battering they were always taking: Gio Linh, Con Thien, the Rockpile, Khe Sanh. It seemed to him that that was where the real war was—where the big NVA units were; some of them even had tanks, he had heard. "No more squad-sized patrols," the captain said. "And we dig in every night—you never know when you're going to get mortared up there."

The marines struck their tents and packed their gear. Amtracks, led by tanks, carried them to battalion headquarters where they spent the night in wooden hooches. The next day trucks took them to Da Nang. They were loaded up again, this time on C-130 aircraft, and flew to a not yet completed airstrip outside Quang Tri City, the province capital.

It was overcast as the lieutenant and his men got off the plane—the monsoon started earlier up here; it was the first overcast day the lieutenant had seen in Vietnam. The land was flat and sandy; in the distance were palm trees and hooches. The men said little as they waited at the edge of the airstrip for trucks. The sky seemed ominous to the lieutenant, and he readied himself to shout at his men to take cover. What would a mortar attack be like?

The trucks arrived and took the marines to their new home, Hill 25, four kilometers south in open, rolling terrain. The lieutenant's platoon set about digging holes and filling sandbags, making fighting positions on their part of the perimeter. The soil was much harder here, stony, and it took hours to dig the holes. The second night it poured, and the holes filled with water; the hill became muddy. The entire company went on a two-day patrol and at night the captain made the men dig holes again. Coming back a sniper shot at them but missed. Another company in the battalion, out on patrol, ran into mines and lost six men wounded, two of them without legs.

The lieutenant's platoon received some replacements, among them two corporals, one fresh from the States and one from another platoon in the company. The lieutenant made them both squad leaders. Corporal Shields was demoted to fire-team leader.

The battalion had been at its new base camp a week when word came down that it was going on an operation. "Now you'll see some real action," the captain told the lieutenant. "Something always happens on operations—they're a big deal." He sounded enthusiastic.

Berk came to the lieutenant's tent as soon as he heard.

"Sir, I just wanted to make sure you know that Blair isn't going."

"What's that, Berk?"

"Corporal Blair, sir. He's only got three weeks to go. Short-timers that short don't have to go on operations. That's the policy—I just wanted to make sure you know."

"Thank you, Berk. You can go now."

"Yes, sir, but I just wanted to make sure you know."

Corporal Blair, the lieutenant knew, was Berk's best friend in the platoon. He was from the Pacific Northwest, as was Berk, but he seemed quite different: small, dark-haired, pale, quiet. He never caused any problems. He and Berk had met at boot camp and had served together since. But now Blair had decided he had had enough of Vietnam and was going home for good.

Later that day Blair came into the lieutenant's tent. "I'm just asking, sir," he said. "I'll do it if I have to. But I'd appreciate it if you'd find out for me."

The lieutenant went to the company office and asked the first sergeant.

"Sorry, Lieutenant, but he's got to," he said. "The policy is they stay behind only if they've got two weeks to go or less. Berk been bothering you? He was over here, too. I told him to get out."

The lieutenant called Blair into his tent and told him what the first sergeant had said. Blair shrugged his shoulders. His

face was so pale it looked as if he were sick. He had pimples
on his cheeks and forehead. "I guess I go, then," he said. "I
figure they'll need me, anyway—the platoon's so small now."
He smiled. "Don't mind about Doug—I mean Berk—
Lieutenant. He told me he came over to see you. Berk's
always trying to protect me."

But Berk didn't accept the decision. For the next two days,
whenever the lieutenant was within hearing, Berk com-
plained loudly: "Blair shouldn't have to go—that's not right."
There were no more hog calls.

The battalion prepared itself. Meetings were held, word
passed down, tactics discussed; ammunition and C rations
were handed out, packs were packed. The operation was to
last a week, but the captain said it could go on for a month,
depending on the amount of contact. The lieutenant, like the
captain, decided not to take his shaving gear; he did pack a
carton of cigarettes. The captain gave the lieutenant new
maps for him and his squad leaders. They were going to the
Hai Lang National Forest, fifteen kilometers south, a large
dark green area on the map, full of contour lines and with no
villages. The captain said it was reported to be an enemy base
area, home for two NVA regiments. The marines' mission
was to find and destroy as many enemy as possible. The
lieutenant's battalion was to advance through the forest
parallel to another battalion. The lieutenant's company was
to be in the lead. The lieutenant's platoon, still the smallest,
would be last in the company column.

On the morning the operation began, the battalion assembled on a nearby hill. One marine from the lieutenant's
company was missing—from the first platoon; he had "gone
UA"—unauthorized absence—early that morning, the platoon commander said. The marines waited and then helicopters appeared, seeming to fill the sky. They touched down for
a few seconds, raising dust, then lifted off, taking marines
with them.

A few minutes later the lieutenant's helicopter touched
down again on a grassy hill and he and his men jumped down.
There were the whirl and rush of helicopter blades, the sound
of marines shouting orders, and a television cameraman on
one knee filming the scene; but no enemy.

The lieutenant and his men started to move out, following
the rest of the company, toward the battalion's objective, a

point on the map twenty kilometers away. Around them was tall, thick vegetation.

The going was slow; the column paused as often as it moved. The marines at the front had to cut their way through with machetes. The sun was out, but most of the time the lieutenant couldn't see it because of the canopy of foliage above. The air had a sweet odor of tropical vegetation mixed with the smell of rot. Someone passed the word down the column to watch out for land leeches. The lieutenant wondered how they could ever see the enemy in terrain like this.

The column came to what was supposed to be a tiny stream, according to the map, but was instead a fast-flowing river, about ten meters wide and five feet deep. The marines had to use ropes to cross it. Some marines, afraid of the water, had to be yelled at and then pushed. That night the companies set up on adjoining hills, digging holes in the hard, stony soil in case of enemy attack. They had traveled only four kilometers. Word was passed that the other battalion on the operation had found an NVA hospital that looked recently abandoned.

There was no attack that night and the next morning the marines began their march again. It was the same slow movement, with the lead marines hacking out a trail with machetes. Just after noon they came across a trail that seemed to run in the same direction they were headed, and the captain gave permission to follow it. The column moved faster now.

Berk surprised the lieutenant—after all the talk about how good he was in the field. The lieutenant had told his platoon that noise discipline was important—the captain had said that sounds carried in that kind of terrain—yet Berk was constantly talking loudly to the marines around him, like a spoiled child not getting enough attention. He bragged that he had been in jungle like this before, on his first tour: he knew what it was like. Everyone else was wrong, he said, sounds didn't carry—that was why the NVA stayed here. According to him it was stupid for the marines to be in here in the first place—there was no room for maneuver, and if one part of the column was attacked, the rest of the marines would be useless. They were going to get the shit kicked out of them, he said, just like the other time. The marines near

Berk in the column remained quiet. Three times the lieutenant ordered him to shut up.

In the middle of the second afternoon the sound of firing
interrupted the quiet. It came from somewhere in front and
sounded like several strings of fireworks going off all at once,
the lieutenant thought; as though there were a celebration.
The marines near the lieutenant were instantly alert; they
clutched their rifles tighter and looked around, as though able
to see farther. Nobody said anything. The firing stopped.
Word came down the column: *"Ambush."* Then there was a
radio message: the lieutenant was to bring his platoon up
front, fast.

"Let's go—move it!" The lieutenant and his men rushed
forward, crouching low.

On the ground, at the head of the column, fourteen
marines from the first platoon lay on the trail. Through the
corpsmen hovering around them with bandages and needles,
the lieutenant could see blood and bits of white bone. Some
of the men were crying out in pain.

"Leg wounds," the captain said. "Every one of them." He
swore. "They had a machine gun set up right on the trail and
we walked right into it. *Damn it!* I *knew* we shouldn't have
taken that trail." He grimaced, then turned to his radiomen
and gave them instructions for the medevac. Off to the side
marines were hacking at the vegetation, clearing a helicopter
landing zone. The captain told the lieutenant to take his
platoon and deploy it along a narrow ravine on one of the
company's flanks.

Helicopters came in and took out the wounded. Another
chopper, a Huey gunship, circled high above and fired rockets
at suspected enemy positions. The rockets made loud *phit*
sounds, like Roman candles.

Just after the last chopper left, just as it was beginning to
get dark, firing broke out again. From the lieutenant's
position it again sounded like strings of fireworks going off.
But this time it didn't stop; it got heavier.

The captain called the lieutenant to his position at the edge
of the LZ. The lieutenant rushed up and got down on his
stomach next to the captain. Bullets flew by over their heads.
The lieutenant's heart was beating fast.

"It looks bad," the captain said. "It looks like there's a

bunch of them out there." There was excitement in his voice, as though he was glad about what was going on. He turned and shouted to one of his radiomen, then turned back to the lieutenant. He told him to bring his men up, leave the machine gun and another squad there for reinforcements, then take the rest of his platoon up a hill next to the LZ.

"We've got to have that hill," the captain said. He stared intently at the lieutenant. He said he didn't know whether the enemy was up there or not.

In the semidarkness the lieutenant gave orders to his squad leaders. His men began hacking out a trail at the base of the hill; the firing near the LZ increased. Then Berk came up to him.

"I'm not going up that hill, sir," Berk said.

"What do you mean, Berk?"

"I mean it, Lieutenant, I'm not going up that hill! I'll stay down here and help the corpsmen with the wounded."

"What is it, Berk?"

Berk jerked his head to the right and left; he seemed unable to control himself. His large round face looked very young under the rim of his helmet. "Something's going to happen, Lieutenant, I can feel it . . . I can't do it any more . . . It's been too much . . . I'm not going up that hill."

It was getting dark. The lieutenant tried to think of what to say, but Berk moved away. "Berk!" he yelled, but Berk was out of sight.

The lieutenant started up the hill. Below him, amid the din of rifle- and gunfire and explosions, he could hear marines shouting at one another. The lieutenant hollered at his men to work faster. The shouts below turned to screams and then to shrieks of obscenities, hurled against the enemy. The lieutenant had never heard men sound like that before. He yelled even louder at his men. It got dark. The lieutenant kept wondering what he would do if the captain and his men were overrun.

They got to the top of the hill. There seemed to be no enemy. Below, reinforcements arrived and the firing subsided. The lieutenant's platoon set up fighting positions from the top to the base of the hill in case the enemy attacked again. In his fighting hole early in the morning the lieutenant listened to the casualty reports on the platoon radio. Thirty-

eight marines had been wounded, ten killed. One of the dead
was Blair.

The next day the dead and wounded were evacked and the
company was resupplied with food, water, and ammunition.
The company, along with the rest of battalion, started moving
back. They hadn't even come close to reaching their objective, but someone in some headquarters had decided they had
had enough.

That evening the company set up on another hill. The
lieutenant assigned his squads their night defensive positions
and the marines dug in.

The lieutenant went over to Berk. Corporal Shields, next to
him, was opening a can of C rations. The lieutenant sat down
"How are you doing, Berk?" The lieutenant held out a pack
of cigarettes. Berk shook his head. His eyes and cheeks were
wet with tears. The lieutenant looked at Shields. Shields
glanced away, then got up with his C ration can and moved
over to a position nearby.

"Not good, Lieutenant," Berk said. "I've had it. Blair's
dead. Blair was my best buddy and he shouldn't have died."

The lieutenant looked at Berk's big, red, freckled face. Two
thick white streams came down over his upper lip.

"I saw him, Lieutenant," Berk said. "He died right away
and I was there, I kept going back to him. I was helping out
with the wounded but I kept going back. I wanted to die, too,
Lieutenant—I kept waiting to get hit." He sobbed. "Blair was
like a brother, Lieutenant, closer than a brother—the closest
I ever had. My parents are split and my old man's a rummy,
anyway. I've got a sister, but she's married and I never see
her. Blair and me were tight—really tight. We went home on
leave and bought some land together—in Oregon. We were
going to do something with it, farm it or something, someday.
That's over now. I'm gonna sell the land, it's not the same."
His shoulders were shaking.

"He was the first person who ever really knew me. Do you
know what that means? To lose someone like that?" He kept
crying, looking at the lieutenant. The lieutenant stared back.
For a moment he wanted to take out his handkerchief and
wipe Berk's nose, to call him Doug. But then Berk sniffed
loudly and wiped it himself with the back of his hand.

"But I didn't get hit and he did. I was next to him, Lieutenant—I laid down next to him. I wanted to die, too."

"I'm sorry," the lieutenant said.

Berk shook his head. "I don't blame you, sir. I know you're an officer and you've got your duties, you do what you've got to do. But I'm getting out. My papers for extending haven't gone through yet and I'm gonna rip them up. This isn't right, when Blair gets killed and he only had three weeks left. I've been thinking, Lieutenant—since he got killed, I've been thinking. I can see things that I couldn't see before. I know a Congressman back home who's against the war and I'm gonna go and tell him all about it. I've got a whole lot to tell him, too. I'm gonna fight against this war, Lieutenant. I'm not gonna fight the gooks any more."

The lieutenant passed him the pack of cigarettes again. Berk took one and the lieutenant lit it for him.

"I know there's not much I can say, Berk. I didn't know Blair well—I don't know anyone over here well. But Blair was a good man, I could tell that. I just want to say one thing: you're only a buck private, Berk, but you know, and I know, that a lot of the men in this platoon look up to you. Don't let them down now; this operation isn't over yet."

Berk shook his head. "I don't care, Lieutenant—no matter what you say. I don't care. The only thing that's keeping me going now is Larry"—he nodded toward Shields. "Larry's had it, too, Lieutenant; he can't take it any more. We've been through a lot together and now we're just gonna help each other stay alive. That's all."

The lieutenant looked at Shields, who was spooning C rations into his mouth, staring blankly. The lieutenant stayed quiet a moment, then got up and left.

The next day the battalion continued back. Word came down that helicopters weren't available to take the marines out, they'd have to hike all the way to base camp. Late in the afternoon they recrossed the river they had had to ford with ropes. This time no one needed any pushing.

That evening, after the company had dug in for the night, there was another ambush. An eight-man detail that had gone to get water from the battalion CP got hit on their way back.

It was quick, about ten seconds. Four marines were wounded, two killed. The water cans lay on the trail full of holes. One of the dead was from the lieutenant's platoon, an eighteen-year-old PFC who had arrived in-country two weeks before. He had been a good-natured marine who joked about himself and made friends quickly.

Then someone started screaming. It was Johnston, from the lieutenant's machine-gun squad, the only one from that squad who hadn't been wounded. *"No, no!"* he shouted. *"Want to get out! Can't take it! No more! Don't shoot!"* He started weeping. The men near him turned away. A corpsman injected him with morphine; battle fatigue, the corpsman said.

It poured that night. The monsoon was beginning. Many times the lieutenant woke and shifted position in his fighting hole, but it filled with water and he got soaked. In the morning he felt sick; a corpsman took his temperature: 103°. The lieutenant had stomach pains, too, and couldn't stop crapping.

"Dysentery, looks like," the corpsman said, "probably from drinking bad water." He went to tell the captain.

The company waited while medevac helicopters came in and took out the dead and wounded from the ambush the night before, as well as the marine with battle fatigue. The lieutenant, sitting near the edge of the LZ, heard the captain and the corpsman talking. Their voices seemed far away.

"I think he should go out too, sir," the corpsman said. "He's pretty sick. He's just going to get weaker and weaker."

"All right," the captain said, "he'd better go." His voice sounded sympathetic, almost tender.

The lieutenant raised his head. The captain was standing right over him, his thin face dark with stubble. "I'm sorry, Skipper," the lieutenant said.

The captain smiled. "It's not your fault, Jim. You get a rest—see you in a few weeks. Your platoon'll be waiting for you when you get back. You've got my word."

Five days later the lieutenant got a ride from the division med station at Dong Ha to the battalion base camp on Hill 25.

As soon as he got there he reported to the captain. The captain, sitting on his cot in his tent with a copy of *Stars and Stripes,* looked surprised.

"I figured you'd be gone about three weeks at least," he said. He was clean-shaven and wore a green T-shirt that looked new.

The lieutenant explained that the doctors needed beds. He was weak, he said, and had to take pills every day. He showed the captain the four little bottles of pills he had, each a different color.

"Seen this yet?" The captain held up the newspaper. The headline read, "Marines Battle NVA in National Forest."

The lieutenant nodded. "Yesterday."

The captain swore. "The guy who wrote it wasn't even there. It doesn't say anything."

The lieutenant asked how the rest of the operation had gone.

"Got hit once more after you left," the captain said. "Snipers. A couple men got hit, but they'll be okay. All in all lost about half the company—but we've already got some replacements. It'll take time, but we'll get back on our feet." Now he sounded enthusiastic again.

The lieutenant asked about his platoon. The captain appeared embarrassed. "I want to explain," he said. "That day we got back here there were three new second lieutenants waiting to join us, fresh over from the States. I . . . I gave one of them your platoon—just to break him in. I figured you'd be away a lot longer. I figured you'd need a rest."

The lieutenant nodded. He felt tired, he wanted to sleep. "That's all right, Skipper," he said.

The captain seemed not to hear him. "Let's wait till you get better," he said, "and then we'll decide. You still look pretty weak—you've lost a lot of weight. If you want your platoon back you can have it, you've got my word. In the meantime you'll be my XO."

"Aye, aye, sir." Then the lieutenant asked. "How about Berk?" He told the captain what Berk had told him.

"Berk's okay," the captain said. "I took him out of the field; he's only got about three weeks left." He said he had given Berk a job helping the company supply sergeant. "I took Shields out, too." He shook his head. "I had to. He's really had it."

Four weeks later the lieutenant was on the back of a truck, on his way to a meeting at regiment as a stand-in for the captain. The lieutenant had recovered from his dysentery, but was still the executive officer of the company.

Berk approached the truck, a seabag over his shoulder.

"Can I have a lift, sir?"

"Where are you going, Berk?"

Berk grinned. "Home, sir. This is the big day. Got to go by regiment first."

"Come on up."

It was a hot, sunny day. The truck traveled swiftly on the highway, past little children in filthy clothes who held out their hands and begged for money and cigarettes. The vehicle raised dust and villagers dodged out of its way. That same smell was in the air—burning firewood, cheap tobacco, animal dung, dust. The lieutenant felt as if he had lived with it for a long time.

Berk shouted over the noise of the truck. "Keep your eye on the kids, sir—sometimes they lob in grenades."

The lieutenant nodded and looked out. The truck neared regiment and slowed down.

"What are you going to do now, Berk?"

Berk smiled. "Going to college, sir."

"You're what?"

"Yes, sir."

"I thought that was for sissies."

"Yes, sir, it is—and I'm gonna be a big hero for all those sissies, talking against the war. The chicks are going to love me—I can see it all now. *Oooouuuuueeee!* Hey—this is where I get off!"

The truck was passing an olive-green tent inside the regimental compound with a red-and-yellow sign in front: "s-1." The lieutenant leaned around to the window of the cab and told the driver to stop. Berk jumped down and the lieutenant, using both arms, handed his seabag down to him. "So long, Berk. Stay out of trouble."

Berk shook his head. "No way, sir. Good luck to you, Lieutenant. You're okay, hope you make it. How much time you got left?"

The lieutenant thought for a moment, but before he could answer Berk continued. "I'll tell you one thing, sir: I'm glad as hell I'm getting out. I'm gonna have a good time when I get back." He grinned. It was a big grin on his wide young face. He picked up his seabag with one hand as if it weighed nothing, threw it over his shoulder, and waved to the lieutenant with his other hand. The lieutenant, still counting the months he had left to serve, waved back and tried to smile too.

4: The Operation

The lieutenant was with his platoon when the firing began. The platoon, strung out in a shallow ravine dense with tall vegetation, was protecting one of the company's flanks. The firing came from where the rest of the company was, from somewhere the lieutenant couldn't see near the helicopter landing zone they had cleared that afternoon. What was it this time, another ambush? Or was it only a sniper and all that firing was being laid down by the marines? The men in the lieutenant's platoon knelt and lay silent, their weapons ready, listening to the noise. It was just beginning to get dark.

A message came over the radio for the lieutenant to get to the captain's position—fast. He moved rapidly along the ravine, around the trees, vines, branches, and men. His radioman followed. Outside the ravine they ran down the short trail that led to the LZ.

The captain was at the end of the trail, lying in the dirt, shouting orders to his two radiomen close by him. The lieutenant got down on his stomach next to the captain. He still couldn't tell where the firing was coming from, but he told himself he didn't need to know—not yet. The steady crackle of shots sounded different to him this time. It seemed purposeful, as though it wasn't about to stop. He fixed his eyes on the captain and prepared himself to take and carry out orders.

"What is it, Skipper?"

"It looks bad," the captain said. "It looks like there's a bunch of them out there." For a moment he smiled.

The lieutenant felt reassured, immediately, in spite of what the captain had said. The captain seemed almost to welcome the situation—and the lieutenant into it.

"What do you want me to do, Skipper?"

"I want you to get your guns up here—we've got to have some guns. They've already knocked ours out."

"Aye, aye, sir. Chapel, call Sergeant Jackson and tell him to send Foreman up with the guns. On the double."

The radioman called back to the platoon.

"Now," the captain said, "I want you to listen closely. Here's what you have to do: first, you've got to get your platoon up here and give me one of your squads. I need more men. We're already taking casualties."

"Aye, aye, sir."

"Hold on, I'm not finished. Do you see that hill?"

The lieutenant looked to his right in the direction the captain pointed and saw a hill about thirty meters high and about that far away.

"Yes, sir."

"I want you to take the rest of your platoon and go up that hill, then set up positions from the top going down the other side. That's where third platoon is, on a trail that goes around the base of the hill. You've got to form a line of defense from the top of the hill down to the trail. Do you understand?"

"Yes, sir. Anybody up there?"

"I don't think so. Not yet. That's why you've got to get up there fast. It's the highest ground around here. If they take that hill we've had it."

"Roger, will do."

The captain turned to take a message from one of his radiomen and the lieutenant spoke to his. "Chapel, call Jackson again. Tell him to get the platoon up here fast."

Corporal Foreman and the machine-gun squad appeared, crouched low and running up the trail. Foreman was the squad leader, but he was carrying one of the guns himself. He asked the lieutenant where to go, and the lieutenant told him to wait for the captain's orders. Foreman nodded and got down low on one knee, staring toward the firing, his jaw muscles tensed. The lieutenant was surprised; he had never seen Foreman like this. He knew him only as someone who was always laughing and smiling, boasting about how many gooks he had killed. Now Foreman had the mean, determined look of a schoolboy about to get into a fight.

The captain put his arm around Foreman's shoulders and shouted into his ear. Foreman turned and yelled at the four marines behind him. Then, with Foreman's short, powerful body leading the way, the squad charged ahead to the left and out of sight.

Chapel asked the lieutenant whether the men should bring their packs or leave them in the ravine. The lieutenant thought for a moment. They were on a big operation, far from their base camp, in the Hai Lang National Forest, and had brought a lot of gear. They would have to act fast, he knew. What if their position were overrun?

"No—no packs," he said.

"Make sure they bring their machetes," the captain said. "You'll have to cut your own trail on that hill."

The lieutenant gave the order. The captain turned to him again. "Now do you know what you have to do, Jim? Are you sure you understand?"

It seemed to the lieutenant that the captain's voice had changed. The confidence, the sense of sharing were gone.

The lieutenant looked at the captain and spoke firmly and evenly. "I understand, Skipper. I'm going to take my platoon up that hill and then down the other side, link up with third platoon. I'll set up a line of defense from the top of the hill down to their position."

"All right," the captain said. "I'm counting on you. This is important—we've *got* to have that hill." He turned back to his radiomen.

The lieutenant's platoon came up the trail. He led them to the right, toward the hill, then called together his squad leaders and Sergeant Jackson. He thought for a moment about which squad to leave with the captain. There was one squad leader the lieutenant hardly knew—Norris. He was the transfer from another platoon and he was supposed to be good.

"Corporal Norris. Take your men and report to the captain."

"Aye, aye, sir."

The lieutenant, shouting above the firing, told the two other squad leaders and Jackson what they had to do. He picked Corporal Thompson's squad to lead the way. Thompson was new in-country, but he was older than the other

squad leader. He looked like a good squad leader, the
lieutenant thought, with his square jaw and insistent stare.

"We've got to get up there fast, Corporal Thompson," the
lieutenant said, "but there's no trail—we've got to cut our
way. Your first two men will need machetes."

"Aye, aye, sir. Are there any gooks up there?" Thompson's blue eyes were wide open. His voice showed no
emotion.

"I hope not," the lieutenant said. "That's what we have to
do—get up there first. Brief your men and let's get going."

Two marines from Thompson's squad led the way. They
picked a point at the base of the hill and then started hacking
at branches, vines, and slender trees. The first marine cut an
opening just wide enough so he could move ahead, then the
other marine enlarged the path. Thompson was behind them
and then came the lieutenant and his radioman.

"Get them moving, Corporal Thompson," the lieutenant
said. "Faster!"

Thompson spoke to the lead marine. "Let's go, Malone,
move it."

It was getting darker and the firing had increased. The
lieutenant watched the two marines hacking away ahead of
him. It seemed as if they weren't making any progress at all.

"Let's go, Thompson, get those men moving!"

Thompson spoke to his men again, but there seemed to be
no force in his voice. The lieutenant knew Malone and knew
he needed pushing.

"Come on, Malone, move out! Let's get going!" Why had
Thompson chosen Malone?

The firing below was intense. But amid the bangs and
whirrs and *rat-a-tats* the lieutenant could hear voices shouting orders. He remembered how they had had to shout like that
in training. Now he understood, he thought: there were times
one had to sound that way. He looked ahead and saw Malone
in the semidarkness hacking away at the vines and branches
as if he had all the time in the world.

"Goddamnit, Malone, *move! Faster!*" The lieutenant felt
his voice become deeper, more powerful. "*Faster!*"

Suddenly it was dark. The lieutenant could no longer see
the top of the hill through the thick growth around and above
him. For a moment he remembered how it had looked from

the LZ below, when he was telling the captain he knew what
he had to do.

"Which way, Lieutenant?"

"Just keep going!" He was sweating heavily and he felt
thirsty. "Keep going up, toward the top!"

The sounds from below now were different. The lieutenant
heard no more shouts from firm, deep voices. He heard
screams—high-pitched, hysterical. *"Corpsman! . . . Help!
. . . Oh, Jesus! . . . Please . . . Corpsman! . . . Oh, God!
. . . Please!"* It occurred to him that men were dying down
there.

"Keep moving, Malone—FASTER!"

But where was the top? It seemed to him that they could go
many different ways and still be going up. If he could only *see*
the top—just for a moment! What if they couldn't find it?

He heard a new sound from below—shrieks, hateful and
obscene, hurled against the enemy, as if the marines knew
personally whom they were fighting. The lieutenant thought
the swearing wasn't hate-filled enough, or that it was the
wrong kind of hate: the bitter, desperate hate of men who
knew they were going to die. Were they? What if they were
overrun? What would he do then? Stay up on the hill and
fight the enemy? Or go back and try to save the marines down
there, not knowing whom they'd be shooting in the darkness?
The lieutenant had a picture in his mind of complete chaos:
no one in charge, no one knowing what was going on,
everyone screaming for his own life. *Please,* he thought.
Don't get overrun.

Suddenly they were in a small clearing where they could
move around without the machetes.

"Is this it?" the lieutenant asked. "Is it the top?"

Thompson answered, "I'm not sure, Lieutenant, could
be." His voice was still dull, unexcited.

The lieutenant looked around. The ground seemed flat.
Yes, he thought, it would do as the top.

The five of them stood in the little clearing—the two
marines with machetes, breathing hard, taking gulps from
their canteens; Thompson standing like a dummy; Chapel,
the radioman, drinking water and listening to what was going
on over the radio. The lieutenant felt that, before he did
anything else, he had to drink some water. He pulled out one

of his canteens, but it was empty; he pulled out the other, and it had just a little in it. He remembered the streams they had crossed that morning, all the chances he had had to fill up, but hadn't. He told himself he would take only a small sip and save the rest. But suddenly he put the canteen to his lips and drank it all. When he finished he was still very thirsty.

Malone spoke—a loud whisper: "Lieutenant, I hear something! I think it's gooks—I think they're up here!"

Damn him, the lieutenant thought, why did he have to panic now? He couldn't be right—he and his men had got here first.

"Where? Are you sure?"

Thompson broke in. "It's only the sounds from below. They carry up here." That calm voice. Didn't anything excite Thompson? But he was right, it was only the voices from below, winding up the path they had made. The lieutenant had been told that sounds carried easily in this kind of terrain.

"No," Malone said, "I can hear them. Listen. Over there!"

The lieutenant listened. He might have heard something, he might not have. Were they up here or weren't they? Malone said yes; Thompson, no. Whom to believe? But they couldn't just argue, they had to be sure. They had to *know*. The lieutenant didn't think so. He didn't want it so. He would show Malone. He stepped away from the others and headed in the direction Malone's rifle pointed. The clearing extended a few feet farther and he went to the edge of it. He stopped and listened. Then he walked back.

"There's nothing. It was just the sounds carrying."

The lieutenant felt better. They had reached the top first—he had proved that by walking out there alone and exposing himself. Now they had to go down the other side of the hill, set up positions, and link up with third platoon. But where was the other side?

The lieutenant went over to Chapel, who had his ear to the radio. For a moment the lieutenant thought of asking him for some water.

"Chapel, tell Six we're at the top, then tell Three we're coming down to link up. Tell them to watch out for us."

"Aye, aye, sir, but it's gonna be hard to cut in. Net's all tied up between One and Six."

"How're they doing down there?"

"Sounds pretty bad. They've got the mortars working, though. Delta should be here pretty soon."

"Delta's coming?"

"That's affirmative, sir."

That was better. D Company to reinforce. They wouldn't get overrun now.

Now, from down below, he could hear them chanting, "*Del-ta! Del-ta!*" Like cheering a team in a game. No, the lieutenant thought, not like that. More desperate. But with hope, too: they were going to make it, with Delta coming. Delta! *Del-ta!*

Someone came into the clearing.

"What's the holdup, Lieutenant? Aren't we supposed to be setting up positions?" It was Sergeant Jackson.

"Jack—good to see you!" The lieutenant's words rushed out. "Yeah, we've got to get down there—link up with third platoon. We're trying to call them now, tell them we're coming." It *was* good to see him. Jackson was young for a platoon sergeant—all the men called him Jack—but he had a lot of experience.

"How's your water supply, Sergeant Jackson?"

"Pretty low, sir. The whole platoon is low. We've got to go easy on it." Was there disapproval in Jackson's voice? The lieutenant looked, but in the darkness he could barely see Jackson's flat, black face.

"Right. We've got to go easy."

Sergeant Jackson turned to Corporal Thompson. "All right, Thompson, start your men moving—there." He pointed to a spot on the edge of the clearing. Malone and the other marine started hacking. "That's right—let's get moving!"

"That's good, Sergeant Jackson, that's good." The lieutenant turned to his radioman, "Chapel, have you got through to Three yet?"

"No, sir; net's still all tied up."

"Well cut in and tell them, damn it! I don't want them shooting at us."

"Aye, aye, sir."

The lieutenant stood at the edge of the clearing, breathing heavily. Slowly and quietly, the marines in his platoon filed past, across the clearing and down the other side. For a moment he thought of stopping one or two that he knew better than the rest and asking for water. But he couldn't see their faces. He listened to the sounds below. There was still firing, but no more yelling. Delta had arrived.

Suddenly the lieutenant realized that the marines going past him couldn't see who he was either. He had a strange, uncomfortable feeling, standing there in the darkness unseen, of not being able to move, of being left behind.

"Come on, Chapel, let's get going." They joined the line and started down the hill.

The lieutenant let Sergeant Jackson place his men in positions going down the hill to the third platoon. The lieutenant, Chapel, and the platoon corpsman took a position near the top. There was some occasional firing down below by the LZ, but it was merely marines shooting at shadows and noises. The lieutenant stood a two-hour radio watch and then, exhausted and thirsty, went to sleep.

The next morning the lieutenant gave instructions to Sergeant Jackson. The men were to return to the ravine in three's, get their gear, come back to their positions on the side of the hill, and stay there until the lieutenant received orders from the captain.

The lieutenant walked down the hill along his platoon's positions. In three's and four's his men huddled in the shallow holes they had dug the night before. They asked the lieutenant questions: "What are we going to do now, sir? . . . Are we staying here tonight? . . . Are we going forward or pulling back? . . . Do you think they'll attack again?" The lieutenant said he didn't know. Some asked whether he knew the name of the operation they were on. The lieutenant didn't know that either.

At the bottom of the hill, on a trail that led to the helicopter landing zone, were the marines who were left from the third platoon. Their holes were deeper than those of the lieutenant's platoon, and they each held six or seven men, close, as if it were cold and they needed warmth. "When are we getting out of here, sir?" The lieutenant said he didn't know.

In the LZ there was activity all around. On the edges of the clearing marines were hacking away with machetes, enlarging it. To one side, a marine was stacking up a pile of equipment

—flak jackets, helmets, cartridge belts, ponchos, shoulder straps, packs. It was already six feet high. Other marines were rummaging through it. Next to the pile, laid out in a row, were two dozen enemy weapons—rifles, machine guns, grenades, rocket launchers.

At the other side of the LZ was a line of wounded marines waiting to be evacuated. Some stood on crutches, some lay on stretchers. The stretcher cases were at the head of the line. Corpsmen were busy filling out tags for each one.

The lieutenant found Norris, the leader of the squad that had stayed behind in the LZ, standing toward the back of the line. He was bareheaded and one of his arms was in a sling.

"Hello, Lieutenant," he said. "Oh, sure, I'll be all right; it's not much of a wound." Norris spoke politely, with a slight Southern accent. He seemed to be trying to smile.

"I heard Blair and Garcia got it," the lieutenant said. "I'm sorry, I'm real sorry."

Norris nodded. "It was bad, Lieutenant," he said. "They got it and the rest of us are wounded. The whole squad. Blair got it right away, before we even got into it—he never even knew what happened." His voice was soft, almost apologetic.

The lieutenant put his hand on Norris' good shoulder. "I'm sorry," he said. He thought what little time Norris had been with the squad. Did that make it easier or worse? "You did a good job, you and your men. I'm sorry." He started to move away. Norris turned back to face the front of the line, as if waiting to buy a ticket.

Farther up the line the lieutenant found one of his men from the machine-gun squad. He was a short, nineteen-year-old lance corporal with a thin face and large nose. He had a bandage around one of his calves and was leaning on a stick.

"Foreman? He got hit bad, Lieutenant—he's already been evacked. All of us got hit, except Johnston, but Foreman got it the worst."

"I'm sorry," the lieutenant said.

"Don't be sorry for me, Lieutenant," the marine said. "I'm glad I got hit—I'm getting out of here. This is shitty."

The lieutenant tried to think of something to say, but the lance corporal went on. "What's the point? Those guys got zapped for nothing. What the hell are we doing out here, anyway? We can't fight Charlie out here—this is where he lives. First they ambush us, then they kick the shit out of us.

It's stupid. I'm glad I got wounded." He sounded as if he had waited a long time to speak like this, as if his wound had erased their difference in rank.

As the lieutenant walked away, the marine called out, "Sir—do you know what the name is for this operation?"

The lieutenant shook his head.

He walked by the dead. They were covered with ponchos and laid out in two rows of five; a corpsman was tagging them. The corpsman had pulled the poncho off of one and was looking for the dog tag. It wasn't around the neck where it was supposed to be.

"This one from your platoon, Lieutenant?"

The lieutenant looked down from above the dead marine's head. The short black hair stuck straight up. The mouth was open and the lieutenant could see gold fillings in the lower teeth. The man's skin was yellowish.

The lieutenant shook his head. Then the corpsman found the dog tag around the marine's ankle.

"Garcia," he read.

"Garcia? I know Garcia." The lieutenant walked around and looked from the front. "Yeah, Garcia. He's from my platoon. He was a good man."

Off to one side, lying askew, were the bodies of three Vietnamese. On their faces were expressions of horror. It looked as if they had just died, as if they hadn't been part of the fighting the night before. The lieutenant realized they were the only things in the LZ that hadn't been placed in some arrangement. Nobody had covered them either, and they were beginning to smell and attract flies.

The captain was in the same place as the day before, where the trail came into the LZ. He was standing, without helmet or flak jacket, giving messages to his radiomen and directing the activities around him.

"Was that it, Skipper—three KIA?"

"Christ, I don't know. That's all they left behind, but we got a hell of a lot of weapons, and that means something." He seemed not to have changed at all, his voice still aggressive and enthusiastic. "I put fifteen in the report," he said. "I told the colonel I think that's conservative and he said all right. If regiment doesn't like it they can put down whatever they want." He swore.

"NVA?"

"Yeah, it was NVA all right. They were smart. I should have realized that ambush yesterday was only a setup—the way they only shot low. They knew if they wounded a few of us we'd have to clear an LZ. Then just when it started to get dark they attacked." He sounded begrudgingly respectful.

"But this never should've happened." He shook his head. "We never should have taken that trail. That was my fault, I know. But they were getting tired up there, working those machetes." His voice lowered. "I guess I was getting a little impatient, too, with the colonel calling me all the time, asking why we weren't moving faster."

Then the captain's enthusiasm returned. "Christ, it was something down here. Grenades coming in all over. I couldn't believe how many grenades there were—right around me. The mortars were here, that's what they were trying to knock out. I don't know how I didn't get hit. But the mortars were amazing, they really helped a lot." His voice became confidential. "For a while it was really close, Jim, I'm not kidding. We damn near got overrun. But it was the first platoon that did it. They were magnificent. Counterattacked three times."

The lieutenant was surprised there had been so much order in what had gone on. He tried to fit the captain's narrative to the sounds he had heard. Which series of screams had been the third counterattack?

"How about Delta?"

"I'm glad they got here, but it was really over by then. Maybe that stopped them from attacking again, though."

The lieutenant hesitated. Then he said, "How many have we lost, Skipper?"

The captain frowned. "Thirty-eight wounded; ten KIA. We're in bad shape. I'm sorry about Blah and Garcia."

The captain told him that he and his platoon had done a good job securing the hill. The lieutenant changed the subject; he didn't want to talk about the hill. He asked the captain how his men had done down here.

"Real well, especially your machine gunners. They charged right into it and kept those guns going. We would have lost it if we hadn't got those guns when we did. I'm not kidding you. Foreman was great. I'm going to put him up for the Silver Star."

"Really?"

The captain nodded. "He did a hell of a job. He was up that trail alone with his gun, must have been hit four or five times but kept it going till we could get some more men up there. If he hadn't kept that gun going they would've swept right over us."

For a moment the picture of Foreman's determined, tensed face charging into battle appeared in the lieutenant's mind. He remembered the pride he had felt—and the envy, too.

"How bad was he hit?"

"Pretty bad, got it in both arms and legs, but I think he's going to be all right. Don't think he'll lose anything, either." The captain smiled. "He was here with me most of the night—the corpsmen dragged him back. Said he was afraid of falling asleep because he might not wake up. Asked if I minded if he talked. Being polite! I said, 'Hell, no, talk all you want.'"

The lieutenant smiled. "Foreman's a talker, all right."

"But you know what he told me? After all that mouth about all the action he'd seen on his first tour, he admitted he had never been in a real firefight before. Said he made it all up. Now he says he never wants to be in one again."

The lieutenant shook his head.

"Really. He told me." The captain's voice became serious. "He told me about you, too, Jim."

"Oh?"

"He told me he thinks you're a good lieutenant."

The lieutenant looked away. The praise seemed out of place to him, here in the LZ, after the talk about the night before. It was just like Foreman, he thought; trying to win the lieutenant's favor. Foreman was always trying to win someone's favor. Still, the captain's words made the lieutenant feel good. He wanted to be liked by his men.

The lieutenant asked the captain about resupply—he said his platoon needed water badly. The captain said that it would arrive in a couple of hours, after they got all their dead and wounded out. The captured weapons would be going out too, but the pile of marines' equipment would be blown with explosives; it was too heavy to take out. He said that the whole company needed water.

"And then what, Skipper?"

The captain frowned. "The colonel told me we're probably

going to pull back. I don't like it—not after a fight like that . . . but I guess we're really hurting."

"Oh, by the way, Skipper," the lieutenant said, "some of the men have been asking—does this operation have a name yet?"

"Medea," the captain said, "it just came over the radio. Operation Medea."

The lieutenant went down to the ravine and got his gear. Then he walked back across the LZ to the hill. It was hot now and the stench in the LZ was worse. The bodies stank and some of the men had taken craps and not buried them; there were flies everywhere.

The lieutenant walked up the hill. Some of his men asked the name of the operation and he told them. A few asked how it was spelled and what it meant.

He stopped at Corporal Thompson's position and briefed him on what was happening.

"And tell your men they did a good job," the lieutenant said.

"Thank you, sir. Uh, sir?"

"What is it, Thompson?"

"It's just that . . ." He paused. "Some of the men were wondering—I mean, about all that yelling at us last night going up the hill—whether it was necessary." Thompson's blue-eyed, staring face looked blank.

The lieutenant sighed; he felt tired. "I know Malone," he said. "He's a good marine, but I know he's got to be pushed. Sometimes it's necessary, that's all."

"Yes, sir," Thompson said. "Thank you, sir."

The lieutenant left and briefed the other squad leaders, then discussed resupply with Sergeant Jackson.

The lieutenant found a place in the shade and sat against a tree, away from Jackson, away from his radioman, away from his platoon. He felt tired and hungry and thirsty. He had a pack of C rations, but he didn't feel like eating anything without water. He lit a cigarette. How could he smoke a cigarette? Could he be that thirsty if he could smoke a cigarette? But he kept on smoking; it made him feel more relaxed, more tired. He thought about how thirsty he was. He counted the number of hours he had been without water and thought about how much he had sweated during that time; he was thirstier than he could ever remember being. He thought about how that marine he had talked to down in the LZ, the short skinny lance corporal with the big nose, would soon have all the water he wanted. He decided he had never liked that marine. He thought about how hard it was going to be—when the water finally came in—waiting to get his while his men took theirs first.

5: The Defectors

It was just coincidence that the Viet Cong official picked the Marine Corps' birthday on which to defect. At least, that was what the colonel told the captain and the captain told the lieutenant. The lieutenant stayed at the battalion base camp on Hill 25 while a platoon from his company went out to pick up the defector. He was a financial official, the battalion intelligence officer had said, and one of his conditions for defecting was that marines be his escorts; his didn't trust the South Vietnamese. It was the kind of assignment the lieutenant would have liked—a chance to use the language—but this time he was glad he didn't have to go out and miss the birthday dinner.

First came the ceremony. The battalion stood in formation, at attention, on the reddish-brown dirt hill that was then their home, while the sergeant major read the Birthday Message from the Commandant. Halfway through, it started to rain, and then it poured. The colonel presented a piece of birthday cake to the oldest and youngest marines in the battalion. Because they were under an open tent, those three didn't get wet. The lieutenant, standing in formation, cursed himself for not wearing his rain suit.

They ate the dinner in the shelter of mess tents, and now the lieutenant thought that getting soaked was worth it. Their battalion had one of the best mess sergeants in the division, and he had made roast turkey with stuffing, gravy, cranberry sauce, mashed potatoes, and string beans. Also there were sliced cold meats and a salad tray with radishes, carrots, celery, and olives. Ice cream and birthday cake for dessert.

The platoon came back in the evening with the defector and, it turned out, his wife. The mess sergeant had saved some food so they got to eat the birthday dinner too.

That night the captain briefed the lieutenant and the platoon commanders in the captain and lieutenant's tent. Ong Xuan, the defector, claimed that he could lead the marines to four large caches of enemy rice. That had been his job, he claimed, supervising the collection of rice from the local villagers for both the VC and NVA. He said the rice was only a couple hours' hike—at most—from the base camp. Regiment wanted to act right away, before anyone had a chance to move the rice.

"What if it's a trap?" one of the lieutenants said.

The captain tried to reassure them. He said that they would use two companies, supported by tanks. There would be amtracks also, to bring the rice back—which would then be given to the refugee program. If the rice was only a couple of hours' march away, that meant it was in open terrain—an unlikely spot for an ambush. "The colonel's going, too," the captain said, "so I guess *he* doesn't think it's a trap."

One of the lieutenants asked why the defector hadn't pointed out the locations of the rice on the map.

"He says he can't read a map," the captain said, sounding as if he wanted to believe it. Then he told them their company was to be in the lead, with the lieutenant acting as interpreter for the defectors.

"I told the colonel about you," the captain said to the lieutenant. "I told him how good you are, working with Vietnamese. Don't let me down."

The lieutenant said he would do his best.

Dobson, the platoon commander who had gone out that day to pick up the Vietnamese, said, "I'll tell you one thing." He grinned. "That guy's wife is a real piece of ass."

Four hours after they left base camp the two companies were still in open, hilly terrain. The sun was out. It was warm, but not hot. The sun and dryness felt good after all the rain of the day before. And no one would ambush them here—not in this terrain. The lieutenant kept checking his position on the map. Behind him the rest of the marines were stretched out in a long, curving green line like a snake, up and down the rolling hills. The lieutenant tried to imagine where the rice would be. Hidden underground? In caves in the sides of one of these hills? Behind the column and to the right a tank and two amtracks sat on a hill, ready to move.

The captain called on the radio and asked how much longer before they got to the rice. The lieutenant asked Ong Xuan.

"Nam phut," he said. Five minutes. The lieutenant told Chapel, the radioman, and he told the captain.

Chapel said, "The captain says we've been saying five minutes every time for the last hour. He says he wants to know how much longer it really is. He says the colonel wants to know too."

The lieutenant asked Ong Xuan again. Ong Xuan smiled. He was tall for a Vietnamese and had a shock of black hair over his forehead that gave him a boyish look.

"Nam phut," he said again. The lieutenant told Chapel.

They descended another hill, crossed a small stream, and suddenly everything looked different. They were no longer in hilly, open terrain; the lieutenant couldn't see around or above him for more than a few feet. He looked at his map. They were at the edge of a large, dark green area, full of contour lines and without any villages. NATIONAL FOREST RESERVE, the map said.

"Uh-oh," Chapel said. "This is the same shit we were in on Medea, Lieutenant: that damned Hai Lang National Forest. This is ambush country."

The captain radioed the lieutenant to halt and came up to his position.

"I'm not kidding, Skipper," the lieutenant said, "he keeps saying five minutes every time I ask."

The captain frowned. "Are you sure? How about Cao Tri—what does he say?" Cao Tri was the company's new Kit Carson scout—a VC defector himself. He didn't speak English but the lieutenant understood his Vietnamese well, and Cao Tri acted as a kind of interpreter.

The lieutenant asked Cao Tri.

"He says the same, Skipper—that Ong Xuan is saying five minutes."

"Ask him again how far it is," the captain said. "Tell him it's been over an hour since he first said it was five minutes. Ask him how five minutes can turn into an hour."

The lieutenant spoke to Ong Xuan again, with Cao Tri helping. The captain's tone and the lieutenant's questions

seemed not to disturb Ong Xuan at all. He listened and
answered politely with the same pleasant smile. His wife
stood next to him. She was barefoot and wore a dirty white
blouse and baggy skirt. She hadn't said anything.

"Skipper, he says he always used to take this route by
himself or with his wife, and that they go pretty fast on these
trails—a lot faster than us. That's why he said five minutes.
He says that we go real slow."

The captain swore; he seemed offended. "I'd like to see
them do this in five minutes," he said. "Look—ask him again
how far it is—but in distance, not time."

The lieutenant asked.

"He says five hundred meters, Skipper."

The captain looked skeptical. "I hope he knows his meters
better than his minutes. I don't like this at all: you know what
happened the last time we were in here. And now we lose the
tanks and amtracks." He looked around at the thick tropical
vegetation and then at the defector and his wife. "But I guess
we've got no choice. The colonel wants us to go ahead."

They continued on the same trail, moving deeper into the
mountainous terrain. It was tough going. The trail was
narrow and curving and it had been cut to height of people
shorter than the marines, forcing them to stoop over. But
Ong and Ba Xuan moved easily, and several times the captain
radioed to tell the lieutenant to slow down. The lieutenant
realized, after a few turns of the trail, that his map would be
no use, and he put it away.

Finally Ong Xuan told the lieutenant to stop. He pointed to
his right. It seemed just more of the same—trees, vines,
branches. The lieutenant looked more intently and suddenly,
as in an optical illusion drawing, an outline appeared of an
elevated hut, ten feet on a side, surrounded by the thick
vegetation.

"Chapel, call the captain and tell him we're at the first
one."

There was a short trail leading to the building and the
lieutenant headed up it, but Ong Xuan grabbed his arm and
spoke excitedly.

"What is he saying?" the lieutenant asked Cao Tri.

"It is dangerous," Cao Tri said. *"Co min."*

The lieutenant stepped back.

"She'll go first," Ong Xuan said.

Ba Xuan walked past her husband and very slowly started up the trail. Suddenly Cao Tri took out his bayonet and followed. After a few feet Ba Xuan stopped, made a gesture and said something. Cao Tri went to where she stood and knelt down. He stuck his bayonet into the ground, slowly, at different angles, then dug up some dirt with his blade and lifted something out of the ground. He stood and did something to it with his fingers, then walked back to Ong Xuan and handed it to him. Then he went back to the woman.

"Chi-com," Chapel said. "Little one. Looks pretty old, too. Wonder how much damage it would do. How come she knows where they are?"

The lieutenant asked Ong Xuan.

"She planted them," he said.

There were two more mines and Cao Tri dug up and defused each of them. He was silent and intent while he worked, but afterward he smiled and showed the mines to the marines at the head of the column.

There was a two-foot space between the walls of the hut and the roof. The lieutenant reached over and in and pulled out a handful.

"This isn't rice," he said.

"Uh-uh." Chapel shook his head. "Salt."

Before dark they pulled back to the open area outside the forest and set up for the night on two adjoining hills, a company to each hill—and an amtrack, too; the tank had gone back. The men set to work digging holes in case of a mortar attack. The colonel called battalion headquarters and had them send out C rations by another amtrack.

When it was dark the colonel came to the captain's position and sat and talked with the captain, the lieutenant, and Ong Xuan. Ong Xuan repeated, through the lieutenant, that he knew where four huts of rice were in addition to the salt. He said they weren't far from the salt. The colonel said that now the plan had changed: they were going to go in tomorrow and blow up the rice and salt. It would take too long to bring it all out by hand. Then he asked the lieutenant whether Ong Xuan thought the NVA might ambush them tomorrow. The lieutenant asked Ong Xuan.

Ong Xuan said he didn't know.

"Ask him if he thinks it's possible," the colonel said.

"Da phai," Ong Xuan said in his friendly way. "It's possible."

The colonel went back to his position and the lieutenant inspected the defensive positions of the company. He heard a lot of talk among the men about how they didn't want to go back in there, how they didn't like being up front, how if it was a trap they were going to shoot the two gooks first. Some talked about how they'd like to screw the wife.

The lieutenant helped Chapel dig their own hole. Chapel had made a bed for himself, using some of the burlap bags that had been on the amtracks to carry the rice in, and the lieutenant decided to do the same. The captain saw what the lieutenant was doing and took some burlap bags for himself. The captain found four sticks, stuck them in the ground around his burlap-bag mattress and put his poncho over them, forming a shelter in case it should rain. The lieutenant found four sticks and did the same.

Before going to sleep the lieutenant joined the three Vietnamese, who were sitting together talking quietly. The lieutenant asked Ong Xuan whether he had a place to sleep and Ong Xuan pointed behind him. He had also made mattresses out of burlap bags. He hadn't bothered to dig a hole.

After the two defectors went to bed the lieutenant asked Cao Tri, "Do you think Ba Xuan is beautiful?"

Cao Tri giggled and said yes.

The lieutenant went to bed. His burlap mattress felt good. It was almost soft enough for him to sleep on his stomach. He thought of the two Vietnamese together, lying on the mattresses next to each other, as if the marines weren't even there. He thought of how different the marines were— digging their holes, eating their food out of cans, worrying about a trap. He decided he wanted to be more like the Vietnamese.

That night it poured. The lieutenant's poncho overhead filled with water and then slumped to one side, letting water run down on him and his mattress. He kept waking and shifting position, trying to find the least wet spot. But the captain's and Chapel's shelters both worked well, and in the morning their mattresses were still dry. Ong and Ba Xuan got up with everybody else and said they had had a good sleep too.

They left the hills and went back into the dense terrain. It rained again, but not hard enough to penetrate the thick canopy of vegetation. The trail became a tunnel of hot sticky air. The lieutenant's glasses fogged up and sweat dripped onto them from his forehead.

"Watch out for leeches," Chapel said. "Land leeches—they come out in this kind of weather."

They arrived at the salt hut. It looked the same as it had the day before and the salt was still there. The colonel decided they would wait to blow it on their way out. He wanted to get to the rice.

They hiked along the trail again until Ong Xuan told the lieutenant to stop. The lieutenant saw the hut immediately. It looked much like the salt hut, camouflaged by the surrounding foliage, except it was bigger. The lieutenant radioed the captain, and Ba Xuan and Cao Tri took care of the mines as before. When the lieutenant stuck his fist into the hut, he pulled out a handful of rice.

"*Gao*," the lieutenant said, smiling, to Ong Xuan.

Marines were placed around the hut for security. Then the lieutenant passed the word down the column for the men to check one another for leeches. Chapel looked him over and said he was all right, and then the lieutenant looked over Chapel. The three Vietnamese sat by the side of the hut and smoked cigarettes; they didn't seem concerned about leeches.

Suddenly Chapel shouted: "Uh-oh! I've got one, I've got one! I can feel it!" He undid his belt and pulled down his pants.

Then the lieutenant swore. "Oh no! I've got one too!" He pulled down his pants.

They didn't wait to burn them off. Chapel grabbed at his crotch and the lieutenant at his ass. They threw the leeches on the ground and crushed them with their boots. They were small, less than an inch long. Chapel and the lieutenant shivered. The marines at the head of the column were laughing, and so were Cao Tri and Ong Xuan, in their high-pitched giggles. The lieutenant looked at Ba Xuan. Her face hadn't changed at all.

The colonel seemed quite pleased when he saw the rice. He

plunged his arm into it and sifted it from one hand to the other.

"That's a lot of rice," he said.

He wanted to know just how much it was. He and the captain and the lieutenant figured the approximate number of cubic feet, and then Chapel, who had once worked on a farm, made a guess at how much a cubic foot of rice would weigh. They decided to round off the figure they arrived at to five tons, which was close enough anyway. If they found three more caches like that the total would be twenty tons. Twenty tons would sound good, they agreed, in the report for regiment. Plus the salt.

Combat photographers had come up with the colonel and they took pictures of the hut. The colonel told them to get a few shots of him standing in front of it—something for his scrapbook, he said. He stood in front of the hut and took off his helmet.

Suddenly Ong Xuan came over to the lieutenant, grabbed his arm, and spoke excitedly—too fast for the lieutenant to understand. "What is he saying, Cao Tri?"

Cao Tri said, "He wants to get in the picture with the colonel."

The lieutenant told the colonel and the colonel smiled and said all right. Ong Xuan went and stood by the colonel and then motioned to his wife. She jumped up and quickly reached behind her neck and let down her hair, then pulled a comb from a pocket of her baggy skirt and used it. Her black hair was straight and shiny, and it came down to her waist. She stepped next to her husband, and suddenly she smiled. It was a big, happy smile. The gray-haired colonel was smiling, too, looking like an uncle next to the two Vietnamese.

The photographers finished and Ba Xuan stopped smiling. She pulled up her hair and tied it again.

One platoon stayed at the hut, along with two of the combat engineers. The colonel stayed, too. He said he wanted to see how the place would look after it was blown. The rest of the marines went ahead on the trail.

They found the second rice cache, and Ba Xuan and Cao Tri handled the mines and the engineers blew the hut up. The lieutenant led the column on.

Ong Xuan told the lieutenant to stop. They were close to

the third cache, he said, but this one was different. There weren't any mines, but there were guards—two of them. He said the marines should creep up and kill them.

The lieutenant radioed back and told the captain the plan, then he assigned two marines to go up the trail and take care of the guards. He lent one of the marines the shotgun he was carrying.

The lieutenant waited. Five minutes later the two marines came back and said there was a guard shack but no guards. They went up to the hut. The lieutenant and two marines searched the guard shack and found a rusty old bolt-action rifle. One of the marines said the guards must just have run off surprised, if they left a weapon behind; that maybe they went to warn others. There was nothing else of value in the shack. Cao Tri found a hat he liked, a crude bamboo helmet. He put it on and laughed and asked the lieutenant how he looked. The lieutenant smiled; the flat, conical shape seemed to fit his wide Vietnamese face.

"Like a VC," the lieutenant said. Cao Tri looked pleased.

The engineers planted the demo. The captain told the lieutenant that it was more important than ever, with those guards somewhere out there, to finish up fast and get out.

They went on the trail headed toward the last cache, the three Vietnamese and the lieutenant leading the way. The terrain had become more rugged and the lieutenant was sweating a lot. They went down one side of a ravine and were going up the other when suddenly he heard shots from somewhere not far ahead. The lieutenant got down. He looked up but his glasses were fogged. The word *ambush* went through his mind, and he called behind for the rest of the platoon to come up fast. There was more firing; he heard rounds go over his head. Next to him Cao Tri, crouched low, held his rifle over his head and fired on fully automatic. Chapel shouted that the captain was on the radio and wanted to know what was going on.

Cao Tri stopped firing. He pulled on the lieutenant's arm and shouted: *"Thuy quan luc chien! Thuy quan luc chien!"*

The lieutenant put his hands to his mouth and yelled: *"Hey, Marines! Hold your fire! It's Charlie Company!"*

Then there were voices from in front. *"Hold your fire! Hold your fire!"* The firing stopped and the lieutenant went up the hill.

"God Damn, Lieutenant, I'm sorry about that"—it was a squad leader from the other company, the one behind the lieutenant's in the column—"but I sure as hell thought that was a VC coming up the hill." He pointed at Cao Tri, who was still wearing the captured helmet.

"That's all right, Corporal," the lieutenant said, "I understand. Looks like the trail doubles back here. It's okay—nobody's hurt. I'm just glad you're such lousy shots."

"Yes, sir."

The lieutenant smiled. "I'm glad he is, too." He nodded toward Cao Tri.

The lieutenant told Chapel to radio the captain what had happened. Then he went over to Cao Tri. He thought Cao Tri would get a laugh out of it, but Cao Tri wasn't smiling. He was standing by himself, frowning.

"What's wrong, Cao Tri?"

"They shot at me—the marines shot at me."

"But Cao Tri, it was a mistake. They said they were sorry."

"They shot at me."

The lieutenant told him again that the marines were sorry. For a moment he thought Cao Tri was going to cry. Suddenly he grabbed the helmet off his head and threw it on the ground. Then he stomped on it, jumping up and down. When Cao Tri finished he looked up and smiled.

They got to the last cache. It looked just like the others, with a short trail leading up to it, but this time Ba Xuan didn't move.

"What is it?" the lieutenant said to Ong Xuan. "Are there mines on the trail?"

"I don't know," Ong Xuan said. "Someone else took care of this one."

The lieutenant asked him what they should do.

Ong Xuan shook his head. "I don't know," he said, looking as though the problem didn't concern him.

The captain called over the radio. "He says to hurry up," Chapel said. "It's getting dark."

"I know it's getting dark." The lieutenant looked at Ong and Ba Xuan. They were standing on the trail, staring off. "Tell him we've got a problem. They don't know where the mines are." The lieutenant turned to Cao Tri and asked him to talk to the two Vietnamese, to tell them that they had to hurry, the captain wanted to get back. Couldn't she try and lead them?

Cao Tri spoke with them. He said to the lieutenant, "They say they won't go. They don't know where the mines are. She didn't take care of this hut."

The lieutenant looked at them again, at their patient, indifferent faces.

"The captain says to hurry up," Chapel said. "He says to figure something out. The colonel wants to get going."

The lieutenant looked around. A combat engineer with demo stood nearby, ready to blow the rice; he and the other marines at the head of the column were all looking at the lieutenant. For a moment the lieutenant thought of sending one of them up the trail first. No, he couldn't do that, he told himself. But what could he do? It was still humid and he was sweating a lot.

Suddenly he turned to Cao Tri. "You go."

Cao Tri frowned. He had the same expression that he'd had after the marines shot at him: a pained, unhappy look, as though his feelings were hurt. He turned away from the lieutenant without a word.

"Please," the lieutenant said, "you're the only one who can do it. You have to." He tried to think of what he would do if Cao Tri said no. He couldn't think of anything.

But he said, "I'll go, too. I'll be right behind you."

Cao Tri still didn't say anything. He took out his bayonet and started up the trail, walking very, very slowly. He was stooped and bent over, his face only about two feet from the ground. The lieutenant was five feet behind, and the marine engineer with the demo was behind him. The lieutenant watched where Cao Tri put his feet each time he stepped, and when the lieutenant stepped he tried to remember where that had been, at the same time watching where Cao Tri was stepping now. His eyes flicked back and forth and it was hard to remember; all the places on the trail looked the same. But he kept going, as if pretending he knew where to step. He thought of how small the mines were, how they wouldn't do that much damage.

He took one more step and was at the hut.

The marines reassembled in the open terrain on the two hills where they had spent the previous night. It was now dark. They could have stayed for a second night, but the colonel decided they should head back now. The lieutenant figured they'd get back around midnight. He was tired. He had hiked a long way in the last two days.

He said goodbye to Ong and Ba Xuan. They were going to ride back on one of the amtracks that had stood on the hill for two days.

Ong Xuan said that they planned to go to the National Police in Quang Tri City. Now there would be no doubt about his story; he even had the photographs to prove it. Under the government's *Chieu Hoi*—Open Arms—program, they would both get a lot of money.

He and his wife smiled when the lieutenant wished them luck. Ba Xuan reached into the pocket of her skirt and pulled out a brown lump and gave it to the lieutenant. She said it was to eat. The lieutenant took a bite. It tasted like maple sugar candy. He thanked her and tried to give it back, but she said it was for him.

Cao Tri came up to the lieutenant and said he wanted to ride on the amtrack too. The lieutenant shook his head. "No, Cao Tri, you can't."

"But *Thieu-uy,* I want to—they are." He pointed to Ong and Ba Xuan. "I don't want to walk." His voice was whiny.

"I'm sorry, Cao Tri," the lieutenant said, "you have to walk back. We all do—the whole company. Even the captain. You're part of the company now."

"But I don't want to," he said. "I'm too tired. I want to go back with them. Ask the *dai-uy.*"

The lieutenant asked the captain.

"Negative," the captain said, "tell him he has to go with us." But as they were about to move out, the captain said to the lieutenant, "All right. Tell Cao Tri he can ride. I guess he did a pretty good job for us today." He sounded as though he were giving in to the lieutenant, not to Cao Tri.

"He did, Skipper," the lieutenant said, "and he'll come around. After all, he's only sixteen years old."

Cao Tri smiled when the lieutenant told him, and told the lieutenant to thank the *dai-uy.* Then he climbed on top of the amtrack and sat with Ong and Ba Xuan and the colonel. The four waved to the lieutenant as they rode by.

The marines started the long hump back. That was about

all the lieutenant had to do now—walk. There was no more talk about ambushes.

At one point Chapel walked along beside the lieutenant. They talked about how it had gone that day, about how surprised the NVA were going to be when they went looking for their rice. Then Chapel said, "The men were talking about you today, Lieutenant."

"Oh?"

"They said they thought you were crazy, the way you were running around up in front all day with those gooks. Especially the ones who were on Medea. They thought you were crazy."

The lieutenant smiled and didn't say anything.

Later the word was passed down the column that the mess sergeant was going to have a fried chicken dinner waiting for them when they got back. On the colonel's orders.

6: The Silver Star

It was late in the morning and overcast. The company was moving across open rolling terrain covered with thick vegetation that came up to their waists. The marines up front had to cut a trail with machetes.

Then they came across what appeared to be a dirt road and followed it. The lieutenant, near the rear of the column, shouted at the men around him, "Keep your interval! Five meters! Spread it out!" In a few minutes the marines again bunched up and again the lieutenant shouted.

From somewhere ahead there was the sound of an explosion: a flat, hollow-sounding thud that seemed to come from a long way off, yet at the same time was quite distinct. The marines near the lieutenant kept marching. Nobody said anything.

Then, one by one like the cars of a train, the column stopped, each marine moving a little closer to the man in front.

"Keep it spread out!"

The word came down the column: *"Freeze, mines!"* It was like a race, the marines against the message, with the message always winning. The lieutenant turned his head and passed it to the marine in back of him, who had already heard it.

There was another explosion. The same hollow-sounding thud that could have been far or close. The lieutenant swore.

Another message came down: *"All corpsmen up front!"*

It must be bad, the lieutenant thought, if they needed *all* the corpsmen. One of them brushed by the lieutenant as he hurried ahead.

The word the lieutenant had been waiting for came down:

"Charlie Five up front!" He began moving as soon as he heard it, going past the message as it was still coming down. He moved as the corpsmen had, walking fast, not running, trying to stay on the ground that had already been walked on, rubbing against the marines as he passed them. He thought about the yelling, the confusion, the cries that he would hear when he got up there. What would he have to do? But he was glad to be going, instead of standing back here with the others, not knowing what was going on, doing nothing but repeating messages that had already been heard.

It was like suddenly being back with people. Here there was noise—activity. The lieutenant saw the captain first, standing in a clearing next to the path, tall, thin, familiar, the only one not wearing a helmet. He seemed to be the center, connected to all the people around him as if with invisible strings.

"Skipper!"

The captain turned. "Jim! Jesus, I'm glad you're here!" He swore.

"How bad is it?"

The captain swore again. "It's a mess." Next to him his radiomen talked into their handsets in excited, high-pitched voices. "Six of them—damn it! As soon as I heard the first one I knew it—we were on a mined path. I *knew* I shouldn't have let them take it!" He clenched his fists. "And then before I could get up here the other one went—tripped by someone trying to help the others. *Damn it!* That's the way it always is—they don't know enough to stay where they are! Two of them are in bad shape—they've both lost legs. We've got to get them out of here and get off this trail before we trip any more." He swore.

The lieutenant looked past the captain at three marines hacking at the bushes on the edge of the clearing. The clearing was in a slight hollow. "This going to be the LZ, Skipper?"

"I guess so, but I don't like it. The choppers might have a hard time coming in. I'd like to find a better one."

"Want me to look?"

The captain hesitated. "No," he said, "I want you here." He glanced around the clearing. The gunnery sergeant was by himself, kneeling on one knee at the far edge of the clearing, watching what was going on, as if waiting for the right time to act. Branches and leaves stuck out of his helmet. The captain called him over. "Listen to me, Gunny. I want you to take a look over that rise and see if there's a better spot for an LZ—one that won't take too long to get ready."

The gunny turned and looked. It was a small rise, a few feet high, just in back of the clearing. "Aye, aye, Skipper."

"Be sure and stay off that trail."

The gunny turned and walked away.

One of the corpsmen, huddled over the wounded on the trail next to the clearing, called out, "More bandages! We need more bandages!" The message went down the column.

The lieutenant saw the lead platoon commander shouting at his men at the front of the column to stay off the trail.

"Lieutenant Dobson—Tom!"

Dobson turned and lumbered over to the lieutenant. He was of medium height and not very stocky, yet he walked as if he were built like a gorilla.

"Who got hit?"

Dobson blurted out the last names of six of his men. He shook his head. "Miller and Leonard got it bad," he said. "I think they're going to lose their legs." He stared up at the lieutenant. His mouth was open.

"I'm sorry," the lieutenant said.

"Jesus," Dobson said. His forehead wrinkled and he looked puzzled. "It happened so fast, just like that." He shook his head. For a moment he smiled. "I almost got hit myself. If Hill in front of me hadn't been standing where he—"

There was another explosion. It came from over the rise in front of them. It was louder than the first two, but not that much louder, the same hollow-sounding thud that suddenly happened and then passed, as if it were perfectly natural. The lieutenant felt himself shudder. In his mind was a picture of the gunny walking away over the rise, pushing the vegetation aside, like someone trying to walk fast through water.

"Stay where you are! Stay where you are!" The captain went ahead with a corpsman over the rise. A few minutes later he came back and shouted for another corpsman and two marines to come up with a poncho and bandages. "And stay off that goddamn trail!" The captain's face was pale. He paused and looked around the clearing, as if trying to decide what to do next. He saw the lieutenant.

"Goddamnit—Jim! Come on—what's the matter? Why aren't you getting them to finish the LZ? You know that's your job! And is the medevac report all set? Are the wounded ready to go out? Come on—don't let me down now!"

"Aye, aye, *sir!"*

The lieutenant shouted at the marines hacking at the brush on the edge of the clearing to work faster. Then he called out to Dobson. "Lieutenant Dobson, I need some more of your men to help clear this LZ!"

"But we don't have any more machetes."

"They can use their e-tools, damn it! Come on—get them up here."

He checked with Chapel, who was now one of the captain's radiomen, about the medevac report. It was all set, Chapel said, the choppers were on their way. The lieutenant made sure Chapel had the right smoke grenade, then he walked over to a corpsman and asked whether the wounded would be ready.

"Just get the choppers here, Lieutenant, we'll have them ready."

He went and yelled some more at the marines clearing the LZ. How big did it have to be? he wondered.

Suddenly the helicopters appeared, two of them, small in the distance. The marines stopped swinging their machetes and entrenching tools and got out of the way. Everybody else went to the edge of the LZ and crouched down. There was no more yelling.

Chapel threw a smoke grenade into the middle of the clearing and thick, bright yellow smoke rose. A breeze caught it and it thinned.

The first chopper descended, scattering the smoke. The noise and wind were like a sudden hurricane, making the lieutenant turn away, clutching his flak jacket and helmet. The chopper landed. From the corner of his eye the lieutenant could see corpsmen carrying wounded.

For no reason, the lieutenant turned around. A marine was being carried by on a poncho. For a moment the lieutenant didn't recognize him. It was the gunny. He didn't have his glasses on; otherwise there was the same slightly tired, almost sad look on his face that he had always seemed to have. The lieutenant noticed the red indentations the gunny's glasses had made high on the bridge of his nose. Then he saw that most of the gunny's legs were gone. He turned away.

The first chopper left and the second came down and took the rest of the wounded. The column started moving. The lieutenant waited and then fell in behind the marine he had been following earlier. They stayed off the dirt path, making their own trail. For a time the marines around the lieutenant were better at keeping their interval and he didn't have to shout as much.

In the afternoon they joined up with the rest of battalion. They hiked and hiked, got to a certain point, spent the night, and then they hiked back.

Two days later word came down that the battalion was moving again. It had been assigned the defense of the new airstrip outside Quang Tri City. The men struck their tents, loaded their gear on trucks, and went to their new home, a flat, sandy piece of land adjacent to the airstrip just east of Highway One and west of the Thach Han River. Each company had a portion of the perimeter to defend and patrols to run every few days.

A week after they hit the mines, a marine came into the tent the captain and the lieutenant shared, introduced himself, and said he had just returned from Da Nang, from the same hospital where the gunny had been taken. "I thought I'd come by here first, Captain. I knew the gunny was from your company." He was a tall, dark-haired marine who sounded subdued and respectful. He said he had been wounded on Operation Medea and was on his way back to his own company. The captain thanked the marine and invited him to sit down on his cot. The lieutenant gave him a cigarette.

"I guess you heard," the marine said. The captain nodded. "He tried, Skipper—hung on for thirty-six hours after they flew him in. He just couldn't make it; died from loss of blood."

"*Loss of blood?*" Suddenly the captain appeared angry with the marine. "What the hell do you mean, loss of blood? If he was there for thirty-six hours, why the hell couldn't they get him enough blood?"

"I don't know, Captain." The marine sounded patient. "I really don't. I thought it was kind of strange myself. You don't usually die from loss of blood, once you've made it to the hospital. Maybe he had a funny type, I don't know. But he was in bad shape."

"God, he really was." The captain let out a breath and turned to the lieutenant. His anger seemed to have passed. "I've seen men lose limbs before, but I've never seen anyone as bad as that—and still live. God, he looked bad. Both legs gone and one of his arms—the whole limbs, I'm not kidding. Why the hell did he go on that trail?—I told him to stay off it. I guess he wanted to get a better look at what it was like on the other side . . . or maybe he just forgot."

The captain was silent for a moment, then went on. "He really looked like a goner, I'm not kidding. God—I almost wished it for him! I had to force myself to look at him. And he was trying to *talk* to me! You know what he said? 'I'm sorry, Skipper, I'm sorry.' What the hell was he sorry to me about? Maybe he thought that some of the others got hit by the same mine; I don't know."

After another silence he looked up. "I want you to write him up," he said to the lieutenant. "I want to see he gets a medal. That's the least we can do." The captain stared at the lieutenant, frowning, as though expecting an argument.

"All right, Skipper. What do you want to write him up for?"

The captain continued to stare. Then he said, "The Silver Star."

The lieutenant looked at the marine, then back at the captain.

"And I want you to do a good job," the captain said. "Do you understand?"

The lieutenant answered in a soft voice, "All right, Skipper, I understand."

The marine got up, shook hands with them and left.

That afternoon the lieutenant sat at the small, portable field desk in his tent. It was raining outside and the light was dim, so he had lighted a Coleman lantern. A pad of lined yellow paper lay on the desk in front of him, and he tried to think of what to write. In his mind he kept seeing a picture of the gunny being carried toward the helicopter on a poncho, looking slightly sad and a bit tired, as if what was going on had nothing to do with him. How had he looked, the lieutenant wondered, when the captain had seen him; when the gunny told the captain he was sorry. The lieutenant shuddered. But did the captain really think he deserved the Silver Star?

The lieutenant thought he understood. He had often seen the special relationship that existed between company commanders and their gunnery sergeants. The gunnies were like right-hand men, older and more experienced. They could get rough with the troops in a way an officer couldn't, and they could get closer to the men, too. The company's previous gunny had been a tall, stout man with a gruff voice and a theatrical manner who had liked to keep marines afraid of him—including new lieutenants.

The new gunny had been different. The lieutenant remembered when he had first joined the company, shortly after Operation Medea. He had come from another company in the battalion, where he had been platoon sergeant. He had spent almost two years in the field and had a reputation for being an expert in fighting VC. Yet he had looked more like a college student than a marine, the lieutenant thought—a thin, pale face, wire-rimmed glasses, and a blond handlebar mustache that seemed too wide for his face. Only a few years older than the lieutenant, the gunny was one of many marines who had been promoted fast because of the war.

He had been quiet too, not shouting all the time like other gunnies; he had seemed to have an inner assurance and didn't need to make the troops afraid of him. When the company was on patrol, he always camouflaged his helmet with branches and leaves, and whenever the column stopped, the gunny would get down on one knee and remain silent, watchful, until the column started moving again. It had seemed to the lieutenant that the gunny was someone from whom he could learn a lot.

The lieutenant leaned forward in his chair and peered down at the yellow paper again. He remembered all the citations he had to write following Operation Medea, after the captain had made him executive officer. It was like writing research papers: taking the accounts of others and trying to piece them together, writing about what happened as though he had seen it himself. But he didn't want to write about the experience of others; that wasn't what he had come here for. He had told the captain then he couldn't do it.

"You do it," the captain had said, scowling. "This is

important. Those men performed in battle and they've got to know someone appreciates them—this is about all they'll get."

And so the lieutenant had done it, staying up late, smoking cigarettes, making revisions—the way he used to do in college when he'd put off writing a paper until the night before it was due. When he finished, the captain told him he had done a good job.

But what had the gunny done? Only three marines from Medea had been written up for the Silver Star, and they had all been in direct combat with the enemy.

Finally, he started to write. He knew that the patrol they had been on that day was part of a big operation, one that had a name. Maybe mentioning the name would help. He figured it would also help to say that the company had suddenly found itself in the middle of an enemy minefield, that the six marines who were wounded would die if they didn't get medical attention right away, that the company was already out of battle dressings; that suddenly the gunny came up to the captain and volunteered to go forward into the enemy minefield to look for a site for a landing zone; that the gunny hit a mine but the landing zone was found; that the helicopters came in and took out the wounded; that most had lived, but after a thirty-six-hour fight against death, the gunny died.

He finished, put on his rain suit and went outside and crossed the flat sandy area to a GP tent on the other side of the base that housed the company office. The weather was rainy, windy, and cool, but inside the tent it was warm. Clerks were busy at field tables covered with papers, files, typewriters, manuals, record books, ashtrays, coffee mugs. The lieutenant gave the citation to Corporal Henry, the chief clerk, to type up. The first sergeant was there too, sitting in his folding lawn chair next to the kerosene heater, sipping coffee and reading *Stars and Stripes,* and he and the lieutenant talked about how bad the weather was and how the first sergeant could use something to drink.

That evening at dinner the lieutenant sat across from the captain in the officer-and-staff-NCO mess tent. "I went by the company office," the captain said, "and read your write-up on the gunny."

"Oh?"

The captain looked at him hard. "It's good," he said. "It's real good. It's the best you've ever done."

The lieutenant thought about the way he had written it, the simplicity of his sentences—yet the sense of drama he felt he had achieved. Yes, he thought, it was a good write-up. "Thank you, Skipper," he said.

The company received some replacements, among them a new gunnery sergeant fresh from the States. He moved into the tent that the captain and the lieutenant shared, taking over the old gunny's cot. The new gunny had been in the Corps almost twenty years and he seemed like a typical marine gunny, with a short chunky body, sloping shoulders, and thick arms. His hair was shaved close. Almost immediately he started yelling and swearing at the troops.

"Looks like we've got a good gunny," the captain said.

A week later they were sitting in their tent, going through the first mail they'd had in three days. The new gunny had received four letters from his wife. It was raining again and in spite of the trench they had dug around the tent water was running in. The captain and the lieutenant were smoking cigarettes.

The captain handed the lieutenant a letter he had received and asked him to read it. The letter was postmarked from a small Western city. It was addressed merely "Company Commander," not to the captain by name.

Dear Sir:

We have received notice that our son was killed in action. We know from his last letter that he had recently been transferred to your company, and so we are writing to you for help.

Thomas was our only son—our only child—and we were very proud of him. We tried to follow his life closely, including his life in the Marines, although Thomas was a quiet person who often kept things to himself. Perhaps he was trying to protect us.

We do not want to be protected. Perhaps we are being foolish, but knowing our son as we did, we have a feeling—a faith—that his death was somehow useful, that it served a purpose, however small.

We feel we can rely on you—Thomas wrote of you in his last letter with great respect. Can you please help us and tell us how he died? Do not be afraid to be frank.

Thank you, and may God be with you and your men.

> Sincerely,
> Mrs. Thomas Vance

The lieutenant was startled by the letter. He had never thought of the gunny as having parents. But, of course, why not? The gunny, after all, had been only a few years older than the lieutenant. He noticed the handwriting; it was attractive, slanted, easy to read. The woman must be educated, the lieutenant thought; gentle.

He held out the letter to the captain. "That's not going to be easy."

The captain didn't move. "I want you to write it," he said.

"Me?" The lieutenant drew his hand back.

The captain nodded. "These letters never are easy—I know, I've had to write my share. But I think you should do it—you did such a good job on the write-up. And besides, you probably knew the gunny at least as well as I did."

"Can I tell them he's up for the Silver Star?"

"Negative," the captain said. "It's against regulations—not until it goes through."

The new gunny looked from the captain to the lieutenant.

Later that day, alone in the tent and again seated at his portable field desk, the lieutenant reread the letter. She was right, he thought, the gunny *had* kept to himself. The lieutenant recalled how he had looked forward to getting to know the silent young NCO who had been in the field so long, who seemed so different from the other gunnies. This one, the lieutenant remembered thinking, he could be friends with.

Only once had the gunny spoken about himself. It was at night, after the lieutenant and the captain had been talking in their tent. The captain had received a letter from an old college friend—a fraternity brother—and had read it aloud. The friend was still a bachelor and had a job as a stockbroker, making a lot of money; he had many girlfriends. The captain spoke wistfully about the times they had had, the drinking parties, the pranks, the girls they slept with. The lieutenant had told a few stories about his college days too. The gunny, sitting on his cot, had remained silent, cleaning his pistol.

The captain had gone to bed. The gunny had gotten up and announced that he was going to take a walk around the lines. "I'll go with you," the lieutenant said.

Outside it was cool and very dark. The gunny quickly replaced the tent flap so that no light could be seen. The lieutenant breathed deeply, as though cleaning his lungs. He was smoking a lot lately, nearly three packs a day. The gunny set out on his walk and the lieutenant followed. At each position the gunny would have a few words with the man up, while the lieutenant stood back and to one side. When they finished their circuit they stopped outside their tent, next to the barbed wire.

Suddenly the lieutenant asked, "What about you, Gunny? How come you didn't go to college? How'd you end up over here?"

The gunny was silent, gazing out over the wire. Beyond, the lieutenant knew, was a wide gully and then a village, but now nothing could be seen; no lights showed. For a moment the lieutenant imagined that the gunny was looking for VC trying to creep toward their lines—Intelligence had reported the possibility of an attack soon. The gunny reached up and twisted the end of his wide mustache. "I did," he said. He had a slight twang and a compressed, matter-of-fact way of speaking that the lieutenant liked.

"Really?"

"Yes, sir." The lieutenant wanted to tell the gunny not to call him "sir," but he knew he shouldn't. "But not like you and the skipper. I mean, I guess I didn't get much out of it." He sounded almost apologetic. He told the lieutenant he had become disgusted with classes, professors, and students who spent all their time in the library worrying about grades. None of that had seemed real to him. No; he felt he was meant for something different, something special. One morning he woke and decided to join the Marine Corps. The lieutenant nodded enthusiastically. He imagined himself and the gunny remaining together, becoming a kind of team.

Then the gunny said, "How about you, Lieutenant?

Sounds like you liked college all right. What made you join the Corps?"

The lieutenant felt confused. He wanted another cigarette. "No, not really," he said. "I mean . . . I really didn't like it at all. I guess it didn't seem real to me either. Not like over here. You know what I mean?"

The gunny rubbed his chin. "I don't know," he said. He sounded tired. "It did before—when I first got over here and we all thought it'd be over soon. But now, I don't know. It just keeps going on."

The lieutenant waited, but the gunny said no more. The lieutenant suddenly realized that he hadn't thought about a time when the war would be over; he had assumed he could stay as long as he wanted.

Now, he read the letter again. What was he going to say to these people? Somehow it seemed not right to him that they, the living, should have to explain their dead to people back home. The lieutenant thought that men in war shouldn't have a home, or that war should be their home. Wasn't it best to keep to themselves what they did in war? Did the gunny's mother really want to know?

The lieutenant thought back to the only time the company had made contact when the gunny was with them. It had been a damp, overcast day and the whole company had been out on patrol. The marines had paused on a low, open hill facing a gully about two hundred meters wide. Beyond the gully the ground rose again, forming a low ridge topped by a thick clump of bushes.

"I don't like the looks of it," the captain had said. "Let's prep it before we go across." The mortarmen quickly set up their tubes, grateful for the chance to use up some ammo. After two rounds they found the correct range and then put a dozen shells into the bushes. The company moved across and up to the top of the ridge. It had worked! In the bushes they found a dead VC with a carbine and a pistol. They also found the sandals of another. Perhaps there had been others waiting in ambush too. They would have had easy shooting.

"Way to go, Skipper! Good call!" It was Sergeant Harris, the mortar squad leader. He had a Boston accent and pronounced it *Skippah*.

The captain was beaming, as were the mortarmen, who

chalked up another kill. The captain took the dead VC's pistol, a 9 mm automatic, and told his radioman not to report it; the captain grinned mischievously at the lieutenant and put it in his pack. The mortarmen stripped the body to see where the fragments had entered. The rest of the men crowded around to have a look.

The gunny went through the pockets of the dead man's uniform and found a sheaf of documents. "Looks like he was an officer," he said. The captain agreed. They would turn the documents in to Intelligence. He passed the word to get ready to move out.

"Wait a second, Skipper," the gunny said. "There's something we ought to do."

The captain asked what he meant.

"We shouldn't just leave him like this," the gunny said. "We ought to blow his head off—with the shotgun." He explained that the other VC who had been on the ridge had probably scattered in all directions, and that if any of them came back they wouldn't be able to tell who got killed. Since the dead VC was probably an officer, the confusion might be important. "Plus it puts a scare in them," the gunny said. "Makes them wonder if it's going to happen to them." He brought his hand up to his mustache and twisted the end of it.

The tactic of blowing off the VC's head seemed to be another thing the gunny had learned from his experience in the field, like camouflaging his helmet and dropping down on one knee each time the column stopped.

The captain didn't respond; for a moment it appeared as if he hadn't heard the gunny and that the suggestion would be lost. The men were talking about how surprised the VC must have been; how too bad it was that they hadn't killed more.

The gunny spoke up again, in his twangy matter-of-fact way. "We ought to blow his head off, Skipper—with the shotgun."

The captain stood looking down at the dead man. His skin was very white, smooth and unblemished except for three small holes in the chest and stomach. How would the body look, the lieutenant wondered, after the shotgun blast?

The captain replied. "No, Gunny," he said, lightly, as if it made little difference one way or the other. "No, I don't think we'll do it." His eyes remained averted, not looking at the gunny.

The gunny simply stood there, his helmet covered with leaves and branches. It looked like a heavy tribal headdress above his thin, pale face. His expression didn't change at all. The lieutenant put the safety back on the shotgun he was carrying and turned away.

The lieutenant had changed his mind. Now he thought it was lucky that the captain had made him write up the gunny. He couldn't tell the parents about the write-up, but he could paraphrase from it to help him with the letter. He walked across the base camp to the company office and asked Corporal Henry for a copy of the citation.

Corporal Henry grimaced. He was a twenty-year-old marine who usually wore the pained, suffering expression of someone much older. "Didn't you take it back to work on?" he said. "I haven't seen it around here since you brought it in."

"You mean you haven't typed it up yet and sent it out?" Another clerk nearby looked up at the lieutenant.

"No, sir," Henry said. "We've been doing nothing but these record books. We're about a month behind. I thought you took it back to work on it some more."

"I thought you did, too, Lieutenant"—it was Peaches, one of Henry's assistants. He had red cheeks and looked and sounded about twelve years old. He always agreed with Henry, the lieutenant knew.

"It was finished! It was finished when I gave it to you—you should have sent it out two weeks ago."

"I don't think it's here, Lieutenant," Henry said. "It could've got lost; we've had so much work to do—"

"*Lost!* Are you shitting me?"

The two clerks regarded the lieutenant warily. He realized they had never seen him angry before.

Peaches said, "We typed up all the other write-ups and sent them out, sir, the ones from Medea—"

"I don't give a *damn* about them. I want to know where this one is." The lieutenant glanced over at the first sergeant's empty lawn chair, then back at Henry. "Where's the first sergeant?"

"I don't know, sir," Henry said. "He's not here."

"I know he's not here."

The lieutenant left the tent and went back to his own and told the captain what had happened.

"Goddamnit, that makes me mad!" The captain glared at the lieutenant. "This isn't the first time those turds have lost something. But it's never their fault—no, they think they're kings over there. I'm going to take them out on patrol one of these days and see how they like *that*." He picked up his helmet. "I'm going to find the first sergeant. He needs a good boot in the ass, and it's about time he got it." He left the tent.

The lieutenant smiled. His own anger was gone now. He had heard the captain talk like that before, about "those turds" in the office and how he was going to take them out on patrol; how he would give the first sergeant a "boot in the ass." Yet things hadn't changed. The clerks still acted as if they had the hardest jobs in the company; they were always behind in their work.

A day later the write-up remained lost and the captain told the lieutenant he would have to do it all over again. The lieutenant went to his tent and tried to reconstruct what he had written the last time. He wrote a few sentences, but they didn't seem as good. He tore off the sheet of paper and stared vacantly at the pad.

Suddenly pictures appeared in his mind: of marines lying in an enemy minefield, wounded and dying; of corpsmen saying they had no more bandages; of the gunny, a look of determination on his face, coming up to the captain and volunteering to search for an LZ; of the gunny lying beside the LZ, wounded, telling the captain to take the others out first.

The citation took only a few minutes to write. The lieutenant then wrote the letter to the gunny's parents.

That evening he saw the captain in the mess tent.

"I read your new write-up," the captain said.

"What did you think?"

"It's good." The captain sounded matter-of-fact. "But I made a few changes."

"You did what? Sir?"

"Take it easy, Lieutenant. You're not the only one who knows how to write citations—I've done quite a few myself."

"Yes, sir. I understand."

"It was a little *too* good, that's all." Now the captain smiled. "But you did a good job, Jim. I appreciate it."

"I just hope it goes through."

The captain nodded. "It will. I've got a friend at Division Awards in Da Nang and I'm going to write to him. I'll do everything I can. I guarantee you."

The next day the lieutenant stopped by the company office and this time typed up the citation himself.

7: The Captain

The company left the airstrip on patrol early in the morning, just before first light. In the cool, damp air the marines moved through rice paddies and fields and then up into rolling, open hills. The lieutenant stayed near the rear of the column with the mortars.

They passed near a small village that the captain said was supposed to be deserted—in a free-fire zone. He sent one platoon to check it out while the rest of the company remained on a piece of high ground overlooking it.

Suddenly there was firing below. Three shots, then a barrage of automatic-weapons fire.

"Sounds like a sniper," Chapel said. The lieutenant agreed. He recognized the pattern too: first the sniper shots, then the marines returning fire.

Chapel radioed the platoon down in the vill. "One of the men's been hit, Skipper," he reported. "They're putting fire on the hooch where the sniper shot from, but it looks like he's beat it."

"KIA?"

"Affirmative."

The captain swore. He ordered the mortarmen to drop some rounds into the other end of the village and beyond it—where the sniper had possibly fled. The mortar squad had set up as soon as the firing started and they were ready.

"How about some Willie Peter, Skippah?" It was Harris, the mortar squad leader.

"Yeah, goddamnit, give it to them." The captain was angry. "This vill isn't supposed to be here, anyway."

The lieutenant went back to the mortars to watch. The new

gunny was crouched behind them on one knee. He was looking around as though searching for something. His face was pale and his jaws were working hard on the gum he was chewing.

"How're you doing, Gunny?"

"All right, Lieutenant." The gunny didn't look at him.

One of the white-phosphorous rounds plunked down through a thatched roof in the village and exploded. A wisp of white smoke drifted up through the roof and the marines on the high ground cheered. Then flames shot up and the marines cheered again. The captain looked at the lieutenant and grinned mischievously.

Other houses caught fire. A small group of Vietnamese headed out of the village, away from the marines. The lieutenant could faintly hear the high-pitched chattering and squawking of the villagers and their animals.

"This vill isn't supposed to be here, anyway," the captain said again, this time without the anger.

As the platoon returned to the high ground, Chapel radioed for a medevac. It would take awhile, he said, since there was no emergency.

The lieutenant looked at the dead marine as the troops carried him to the LZ. They had him slung in a poncho, propped up, as if to stare back at everyone he passed, except that his eyes were closed. His face looked pale and cold; it seemed like the kind of day it was—chilly, gray, dismal. Below his left eye was a small black hole.

Lieutenant Dobson, the platoon commander, came up toward the lieutenant with the rest of his men.

"Tom," the lieutenant said, "I'm sorry."

Dobson looked up. His face was pale too. "That fucking gook," he said.

After the helicopter took the body out, the company continued the patrol. They set up on a hill for the night. It rained, and when they went back to the airstrip the next day many of the men had colds.

Three days later the captain came back from a briefing with the colonel and his staff and called a meeting of his own. The platoon commanders, the gunny, and the lieutenant sat around him on the ground and on cots, making notes in their small field notebooks. Usually in these meetings the captain spoke in an enthusiastic, aggressive way as he gave them the word on patrols and supplies, assignments and policies; this time he seemed subdued.

"Also," he said, "there will be a memorial service this Sunday for all the men who died on Medea and since then." Actually, there would be three services, he explained—one for officers and staff NCO, and two for enlisted. "Attendance is voluntary, but I'm sure you'll all want to go."

The captain answered questions, and then the three platoon commanders left to hold meetings of their own.

On Sunday the captain, the lieutenant, and the gunny walked across the sand to the mess tent. The sun was out; a break in the monsoon. It was a familiar walk for the lieutenant, but it seemed different this time, as if he were going to church on a cool, bright autumn day, wearing an itchy woolen suit instead of his dirty utilities. The gunny seemed to feel something different too. Usually he talked and joked a lot in the battalion area, but now he was quiet.

The tables had been taken out of the mess tent and the benches were now arranged like pews in a church. The captain and the lieutenant sat together in the back row, the gunny up front. The captain bowed his head and prayed. In a few minutes all the benches were filled.

The battalion chaplain began the service by reading a passage from the Bible. Immediately the lieutenant wanted to smile at the sight of the bald, red-faced padre, now wearing a white-and-violet robe over his utilities. Scuffed-up boots were visible beneath the padre's robe. The lieutenant liked the padre; he considered him one of his friends in the battalion. Sometimes the padre would visit the lieutenant with leftover communion wine and they'd discuss war and religion. Sometimes the first sergeant would join them, and then he and the padre would tell stories about the battalion executive officer, a major who shaved his head every day and talked very slowly in a voice so low it could barely be heard. They called him "Bald Eagle."

The lieutenant realized he hadn't been listening to the sermon. He stopped smiling.

". . . And may we remember them as loyal, faithful marines who died in the service of their country, as men who fought with honor in the most difficult of times, who failed

not the challenge before them. May we continue to fight with
honor, to meet the many tests. . . ."

In spite of the formal wording the padre spoke in his usual
straightforward, almost singsong tone, not like a priest at all.
He sounded more like a graduate student, the lieutenant
thought—one who liked to hang around with jocks. Once,
after a few glasses of wine, the padre had told the lieutenant
that he wished he were allowed to go out on patrol and carry
a rifle like everyone else.

The padre bowed his head to pray.

". . . And forgive us our sins, through Christ our Lord.
Amen."

He sat down and the regimental chaplain got up. He was a
tall, thin, middle-aged man with long, gangly arms and large
eyeglasses. A Protestant minister, he wore a white robe with
black trim over his utilities. He also began by reading from
the Bible. He sounded much more like a proper chaplain than
the padre, with his dignified, ceremonial tone. The lieutenant
noticed that his boots had been shined. He remembered
something the padre had told him about this chaplain: he was
upset about the men receiving pornographic magazines in the
mail. The padre and the lieutenant had had a good laugh at
that. The lieutenant had met this chaplain once, just after
they had both first arrived in the country. How long ago had
that been? The lieutenant counted the months and weeks,
and it seemed as though it had been much, much longer.

The chaplain was now beginning his prayer. The lieutenant
realized that he had hardly heard his sermon either. That was
the way it had always been when he was younger and went to
church with his parents; his mind would wander.

". . . And give us the strength and courage to see us
through these difficult times. Amen."

The two chaplains announced they would each hold communion. The first row got up and formed two lines. The
lieutenant noticed that the gunny fell into the padre's line.

The lieutenant turned to look at the captain. He was staring
straight ahead and tears moved slowly down his cheek. The
lieutenant turned back and faced the front. The officers and
sergeants were coming up the aisle now, finished with the
bread and wine. Most of them were crying too.

It was the turn of the lieutenant's row. He moved his knees
aside and let the captain and others go by.

Then it was over. The mess sergeant had set up coffee and doughnuts at the rear of the tent and the officers and sergeants were standing around, shaking hands with one another and talking in low, respectful voices. The lieutenant got a cup of coffee and lit a cigarette. At the side of the table stood the padre. He had taken off his robe and now he looked like any other officer except for the cross on his collar.

"Padre," the lieutenant said. They shook hands.

"What did you think?" the padre said. "How did it go?"

"Great," the lieutenant said. "It was a good service."

"Really? Did you think so?" The padre smiled, showing a mouth full of crooked teeth. "How was my sermon?"

"Real good," the lieutenant said. "I liked it."

"Thanks." The padre nodded. "Yes, I think it went all right." He spoke in his direct, slightly singsong manner.

The lieutenant smiled and thought of saying something about the regimental chaplain's polished boots, but the padre's eyes left the lieutenant and darted around the tent. Then the lieutenant realized that Bald Eagle was standing behind him, waiting to speak to the padre. The lieutenant moved aside and the XO stepped forward and shook the padre's hand. Other officers lined up behind him.

The lieutenant joined the three other lieutenants from his company, who were standing on the fringe of the group by themselves.

"You lost some men, didn't you—on Medea?" It was Lieutenant Dobson.

The lieutenant nodded.

Dobson shook his head. "I heard that was pretty bad. How many did you lose?"

"Three."

Dobson shook his head again. "That's rough. I know—I've lost only one and that's bad enough. Casey." He said the name as though it held special meaning.

The lieutenant nodded.

"How does it feel, anyway, to be XO? I mean, not to have a platoon any more—don't you miss it? They're such great kids."

The lieutenant tried to think of what to say. He glanced at the other two lieutenants, who hadn't lost a single man yet. Then he noticed that Dobson wasn't listening, but was waving to his platoon sergeant.

The lieutenant went to get a doughnut and then stood off by himself. The doughnut was glazed and tasted fresh. The talk was becoming louder; it was beginning to sound like a party. The lieutenant lit a cigarette. Suddenly he felt that it was wrong to be standing alone. He walked over and told the mess sergeant how good the doughnut was. Then he saw the captain.

"Ready to go, Skipper?"

The captain nodded.

"Should we get the gunny?"

"No," the captain said. "Actually, there's something I want to talk to you about, Jim. Alone."

They headed across the flat, sandy area toward their tent. The sun was still out and it was almost hot. The lieutenant felt relieved—the way he used to feel after church; as though he could now go home and take off his Sunday clothes.

"There was something else the colonel talked to me about after that last briefing that I haven't told you," the captain said.

"Oh?"

"He said I may be losing the company."

"What?" Both men stopped. "Why, Skipper?"

The captain looked hard at the lieutenant. "The colonel thinks I set fire to that vill on purpose—because of the sniper."

"But that vill . . . you said it was supposed to be deserted —that it was in a free-fire zone."

"Yeah, well, they were talking about making it one. I guess I jumped the gun."

"Oh."

The captain took a deep breath, then let it out. He looked down at the ground. "The colonel says there may be an investigation. Word got back to regiment. Apparently some villager got killed—by one of our mortar rounds."

"What?"

"Yeah. Some woman. It could mean a court-martial. Maybe jail. The end of my career, anyway."

They were silent.

"*Damn it!* What am I supposed to do? Just keep losing men to snipers and mines? I didn't *have* to fight this war. Do they want people to serve over here or not? I never meant to kill any villager." His eyes were watery.

"I believe you, Skipper. I know you didn't mean it. I'll tell them."

They started toward the tent again.

"Anyway," the captain said, "I just wanted to tell you—I mean, there are other companies in the battalion that need lieutenants. If you want a platoon again, I can arrange it."

The lieutenant thought for a moment. "No, Skipper," he said, but the captain seemed not to hear him.

"I mean," the captain continued, "maybe I took you away from your platoon too soon; maybe I was a little selfish. But it's hard, sometimes, running a company—as much as I've loved it. I know I've made some mistakes . . . What I mean is, you've been a help."

"Thank you, Skipper," the lieutenant said.

Later that day the gunny told the lieutenant what he had heard: almost none of the company's enlisted men had gone to the service.

"What? Are you sure, Gunny?"

The gunny nodded. "Yes, sir, that's what the platoon sergeants told me." He stared at the lieutenant, chewing his gum, as if waiting for an answer. The lieutenant didn't say anything. He thought to himself that he had been right when he told the captain he didn't want a platoon again.

Two days later the captain returned from battalion head-quarters and told the gunny to summon the platoon com-manders for a meeting in his tent.

When the gunny had left the captain said to the lieutenant, "Well, this is it: the colonel just told me I'm leaving."

"What? Is there going to be an investigation?"

"Negative." The captain smiled. "It's all right. They smoothed it over with the locals and regiment is going to drop it. Apparently they gave the family a bunch of money. It's going to be a free-fire zone, anyway."

"Then why do you have to leave?"

"I'm due to get out of the field, that's all. Hell, I've had the company for over six months, and that's more than a lot of captains get. They've got captains stacked up in the rear waiting to get a company—if they get back from Vietnam without that in their record books, they've had it as far as making major is concerned." He said he was going to a desk job in Da Nang. "But I'll get back to the field after a while. Some way."

His orders had already been cut, he said, and he was leaving the next day.

After the meeting with the platoon commanders, the captain gave the lieutenant a list of men he wanted written up for medals. Sergeant Harris, the mortar squad leader, was on the list, and so was Chapel, the captain's radioman. The lieutenant suggested Sergeant Jackson, his old platoon sergeant, and the captain agreed to include him. The captain also put Corporal Henry on the list.

"What?" the lieutenant said. "That turd?"

"That's affirmative," the captain said, laughing. "Seriously, he's done a good job—in spite of all I say about him. He works his ass off and you know how much help he gets from the first sergeant."

Early the following morning a marine came into the tent. He was wearing a new flak jacket and utility trousers.

"I'm Captain Reynolds," he said. He shook hands with the captain, the lieutenant, and the gunny. He was younger than the old captain, and shorter and stockier.

"Welcome to Charlie Company," the captain said. "I hope you enjoy running it as much as I did."

The captain said he wanted to show Captain Reynolds the company's positions around the airstrip. "You come along too," he said to the lieutenant.

The three of them went outside. It was a cool, overcast, windy day; it felt as though winter were coming. At each bunker along the lines the captain introduced the new captain to the troops. All the men were friendly and respectful, although a few seemed not to know that the old captain was leaving. While they walked the captain told Reynolds about company personnel:

"The first sergeant is kind of a special problem," he said. "I guess I never really cracked down on him. But he's so damn easy to like—he's one of the funniest men I've ever met. And you have to remember, he had no experience at running a company office before this."

The new captain nodded.

"I'm not sure about our new gunny," the captain said, sounding a little embarrassed. "He hasn't had any experience in the field—which is kind of strange for a marine with nineteen years in. But I've been trying not to judge him too soon. I think he'll come around."

As they approached the last bunker on the lines the captain turned to the lieutenant and said, "How about leaving Captain Reynolds and me alone so we can have a few words to ourselves."

"Aye, aye, sir."

The lieutenant walked back toward his tent. A fine drizzle was coming down now and the wind was blowing both drizzle and sand into his face, making him lower his head and turn away. He had a feeling that he was in a different country; someplace far to the north where nobody had ever been before, on a kind of expedition; and that it wasn't sand and drizzle blowing in his face but snow—there was snow all around.

Why hadn't the captain told the truth about the gunny? the lieutenant wondered. Why hadn't he told him that all the gunny did was chew gum and write letters to his wife, talk about retirement, and make jokes about himself? That every time firing broke out, he froze up?

The lieutenant wondered what the captain was saying about him. *"Maybe I took him away from his platoon too soon . . . hasn't really been tested as a leader in battle yet . . . kind of distant from the men, keeps things to himself. . . .He's been a help, though. . . ."* The lieutenant arrived at the tent and found the gunny sitting on his cot reading *Stars and Stripes*. He asked the lieutenant how it was outside.

The two captains returned. The old captain shook hands with the new one and then with the lieutenant and the gunny.

"We're going to miss you," the lieutenant said.

Suddenly the captain grinned. It was a clownish grin, under his pushed-in nose. "I'll miss you too," he said, "It's going to be tough back there—steak every Sunday, O-club every night, sheets and blankets to sleep on. I'm really sorry to be leaving—ha-ha-ha!" He laughed in a rush, as though beating the lieutenant to it.

He wished everyone good luck and left.

8: Con Thien

The new captain came back from a briefing at the battalion CP with word that the battalion was going to move again.

"Okinawa, sir?" the gunny said. "Or maybe Hawaii?" He laughed, chewing his gum.

The captain shook his head. "Looks like it's our turn to spend a month in the barrel."

"Sir?" The gunny raised his eyebrows.

"Con Thien."

The gunny stopped smiling.

"What's the matter, Gunny?" The captain looked amused. "What do you think we're here for anyway?" He turned to the lieutenant. "Right?"

"Right, Skipper." The lieutenant forced a smile.

The captain sent the gunny to tell the platoon commanders that there would be a meeting. "Actually," he said to the lieutenant, "I was a little scared myself when the colonel told us. But what the hell, we don't have much choice."

The lieutenant nodded. He was still thinking of the pictures he had seen in newspapers and magazines of Con Thien: the gaunt faces of the marines staring out from under their helmets; their haunted, hunted-animal looks. He remembered reading about the hundreds of rounds of incoming the men there had been taking every day. What was that like, he wondered—to live each moment knowing one might die the next? It seemed to the lieutenant that now he was finally going to experience the real war. It was wrong to be afraid, he told himself. As the captain said, what were they here for anyway?

The other lieutenants came into the tent and the captain

gave them the word. They were quiet at first, but after the news had sunk in there was a lot of talk about what it was going to be like. "From what I hear," the captain said, "they're not taking as much incoming up there as they were. It sounds like we're going to spend a lot of time sitting around in bunkers. We'll be running a few patrols too."

It was almost Thanksgiving, and Lieutenant Dobson suggested that if they were still up there for Christmas, maybe they'd get a big newspaper write-up or a story on one of the networks: "Christmas at Con Thien."

After the meeting the lieutenant found Cao Tri, the company's Kit Carson scout, and told him about the move. Cao Tri frowned; his eyes narrowed. "Con Thien—bad place," he said. "Too many North Vietnamese."

The lieutenant told him he didn't have to go, but that if he didn't he would be assigned to another battalion.

Cao Tri's forehead wrinkled. "But *Thieu-uy*, I want to stay with the company."

"Then you have to go to Con Thien."

Cao Tri shook his head. "I don't want to go. Con Thien bad place."

The lieutenant said he was sorry, but that he understood.

The battalion spent the following two days getting ready for the move. They packed most of their gear in seabags to be left behind in storage tents. Not all the battalion was going. The first sergeants, supply sergeants, and company clerks were staying, along with part of headquarters. They would make up battalion rear.

The lieutenant was given a new map and the captain pointed out their new location. NUI CON THIEN, it said in the same small lettering as the other features around it, as though it were no place special. Three kilometers to the northeast, the lieutenant saw, was a broken line: DEMILITARIZED ZONE.

The next morning they loaded up on trucks. One marine was missing—Private Foster, the same man who had gone UA before Operation Medea.

The lieutenant was standing next to one of the trucks when Cao Tri came up to him. He had his pack on his back and was wearing a helmet and flak jacket. A transistor radio was slung over one shoulder.

"I want to go, *Thieu-uy*. I want to stay with the company."

"Are you sure, Cao Tri?"

Cao Tri nodded. "But Con Thien is a bad place," he said, frowning. Then he shrugged and giggled.

The trucks headed north on Highway One. They passed the huge, sprawling marine base of Dong Ha, and then the village of the same name. The main street of the town was crowded with Vietnamese soldiers in many different uniforms —regular utilities, jungle utilities, camouflage-striped ones. And they wore many different head coverings—helmets, soft covers, berets of various colors. Some of the soldiers walked down the street holding hands. There was the same strong odor—burning wood, cheap tobacco, animal dung—that all villages seemed to have.

Then the trucks turned west on Highway Nine and soon they were out in the countryside. It was overcast and cool. In rice paddies villagers in bamboo hats waded with their pants rolled up, showing tanned, sinewy legs. For a while the road followed a wide river and on the opposite bank were tall palm trees and low houses. They looked pleasant, the lieutenant thought, like vacation homes. He thought of one day coming back when the war was over, when he wouldn't have to worry all the time. Cao Tri told him that wealthy Vietnamese used to come up here to hunt tigers.

They turned right off Route Nine and headed north again. There were no villages now and most of the hooches along the road looked deserted. The trucks passed through the Washout, a muddy shantytown outpost full of dirt-covered marines. These men had the look of slum residents, bored and defiant at the same time. The men in the lieutenant's truck talked about the night the Washout had been overrun. An NVA sapper unit had broken through the perimeter and swarmed over the position, shooting, yelling in English, throwing grenades. Almost all the marines were killed or wounded. By the following morning the NVA had withdrawn, as they always did.

Suddenly the lieutenant saw the brown hill, low and wide, right in the middle of flat land, like a solitary hump. NUI CON THIEN. As the trucks got closer he could see the sandbagged bunkers and piles of boxes that covered it. It looked like a junkyard.

They stopped a hundred meters short and the marines jumped down, spread out, and headed toward the hill. A

Chinook helicopter, camouflage-painted, flew by with a cargo net hanging from beneath it, only a few feet above the ground. The chopper reached the hill, dropped the net, and then flew away, still very low.

"That's so the gooks on the other side won't spot it," Chapel said. "If they did they'd call in arty."

The marines passed through an opening in the barbed wire. Another group of marines, also spread out, came down the hill toward them. It was like a mirror image, except that the other marines' utilities looked brown instead of green. They shouted to the new battalion about what a nice place Con Thien was, then went through the barbed wire and boarded the trucks. The lieutenant wondered when the incoming would begin.

At Con Thien everyone lived in bunkers. Along the lines around the base of the hill were three- and four-man sand-bagged bunkers. They were small and cramped, and too low to stand up in. The company command bunker was bigger and was located away from the lines, up on the ridge that ran along the top of Con Thien hill. It had a wooden floor and a ceiling seven feet high, two electric lights, and enough room for nine cots. The captain chose the lieutenant, the gunny, his two radiomen, the company corpsman, two supply workers, and Cao Tri to sleep there. The captain, the lieutenant, and the gunny slept on one side, and on the other, separated by a partial wall of sandbags, were the enlisted man and Cao Tri. In one corner was a large cardboard box filled with cans of C rations left by the previous tenants. There was also a sack of onions.

The first evening the lieutenant heard a couple of *crack*s outside, not very loud.

"There it is," Chapel said. He was standing by the door-way.

The lieutenant went over and peered out. There were cries of *"Incoming!"* from all over the hill. At the helicopter landing zone near the bottom of the hill marines ran for bunkers. The lieutenant heard a quick, shrill whistling noise, then more *crack*s.

"Damn," Chapel said, shaking his head, "sure am glad I'm up here." There was the sound of artillery going out.

It rained that night and all the next day and the hill turned to mud. After a few days, everybody's clothes were filthy. When it wasn't raining the enlisted men worked outside, filling sandbags to reinforce the roof of the company command bunker; they also put them around the one-hole shitter nearby. The captain said he wanted to crap in peace.

The men never strayed far from their bunkers. There was incoming every day, but mostly at the other end of the ridge by the battalion CP and the artillery spotters, or down below by the helicopter landing zones. Sometimes there'd be hits along the lines too.

The lieutenant had little to do. Sometimes he asked Cao Tri to give him lessons to improve his Vietnamese. He also discovered a bookcase full of paperbacks in the aid station, and he brought several science-fiction novels back to his bunker.

Several days after they'd arrived at Con Thien the lieutenant was lying on his cot reading when there was a deep rumble and the bunker seemed to shake.

"What's that?" He sat up straight.

Chapel, at the doorway, said, "Over there, Lieutenant."

The lieutenant went over to the door. North of the hill, in the direction of the DMZ, a row of gray puff balls rose up from the reddish brown terrain. It looked like a scene from a distant planet, the lieutenant thought, some strange, fast-growing vegetation springing up from a desolate landscape.

"Arclight," Chapel said. "B-fifty-two strike."

"But where are the planes?"

"You can't see them, they're too high up. It's all done by computer." They kept looking. Another row of gray puff balls rose up.

"Damn," Chapel said, "wouldn't want to be out there." He and the lieutenant looked at each other and grinned.

On Thanksgiving Day helicopters flew in hot chow—turkey and stuffing, mashed potatoes and gravy, peas—and one by one the platoons of the lieutenant's company lined up next to one of the helicopter landing zones and ate. It was a cool, overcast day, and everybody listened for incoming. The captain and the lieutenant went last.

Otherwise, the marines ate C rations in their bunkers. Each man in the company command bunker had a bottle of hot sauce that he used to spice up his meals. Cao Tri always added a lot to his. Chapel, who managed to stay pudgy even on a C ration diet, took onions from the sack hanging in the corner and chopped them with his bayonet to add to his dinners. The large box containing leftover C rations became full of cans of ham and lima beans that nobody wanted.

In the evening the enlisted men would sit together on their side of the bunker, eating dinner, and talk about high school days, girlfriends, boot camp; about the cars they used to own and the ones they were going to buy with all the money they'd have saved up when they got home: Chargers, Malibus, Sting Rays, XKE's. They talked about how much they hated Vietnam and the Marine Corps—"the Crotch," "the Green Motherfucker." Except Chapel, who admitted he was thinking of going to Officers Candidate School and making a career of it. None of the men seemed to hold that against Chapel, who had been to college almost three years and who seemed to know more about any subject, including cars, than anyone else. Besides, he said he was only thinking about it.

Chapel's best friend in the company, Richman, a supply worker, lived in the bunker too, and whenever he or Chapel got a letter from home they'd always read it aloud to the other. They both received copies of their hometown newspapers and they'd read them to each other too. Chapel was from North Carolina and Richman from Texas, but to listen to them one would think they had grown up together and knew everyone in each other's letters and newspapers.

Once Chapel got a letter from his girlfriend saying she was breaking their engagement, that she had found a new boyfriend. He read aloud to Richman:

". . . I know it seems cruel, but that's the way I feel and I think it's best to tell you now. It hasn't been easy to write this letter. . . ."

"'Hasn't been easy'?" Richman got up and stomped around the bunker, swearing at the girl as though he knew her.

"Damn," Chapel said, shaking his head. His face was red and he looked as if he didn't know whether to laugh or to cry. "I can't *believe* it—she had to wait till I got to Con Thien!"

Cao Tri would sit with the enlisted men and giggle when they talked, as though he understood what they were saying. Sometimes they'd teach him swear words and he'd giggle even more; it sounded as if he were being tickled. But when he played his transistor radio too loud, they'd yell at him, saying they hated gook music.

On the other side of the bunker the captain and the lieutenant would sometimes talk about the war. The captain had read a book about the French in Indochina, and he thought that the Americans were making the same mistake as the French in not being mobile enough. The lieutenant thought the problem was dedication: make everyone stay until the war was over, he said, and then they'd fight it differently. But mostly they'd play gin rummy and talk about college days and sports. The gunny wrote letters to his wife and played solitaire.

At night the lieutenant would lie awake on his cot and listen. The marine weapons on the hill fired on and off throughout the night. Each weapon had its own sound and by the end of the first week the lieutenant knew each one. The mortars and artillery were the most frequent. The mortars were loud pops or even *bong*s, while the artillery was deeper and heartier. The tanks fired with roars and the recoilless rifles were *crack*s, like the sound of incoming, but louder. There wasn't much incoming at night; the enemy seemed to know it would be wasted.

There were also sounds inside the bunker. Snores and the sound of men turning over and words spoken in sleep. A rat might be heard scurrying across the floor. There were high-pitched *bleep*s on the radio and the crackle of voices reporting that everything was all right. Suddenly the captain would shout, "Who's on watch?" and a voice would say, "I am, sir," and give a name. Sometimes in the morning the captain wouldn't remember calling out.

One night the lieutenant got up, put on his helmet and flak jacket and went outside. With the sky completely covered with clouds, it was pitch dark; it was the darkest night the lieutenant had ever seen. It was cold, too; not just cool, but colder than anyone knew it got up here, he thought.

He moved into the blackness and felt with his foot for the piss tube sticking out of the ground. He could hear the firing—a *bong* here, a pop there, and *crack*s and roars; they sounded louder out here, clearer. He gave up searching for the tube and took a piss anyway.

He looked into the blackness and suddenly it seemed as if

everybody else on the hill were asleep. The weapons were firing by themselves; only they and the lieutenant were awake. He felt lucky to be here: as though he were in a very special place, like the top of the world, a place where something very special was going to happen.

Then he moved toward the bunker and the spell seemed to vanish. He thought about incoming. For a moment he was afraid he might not be able to find the bunker; then he touched the wall and found the door, went inside, took off his flak jacket and helmet and got back into bed.

One afternoon the lieutenant was sitting in the bunker reading a science-fiction novel, when Chapel called over to him that Bravo Company had made contact with the NVA while out on patrol. "It sounds like they're in trouble," Chapel said. He was sitting in the corner of the bunker by the radio. "One of their squads is pinned down. They're taking casualties."

The lieutenant went over to the radioman; the captain and the other enlisted men in the bunker had gathered around too, listening carefully, as though to an important baseball or football game. Cao Tri sat on his cot listening as intently as the rest. Bravo's company commander was giving his platoon commanders instructions, trying to maneuver his men so the pinned-down squad could move back to the rest of the company. His voice, aggressive and husky, sounded like a voice from a war movie as he shouted, swore, pleaded, and exhorted his men. *Come on, Bravo Two—keep putting out that goddamn fire—you hear me? . . . What's the matter, Bravo Three—afraid of a few lousy gooks? . . . All right, all right, Two Alpha, calm down, we'll get you out of there. . . . Go ahead—shout! Let the sons of bitches hear you!*

The further down the chain of command in the company, the less confident the voices sounded. The leader of the pinned-down squad sounded the worst: desperate, almost hysterical. In the background were the sounds of weapons firing, explosions, screams for help.

Then another squad got pinned down trying to help the first. In the bunker the enlisted men swore. The captain had his map out, getting a fix on the enemy's position in case headquarters ordered them to go out and help. The lieutenant lit another cigarette. On the radio the voices got louder.

The company commander ordered a platoon to move ahead. A squad leader, nearly crying, said that another of his men had been killed.

A tank arrived, then another. The marines in the bunker cheered; Cao Tri giggled. Finally the NVA pulled back and the pinned-down squads were able to disengage. The company put their dead and wounded on the tanks and the Bravo company commander announced that they were all returning to the hill.

The next day the lieutenant's company had to run its first patrol. Before daylight the men assembled near the opening in the barbed wire. They were supposed to maintain silence, but there was a lot of swearing as they stumbled around in the mud. Once outside on the road, however, the going was better, the road had been built by marine engineers and had a rock foundation. There was a little light now and the lieutenant felt good to be out and moving around.

They patrolled all morning without making contact, and in the afternoon stopped to eat and rest at the last checkpoint on their route, a large grassy area bordered by tall trees and crisscrossed by elevated hedgerows. AGRICULTURAL DEVELOPMENT CENTER, it said on the map. Now there were fresh bomb craters all around. "Arclight," Chapel said. Some of the craters were over ten meters across.

The lieutenant set up a perimeter defense and put some men up in trees to act as lookouts. One of the marines on the ground called out that he had found some fighting holes in the embankments—it looked like a network of enemy bunkers, now abandoned. The lieutenant told the captain, and the captain gave orders for the men to check them out.

The lieutenant joined two of the marines in their search. They came to a cave that had been partially destroyed, a dozen mortar rounds lay in the dirt. A marine picked one up and showed it to the lieutenant: Chinese markings. A few feet away, in the side of the embankment, was a hole about two feet square. One of the marines took a flashlight and crawled into it. He came out with a poncho and a pair of boots. He went back in and came out holding something stringy and black. The three of them stared at it.

"Hair," the marine said. He went in again and brought out what looked like yellow pebbles. "Teeth."

"Is that all?" the lieutenant asked.

The marine nodded. "The bunker wasn't damaged at all, Lieutenant; must've been the concussion that got him." He looked at the bomb crater on the other side of the embankment. "Must have been a hell of a concussion, if it knocked out his hair and teeth. I heard the NVA up here get doped up a lot; now I see why. You think an animal or something ate the rest of him?"

The lieutenant nodded. "Could be. I've heard there are tigers up here."

He went to tell the captain of their discoveries. Just then another marine called out that he had found a body. The lieutenant and the captain went over to take a look.

It was lying in the open, face down, at the bottom of a partially blown away embankment. The body was dressed in a full set of utilities including combat boots. It was all covered with dirt, and looked itself to be part of the earth, like a fossil. The captain told one of the marines to check for a weapon. The marine found a long stick, reached down and turned the body over as if handling a snake. There was movement all over its chest.

"Jesus Christ, what is it?"

There was silence. Then a marine said, "Maggots." There was no weapon and they all turned away.

The lieutenant told the captain about the mortar rounds and hair and teeth they'd found.

"That's good," the captain said. "We'll take that stuff back and turn it in to battalion. This is what they want to know, whether these arclights are doing any good."

A half hour later they set out again on their patrol route and returned to the hill without making contact. But they took one casualty: a marine who sprained his ankle climbing down from a tree.

One morning the lieutenant woke and felt sick. He asked the corpsman to check him over.

"You've got a pretty high fever, Lieutenant. A lot of men have been coming down with something—it's staying in these bunkers all the time and not getting any sunshine. You'd better go to the aid station and get some penicillin."

The next day the company was to run another patrol. The

lieutenant woke early in the morning with the others, and the corpsman took his temperature. It was still high. The captain ordered him back to bed.

Later he woke again. His fever was gone and he felt better. He made himself a C ration breakfast of scrambled eggs and onions, the way Cao Tri had taught him, and then he went outside. He looked in the direction he knew the company had gone but of course couldn't see them. He went back inside and took his Vietnamese phrase book from under his cot. He read a page and then put it back and took out the science-fiction novel he'd been reading. He read. It was about a war in the future, in America after a nuclear holocaust. Indians and the white men were fighting again. There weren't any guns and the Indians were winning. They knew the land, they could see better at night, the animals were their friends.

The lieutenant thought of the company out there. Would this be the patrol on which they ran into the NVA? Was the lieutenant missing the experience he had come here for? He imagined the captain giving orders in a war-movie voice, swearing; the frantic voices of pinned-down squad leaders, hysterical cries of dying men, confusion, nobody able to see the enemy. Would the lieutenant know what to do? He thought about the high-powered rifles each side would try to shoot the other with, the mortar and artillery rounds coming in, the tanks that would finally arrive. The NVA would pull back, the company would disengage, the dead and wounded would ride back. Battalion headquarters would mark the area for an arclight and soon the planes would fly over, too high to see; a computer would release the bombs and gray puff balls would rise from the land. And then they'd see the enemy: some hair and teeth. The lieutenant turned back to his book.

The company returned from the patrol. The bunker seemed to change completely. There were the sounds of boots stomping and marines swearing; the smell of sweat.

"How'd it go, Skipper?"

The captain's pants and boots were covered with mud. His cheeks were red and he seemed fresh, healthy, full of energy.

"Shitty," he said. "Ran into a minefield. Tripped two, took five casualties."

"Any KIA?"

"Negative. Two of them medevacked, but I think they'll be all right—no legs lost or anything like that." He showed the lieutenant on his map where the minefield was.

"Little ones," Chapel said. "Chi-coms, I'll bet—like those ones that Cao Tri dug up that day we got the rice. About the size of a grenade." Cao Tri was standing next to the lieutenant and at the mention of his name he spoke rapidly, scowling.

"Cao Tri's been excited as hell about something," the captain said, smiling at him. "What's he trying to say, anyway?"

The lieutenant asked Cao Tri. "Please, speak more slowly," he said.

"*Thieu-uy*, I knew there were mines. I told the marines— *co min, co min!*"

"But they didn't understand you. They don't know Vietnamese."

"No, no, no—they understood. I know. But they laughed at me."

The lieutenant told the captain what Cao Tri had said.

The captain swore. "I'd like to know who those men were. Hell, *I* would've listened to him. That's a real shame."

The lieutenant agreed. He pictured himself out there, shouting at the company to freeze and nobody getting hurt. He told Cao Tri that the captain appreciated what he had tried to do and that the captain was angry at the marines who wouldn't listen.

"Thank you, *Thieu-uy*," Cao Tri said, but he still seemed dissatisfied when he walked away.

The next day the lieutenant asked Cao Tri to give him a Vietnamese lesson. They sat on the lieutenant's cot and went down a vocabulary list the lieutenant had made up from his phrase books, discussing what each word meant.

Cao Tri was usually easy to understand, the lieutenant thought, unlike most of the villagers he had met. Occasionally, though, the lieutenant couldn't understand him, and then Cao Tri would squint his eyes and twist his mouth up, trying to think of another way to express himself.

After they finished the lieutenant told Cao Tri again that the captain felt bad about the marines' not paying attention to him on the last patrol. "How did you know it was a minefield?" he asked.

"That's what I did," Cao Tri said, smiling, "when I was a VC." He seemed proud.

"How old were you when you joined the VC?"

"Fifteen."

"What were you doing before that?"

"Working in the rice fields."

"Why did you join the VC?"

"They forced me to."

"Why did you leave the VC and fight with us?"

Cao Tri hesitated. He turned away from the lieutenant and twisted up his mouth and squinted, as if trying to think of something the lieutenant would understand.

He got up, turned, and faced the lieutenant, as if preparing to recite. His head was very wide and it looked almost as wide as his shoulders. With the palms of his hands Cao Tri patted his jungle utility shirt and his jungle utility trousers; then he squatted and patted his jungle boots. He pointed to his M-16 rifle leaning against a wall and to his transistor radio next to it and to the carton of Salem cigarettes next to that. He turned and pointed to the large cardboard box full of extra C rations. Then he stood up again and looked at the lieutenant, shrugged, and grinned.

The lieutenant looked quickly around the bunker to see whether anyone had seen. Then he remembered that nobody could understand them anyway. He thought about saying something to Cao Tri, something about purpose and causes, but he decided not to—not now. Cao Tri was only sixteen years old, he thought, and was too young to know better.

Three days before Christmas the captain came back from the battalion CP with word that the battalion was scheduled to leave Con Thien in two days.

"Back to the airstrip, Skipper?" the lieutenant asked.

"Negative. Hill Twenty-five." The captain said he wanted the lieutenant to leave early—that very day—so he could coordinate the company's move with battalion rear.

By late afternoon the lieutenant was ready to leave.

"Have a good trip," the captain said, smiling. "Don't let the first sergeant drink too much."

"Right, Skipper."

The lieutenant walked down the hill to the opening in the barbed wire and in a few minutes a truck came by and picked him up. They drove south, passing the Washout, then turned east on Route Nine. Farmers worked in rice paddies, bent over. The village of Dong Ha was still crowded with Vietnamese soldiers.

At the airstrip the lieutenant jumped down from the truck and made his way to the company tent.

"Hello, there, First Sergeant."

The first sergeant looked up from his desk where he was packing papers into a carton.

"Oh, hello, Lieutenant. What brings you here?" His voice was squeaky.

"Captain sent me down early—to coordinate with battalion rear. Guess you've heard about the battalion moving again."

"Yes, sir, we've been trying to get ready ourselves. You'd think we'd be good at it by now, with all the practice we've had." He laughed. It was like a chirp.

The lieutenant said hello to Corporal Henry and Peaches.

"How was it up there, Lieutenant?" Peaches asked.

"Terrible," the lieutenant said. "You couldn't crap for a month because it wasn't safe to go outside."

Peaches' face got red.

"You got a place for me to stay, Top?"

"Yes, sir, you can stay with me. There's an extra cot. Go on over and I'll be by soon. I've got a little something I think you'll like." He smiled.

It was cold and drizzly and almost dark. The lieutenant crossed the sand and went into the first sergeant's tent. He lit the Coleman lantern. It was a big tent; the supply sergeant and his helpers and the mail clerk lived there, too. Empty ammo boxes lined the floor and empty C ration tins were scattered around, as well as candles, clothes, magazines, packages of Kool-Aid, and bottles of hot sauce. A rope went from one side of the tent to the other and on it hung sets of utilities and underwear.

The lieutenant took off his flak jacket and helmet and sat in the first sergeant's lawn chair. He sighed. He had been looking forward to that: it was the first time he had sat in a chair in a month. At Con Thien there had been only cots or ammo boxes to sit on, and his back always seemed sore. The first sergeant had bought two of these chairs from a Vietnamese street vendor and he took them with him every time the battalion moved; the other one he kept in the office. They were made of aluminum with wide pieces of striped cloth for the back and seat. The back of this one had a tear and the bottom was sagging, but the chair was still comfortable.

The lieutenant looked through the magazines on the floor. Automobile and adventure magazines—all old, the same ones that had been there before. But under the first sergeant's cot he saw something new—a newspaper from the States. The lieutenant picked it up. It was a Sunday newspaper! He looked at the date; it was a month old. He turned to the sports section; he had read all the football scores before. The magazine section had a picture on the cover of lush foliage. The title was, "A Month with Charlie Company in Vietnam." Quickly the lieutenant looked inside. It was a story about another Charlie Company, an army unit far to the south. He started to read.

The first sergeant came in and the lieutenant got up from the chair.

"Well, Lieutenant," the first sergeant said, "looks like you came by at just the right time. I happened to pass by the airstrip today"—he reached into a pack beneath his cot and brought out a bottle of bourbon—"a little something for the Christmas season." He gave the lieutenant an empty C ration can and poured bourbon into it and did the same for himself. Then he sat down in his chair. He looked like an old lady, the lieutenant thought, with his small round face and glasses, sipping tea in her favorite rocker. The lieutenant smiled and asked the first sergeant how he was getting along with Bald Eagle, and the first sergeant swore and told a story about listening for hours to Bald Eagle explaining how they were going to move. They finished their drinks and had another.

They then went to the mess tent. With most of the battalion at Con Thien it was almost empty, but there was a lot of food: pot roast with mashed potatoes, gravy, and creamed corn. The lieutenant went up for seconds and thirds.

They sat with two other first sergeants from the battalion. One of them winked at the lieutenant and asked the first sergeant whether he had heard from his ex-wife recently.

Immediately the first sergeant hit his fist on the table. "That dumb broad!" he said, and ranted about her and the man she had run away with, his ex-best friend, also a marine. "That dumb shit!" The lieutenant and the two other first sergeants laughed through most of the meal.

After dinner the lieutenant and the first sergeant went back to the tent. Baylor, the supply sergeant, was there now, along with his two helpers and the mail clerk. Baylor was actually a twenty-year-old draftee who had just made corporal. He had a small portable record player that he was listening to at the other end of the tent. The lieutenant recognized the music—it was the only record Baylor had. His wife had given it to him, he had once told the lieutenant, to remember her by.

The first sergeant lit the kerosene heater next to the chair. Then he poured more drinks.

"Those airedales have everything, Lieutenant. I'm going to miss it here." His words were slurred.

The lieutenant smiled. "Say, Top," he said, "did you read about us in that magazine you've got?"

"What's that? Did we get a write-up?"

The lieutenant showed him the Sunday magazine. "Sure, didn't you see it?"

The first sergeant looked at the magazine; wrinkled his forehead, then laughed. His laugh had become louder, throatier. He finished his drink and poured another.

"Did you read that, Lieutenant?" He laughed. "'Charlie Company in Vietnam'—I laughed so hard when I read that I thought I would die! One dumb shit shoots himself in the toe trying to get his pistol out of his holster, another is on patrol going through a village and gets bit by a dog, and the third jumps out of his helicopter too soon and kills himself. And that was their action for the month!" He laughed again and started coughing. He cleared his throat. "And what was that dumb reporter doing, spending a month with them? He must be as screwed up as they are."

The lieutenant laughed, too. The first sergeant sounded just the way he had at dinner when he was talking about his ex-wife.

The first sergeant took another drink and lit a cigarette.

"What do you think, Lieutenant?"

"What?"

"You go out to the field. Do you think we're that screwed up?"

The lieutenant smiled. "No, Top."

"How about Con Thien? What do you think of that?"

"Actually, it wasn't that bad. They're taking a lot less incoming up there now. We were lucky—"

"No—I mean, what did you *think* of it?" Suddenly the first sergeant's voice sounded sharp. The lieutenant tried to look into his eyes, but light reflected off his glasses.

"What do you mean, Top?"

The first sergeant swallowed. "What are we doing in a place like Con Thien? Or here? Or any of these places? We're not supposed to be doing stuff like that—that's the Army's job. We're supposed to go in, fight, and get out." He put his hand over his mouth, then took a sip from his tin. "And if they are going to use us like that, why don't they let us stay in one place long enough to get to know it?"

"You're right, there, Top—"

"Something's wrong, Lieutenant."

The lieutenant frowned and stared at the first sergeant.

"Something's wrong, I can feel it." The first sergeant swallowed. "I've got a theory, Lieutenant."

"What's that, Top?"

"I've got a theory." He raised a finger; his lips were taut. "I think that Vietnam is going to be the end of us."

"What?"

"That's right, Lieutenant."

"What are you talking about, Top?"

"That's my theory. . . . I don't think there's going to *be* a Marine Corps after Vietnam. That's what I think."

"Oh . . . Why do you say that?"

The first sergeant leaned forward and swallowed again. "I see the signs, Lieutenant," he said. "I was in Korea, and I remember what it was like. We didn't have hardly any gear at all, but what we had we took care of. These men here lose something, they just ask for another. That's not right." He drank some more and took a drag on his cigarette. "I'll tell you another thing we never did in Korea, Lieutenant." He put his head down and swallowed several times. He looked as if he were talking to someone lying on the floor.

"What's that, Top?"

The words came out: "We didn't steal from our dead."

"What?"

"That's right. . . ."

"What do you mean, Top?" The lieutenant glanced quickly at Corporal Baylor and his helpers, but they seemed not to be listening.

"I know, Lieutenant . . . I'm the one who gets the bodies ready to send back home. I know what goes on . . . and it's not just money they're after, either. It's drugs too. We never had any drugs in Korea." He put out his cigarette and took off his glasses and now the lieutenant could see his eyes. They were black; they seemed to blaze. His eyebrows jutted forward, and it seemed to the lieutenant that it was a face he had never seen before.

"The Marine Corps has been my home for twenty years, Lieutenant," the first sergeant said, "but I don't think I'm going to have it any more, not after this."

He glared at the lieutenant, then dropped his head.

"You all right, Top?"

"*I'm* all right, Lieutenant," the first sergeant said, and then he got up and walked quickly out of the tent. The lieutenant heard loud retching noises; he waited a moment, then went outside.

"You all right, Top?" The first sergeant was hunched over, still throwing up; he looked like a big black ball in the darkness.

". . . *right* . . ." the first sergeant said.

The lieutenant felt for the piss tube and peed. The first sergeant straightened up, groped for the tent flap, and went back inside. The lieutenant took a few deep gulps of air. It was cold. He went back inside the tent. The first sergeant was lying on his back on his cot; his eyes were closed.

The lieutenant sat down on a cot. Music was coming from the other end of the tent—a sad, bluesy song that sounded tinny on the portable record player; the lieutenant knew the words by heart. He could hear Baylor talking about his wife, about how he used to go UA to see her when he was in the States, how he was taken in handcuffs to the plane for Vietnam. The lieutenant had heard the story before. He glanced over at the first sergeant, who was now snoring. Was the first sergeant right? The lieutenant tried to think of what he had said, tried to form an opinion, but his brain seemed not to be working the way it normally did. He thought about going to bed. No, he thought, not yet; he had looked forward to this evening, his first night back. He got up and moved over to the first sergeant's chair. There was a little bourbon left in the bottle and he poured it into his tin.

9: The NVA

The dead NVA lay in a field south of the deserted village next to the river. A four-man patrol led by the captain had killed him in the early evening.

That morning the daytime patrols had gone out as usual, to the south along the river, to the east through rice paddies, and up into the hills. In the late afternoon they returned to the company CP in the deserted village. None had made contact.

Later, the captain said, "I think I'm going to take a walk." The lieutenant asked what he meant.

"Hell, I'm tired of sitting here all day; I need some exercise. Besides, I've got a feeling we've been setting a pattern—patrols in the daytime, ambushes at night. We never have anything out this time of day."

The lieutenant agreed. Since they had first started working this area—over a month before when they moved from Con Thien to Hill 25—they had had a lot of success: twenty-six KIA's and thirty probables. But in the last week they hadn't got anything.

"Good idea, Skipper." The lieutenant thought it sounded typical of the captain; he had been an athlete in college—a hockey player—and he liked being out in the field.

The captain left the lieutenant in charge of the CP and took Chapel, the radioman, and two marines who volunteered. The four walked south on the main dirt road next to the river. It was just beginning to get dark.

Twenty minutes later firing broke out. The lieutenant turned to his radioman. "What is it?"

"The captain wants us to get down there fast," the radio-

131

man said. "They ran into a couple of NVA and there may be more."

The lieutenant called out, *"Saddle up!"* The marines, leaving C ration tins behind, fell out on the road. The lieutenant called out, *"Double time!"* and they jogged down the road, helmets bouncing.

The captain and the other men were hiding in some bushes by the side of the road. They were all right. One of the enemy had been killed, another had got away. They hadn't seen any more. The captain told the lieutenant to take two platoons and make a sweep in the direction of the river while he took the other platoon south and set up a block. The lieutenant spread his men out on line, and they started to move through wide fields bordered by hedgerows.

The body of the NVA was in the middle of one of the fields. He had been shot in the head. Half his skull was torn off and a part of his brain was lying next to him among the chunks of dirt in the plowed field. From the look on his face it seemed as though he had died in the middle of a scream.

There were a few comments—about what a burst from an M-16 can do, comparisons with past kills—but mostly the men were silent. The lieutenant wondered what message or power they got from staring at an enemy dead, yet he sensed it was important to them, a kind of ritual, and he let them stand there and look.

Only Cao Tri showed any expression. After kneeling down and studying the face and uniform, he turned around and chanted gleefully, *"Bac Viet! Bac Viet!"* The lieutenant told the marines what he had said: "NVA."

They resumed their sweep toward the river. It was completely dark now. The captain radioed that they hadn't seen any sign of the other NVA and ordered all three platoons back to the company CP.

In the evening the captain told the lieutenant how it had happened. The four of them had left the dirt road and were walking south through Tan My, the deserted village, when they heard voices off to their right—Vietnamese voices. They got down behind some bushes and the two appeared some thirty meters away, walking toward them. They were dressed in brown khaki uniforms and were talking and laughing, their weapons at sling arms.

"Holding hands too," the captain said, "like a couple of fairies." He said they must have know the company's pattern, all right—NVA weren't usually caught so off their guard. Suddenly they saw the marines and started to run. The captain opened fire.

"I got him," he said. He told the lieutenant several times how he had taken aim and fired a quick burst that hit one of the NVA's in the middle of a stride; the NVA had fallen dead instantly as the other kept running. "That's my first," the captain said.

The weapon the NVA had been carrying was a Chinese-made submachine gun. It made for a good report to battalion, the captain and the lieutenant agreed: the uniform, the weapon—and no casualties of their own.

"We should have gotten that other one, though," the captain said. Now he sounded dissatisfied. "That was really shitty shooting."

"Damn," Chapel said. "I would've got him, Skipper, but Hobart in front of me blocked my sight just as I was about to fire."

Later, lying on the ground trying to sleep, the lieutenant kept imagining the scene. Why hadn't he thought of it? he asked himself—going out in the early evening, breaking the pattern.

The next morning the body was still in the middle of the field. During the night an ambush had been set near it, but no enemy had approached. Now the captain sent a patrol to check out a shallow bend in the river where he suspected the other NVA might have crossed. The patrol leader asked the captain's permission to booby-trap the body with a hand grenade; the captain said okay. He said to the lieutenant, "I want you and Cao Tri to go up to Nhu Le and see what you can find out. Question the villagers. What were those two NVA doing hanging around down here, anyway? Maybe there's a big unit nearby. Somebody must know something."

The lieutenant said, "How about Tich Tuong?"

The captain shrugged. "If you feel like it."

The sun was out, it looked as if it might be a break in the monsoon. The lieutenant decided not to take his rain suit. He and Cao Tri and a four-man fire team set out north on the dirt

road connecting the three villages that lay along the river—
Tan My, Nhu Le, and Tich Tuong.

They stopped for a while at the edge of Tan My and
questioned villagers walking into the village. Although Tan
My was deserted, its former occupants often returned to the
area during the day to tend their fields and collect belongings
they had left behind. It had been just a week since Tan My
had been abandoned. The battalion civil affairs officer had
told the lieutenant why and how the villagers had decided to
leave: they had become tired of being caught in the middle,
he said—taxed for rice by the VC and NVA, beaten when
they didn't give enough, and victimized by the marines'
artillery and mortars. They had held a meeting and voted to
get out—to go to Tich Tuong, a pro-government village to the
north that had both a Popular Forces platoon and a Revolutionary Development Team—a paramilitary unit sent out
from Saigon to win the people to the government. The vote
had been thirty-three families for the move and five against.

The lieutenant's company had provided security for the
move, setting up along the road between Tan My and Nhu Le.
It was a strange scene: the villagers pulling their dismantled
homes behind them in wooden carts with wheels as tall as
they were. They looked like pioneers, the lieutenant thought
—only going the opposite way, back to civilization. There was
a kind of holiday atmosphere: the marines cheered the
villagers with the biggest carts—like floats in a parade—and
the villagers laughed back. Meanwhile, an Armed Propa-
ganda Team from Quang Tri City, the province capital, made
up of NVA and VC defectors, rounded up villagers from Nhu
Le and gave talks through a portable loudspeaker about the
Saigon government. Not all the villagers had been happy.
Some were weeping loudly. The civil affairs officer, watching
the move with the lieutenant, had told him that they were the
ones who had voted against it. The marines lining the road
had jeered them.

Now none of the villagers Cao Tri talked to said they knew
anything about the dead NVA. The lieutenant and his group
headed north. Along the way they passed the ruins of a small
red-roofed pagoda that had once been used as an ambush
site. The lieutenant noticed empty C ration cans in the
graveyard by the pagoda and made a note to himself to tell
the platoon commanders that their men should be less sloppy.

It was warmer now that the sun was higher, and as they neared Nhu Le the road became crowded with villagers who, the lieutenant figured, were taking advantage of this break in the monsoon. Women descended steep trails from the road to wade out and wash clothes in the river; others carried fruit, vegetables, and firewood, bound for the market in Quang Tri City. The marines smiled, as they usually did, at the way the villagers carried their produce—in baskets hanging from long poles balanced on their shoulders. Old men with white hair and stringy beards, dressed in pajamas, stood by the side of the road and talked to one another, occasionally spitting betel-nut juice. Children begged the Americans for money and cigarettes.

Cao Tri questioned a number of villagers and the lieutenant said hello to some he recognized. This was the longest he had ever been in one area of the country, and he felt he was getting to know the village. He liked the small houses and well-kept yards lined with trees and bushes. Some of the trees bore fruit and sometimes the lieutenant picked a lime or a grapefruit or a piece of fruit he couldn't identify to go with his C rations. Once an old woman who lived on the edge of the village invited him and Cao Tri into her home for a meal. She served them rice and a mushy white root like potato. After they ate she showed the lieutenant a photograph she kept hidden. It was of her son in an ARVN uniform. The lieutenant, at Cao Tri's suggestion, left her some cans of C rations.

According to the civil affairs officer, Nhu Le had once been controlled by the VC, but was contested now. The presence of the marines had driven the VC out to the hills to the east and south, but they still returned at night. The goal of the Americans was to make the village safe enough for the pro-government village chief, who now lived in Quang Tri City, to return.

The lieutenant asked Cao Tri what he had found out.

Cao Tri shook his head and shrugged. "Nothing, *Thieu-uy.*"

They headed north again, past an old French fort overlooking the river, up to the bamboo footbridge on the northern edge of Nhu Le.

Cao Tri turned to the lieutenant and squinted. "*Thieu-uy,* maybe we can find out something in Tich Tuong."

The lieutenant looked across the stream. Tich Tuong meant another half hour walk, and now it was very hot.

"Do you think we should go, Cao Tri?"

Cao Tri shrugged. "I don't care, *Thieu-uy.*"

The lieutenant looked at the four marines who stood by the side of the road holding their rifles. They had worn their rain suits and were sweating. The lieutenant knew they wouldn't be happy about a half hour hike in this heat to a friendly village where there was no chance to get any VC.

A girl was walking her bicycle toward them across the narrow footbridge. She was dressed up, with billowy, silky pants and a purple scarf around her neck. She looked as if she was going to a party.

"Look, Cao Tri—isn't she pretty?"

"Yes, *Thieu-uy.*"

The lieutenant smiled and said hello in Vietnamese, but the girl turned away, spoke sharply to Cao Tri, then laughed. She mounted her bike and rode away.

"What did she say, Cao Tri?"

Cao Tri giggled. "She said she doesn't like you, *Thieu-uy.*"

The lieutenant stared in the direction of the girl. "Where was she going?"

"I don't know, *Thieu-uy.*"

The lieutenant made a decision. He could use some exercise too, he told himself; and besides, he had never actually seen Tich Tuong; he knew its location only from the map. He told the marines the plan.

They set out across the bridge. There were gaps in it here and there, and the lieutenant remembered what the civil affairs officer had told him: the Nhu Le villagers had requested the marines' aid in building a new one. They wanted a bridge that would be wide and strong enough for heavy carts and even cars to take their goods to market. The lieutenant had not been enthusiastic. He knew the marines in his company were more interested in finding VC and NVA. The bridge job sounded like one for marine engineers.

On the opposite side of the bridge was a deserted stretch of road. Supposedly it was safe here; nonetheless the four marines walked as if on patrol, five meters between men. The lieutenant was pleased they seemed so well trained.

To the left he could see the river. There was a lot of traffic on it—sampans, low wooden boats. The lieutenant had recently heard from Intelligence that the boats his company had been shooting on night ambushes using Starlight scopes were, in fact, the enemy's. He had told the platoon leaders so they could pass the word down to their men. Some of the squads had put up signs back at base camp on Hill 25 showing their number of kills. None of the other companies in battalion were having anywhere near this kind of success.

As they neared the center of Tich Tuong the lieutenant noticed two young men dressed in black standing by the side of the road—black shoes, black tapered pants, black shirts, black narrow-brimmed hats. One of them was wearing a white scarf around his neck. Both carried carbines.

"Cao Tri—who are they?"

The marines stopped, their rifles at their hips. The lieutenant was confused; he had never seen Vietnamese dressed like that. They looked like stateside high school kids from an earlier era hanging around in the street looking for trouble—except for their weapons.

"It's all right, *Thieu-uy*," Cao Tri said, "they are cadre."

Now the lieutenant remembered; Revolutionary Development Team members all wore black; he had read that somewhere.

As Cao Tri spoke to the two cadre, six more, dressed the same, some with hats and some without, emerged from a nearby house and gathered around him. Two carried carbines and one had a grease gun. The lieutenant told his men that they could rest. They took off their rain suits, sat down under a tree by the side of the road, and drank from their canteens.

The cadre seemed very interested in Cao Tri. They asked who he was and where he came from and how long he had been with the Marines and how long he had been with the VC before that. They seemed interested in his weapon, too. They passed around the M-16 and examined it.

In his best and fastest Vietnamese the lieutenant asked Cao Tri whether any of them knew anything about the NVA they had killed.

Now the lieutenant became the object of their attention. The cadre wanted to know who he was, how he knew

Vietnamese, how long he had been there, where he had fought. The lieutenant tried to answer as best he could, with help from Cao Tri. One of the cadre asked to see the shotgun he was carrying. They passed it around, repeating "shotgun" slowly to each other in English. The one with the grease gun offered to let the lieutenant hold it.

One of the cadre motioned for the lieutenant and Cao Tri to follow him. The cadre led them to a house just off the main road and while the lieutenant and Cao Tri waited in a dirt courtyard the cadre went to the door and called inside. A short, squat Vietnamese appeared. He was older than the others, and wore black pants, a white T-shirt, and no hat. He listened to the cadre, then grabbed the lieutenant's hand and shook it vigorously, talking rapidly. The lieutenant asked Cao Tri to explain.

"He is the leader of the cadre, *Thieu-uy*. He wants to talk to you. The cadre told him that you were the one who killed the NVA."

Before the lieutenant could say anything, Cao Tri and the young cadre headed back to the road, leaving the lieutenant and the cadre leader standing by themselves in the middle of the courtyard.

The cadre leader kept talking. He seemed excited and spoke rapidly with great animation, waving his arms about. One moment his eyes would open wide in amazement, the next he would glower in anger. Next he would smile and take the lieutenant's hand and pat it tenderly. Once the lieutenant turned around to see whether the enlisted men were looking, but they were out of sight.

There were three young men in the village, the cadre leader said, who had grown up close friends. The year before, they had been drafted by the South Vietnamese Army, but they ran away. Months later, word got back to the village that they had joined the North Vietnamese Army. The cadre leader couldn't explain exactly how the villagers had found this out; nevertheless, they knew, and were very upset. It was a loyal village, the cadre leader repeated to the lieutenant several times, and all the other young men joined either the ARVN or the Popular Forces. The families of the three renegades were disgraced—nobody would have anything to do with them.

A month ago, the three returned to Tich Tuong to visit their families. They came late at night—slipping by the marines' ambushes, the lieutenant was thinking. But a neighbor of one of the three told the cadre leader of their return, and he took some of his men and went to one of the NVA's houses They arrived just as the sun was leaving. He tried to run, but the cadre leader and his men shot him dead. At this point the cadre leader raised his arm and squeezed an imaginary trigger, acting out the shooting. The other two, he said, had got away.

Nothing more was heard of them until this morning, when villagers passing through Tich Tuong from the south carried news of the dead man lying in the field. He was one of the three.

But how did the cadre leader know? the lieutenant asked, thinking of all the villagers who had told Cao Tri they knew nothing.

The cadre leader became even more excited. Ignoring the lieutenant's question, he contorted his face and swung his arms about as he talked of the third one—the one who was still alive. That, he said, was the important thing, to kill him too, to make sure that all three of the traitors were dead; then the village would have its good name back again.

The cadre leader took the lieutenant's hand in his and asked him to promise to help the village get the third man. Yes, the lieutenant said, he and his company would certainly help. The lieutenant now talked excitedly too. His voice had risen and he spoke rapidly, with rising and falling tones. The cadre leader told the lieutenant to come back and visit any time he wanted, he was always welcome. He again thanked the lieutenant for killing the NVA

When the lieutenant returned to the road he found Cao Tri still talking to the cadre; he seemed to be enjoying himself. The lieutenant realized it wasn't often Cao Tri had the chance to speak to Vietnamese males his own age. He went over and sat with the four marines and quickly told them the story. They nodded but said nothing. The lieutenant told them to get ready to head back.

Suddenly there was a commotion in the road. An elderly man and woman were trying to get past the cadre, but the cadre were blocking their way. The cadre yelled at the old couple and shoved them, pointing to the lieutenant.

Cao Tri knelt beside him and whispered: *"Thieu-uy,* these are the parents of the dead NVA. They are on their way to get their son."

The lieutenant nodded and the cadre became silent. Now he saw that the old man was carrying a wooden stretcher. It looked homemade; the lieutenant had seen ones like it before. One of the cadre stepped forward and roughly shoved the old woman closer to the lieutenant.

The lieutenant looked at Cao Tri, but Cao Tri was staring silently at him along with the others. He looked toward the four marines but couldn't see them behind the cadre. Then he looked at the woman standing in front of him. She seemed very old. Her gray hair was tangled, her skin was blotched and wrinkled, and her face was wet with tears. Her eyes were thick with a watery film and almost colorless; they looked diseased. She seemed benumbed, as though she had been drugged.

How could the cadre treat her so cruelly? Hadn't she suffered enough? The lieutenant wondered what they expected him to do—yell at her? Hit her? What was this confrontation supposed to mean? For a moment he thought of telling the woman that the cadre were wrong; he wasn't the one who had killed her son, he didn't have anything to do with it. It had been the captain. But did it matter who killed him? Did it matter to her? She seemed barely able to see him.

"Di-di!" He said it harshly, hoping it would satisfy the cadre.

They yelled a few more times at the couple and then let them go. The lieutenant and Cao Tri said their *chao*'s and headed back.

They arrived back at the company CP in the middle of the afternoon. The lieutenant told Chapel to radio the marines down by the body and tell them to remove the booby trap; that a couple of old villagers would be coming by to pick the body up; to leave them alone.

The captain said, "Find out anything?"

"Affirmative, Skipper." The lieutenant told his story.

When he finished the captain's face was blank. "Well," he

said, "at least you got some exercise. I haven't done a damn thing but sit here all day."

Later, when all the daylight patrols had come in, the captain said, "Ready to try again, Chapel?"

"Yes, sir."

They headed south on the dirt road. This time the captain took a whole squad.

10: Liberty

The lieutenant had orders to go to Da Nang on company business. He was to pick up the marine who had gone UA before the company went to Con Thien.

"No rush," the captain told him, smiling. "Take a few days, at least—you need a rest. When you get back you can tell us about all the steak you ate." The first sergeant gave him money to bring him back a bottle of bourbon.

From Hill 25 the lieutenant hitchhiked to the airstrip outside Quang Tri City where he got a ride on a C-130 to Da Nang. Then he hitched to division headquarters, a complex of low wooden buildings on the side of a steep hill west of the city.

The lieutenant walked up a dirt road and then climbed a series of wooden stairways until he got to a building near the top of headquarters. The sun was out, but inside the building it was cool. A sergeant dressed in clean, pressed utilities and polished boots gave the lieutenant directions. He made his way to a small office nearby and walked in.

"Oh, excuse me," he said, "I must have the wrong office. I'm looking for Captain Black."

Captain Black looked up from his desk. His utility shirt was clean and pressed, the silver bars on his collar were shiny, his hair was cut short and neatly combed.

"Jim! How are you?" The captain grinned—a big, clownish grin under his pushed-in nose. He stood up and held out his hand.

"All right, Skipper—good to see you!"

They shook hands and sat down. "What are you doing here? Don't tell me you've been ordered back here too."

"Negative, Skipper," the lieutenant said. "Just back for a few days. I've come to get one of your favorites—Private Foster."

The captain scowled. "That shitbird! I heard they got him—shacked up with some hooker in Da-Nang. Caught him with a stash of marijuana too. If you need someone to testify at his court, let me know. I'd be glad to go back up there for that."

The lieutenant took off his flak jacket. "Gee," he said, "I really didn't recognize you, Skipper—all spiffed up like that. I mean, I never knew you were such a good-looking marine."

The captain smiled. "Okay, okay, get it over with."

The lieutenant looked around the office. "Looks pretty nice back here. Doesn't this air conditioning worry you, though? I mean, that it might be a VC plot—keeping the offices so cold everyone gets sick?"

The captain waited until the lieutenant stopped laughing. "Seriously," he said, "how's the company doing?"

"Good, Skipper." The lieutenant pulled out his map and showed the captain the three villages along the river and told him about all the VC they had been getting on their ambushes and patrols.

"How about the gunny?"

The lieutenant shook his head. "Still the same."

The captain frowned. "I feel kind of bad about that. Maybe I should've done something more. But it's hard—he *is* career, and married and all that."

The lieutenant lit a cigarette. "What about you, Skipper? How're you doing back here?"

The captain lowered his voice and swore. "I thought I'd be getting some rest," he said, "but there's no way. This place is full of majors and light colonels who haven't been to the field yet or who screwed up, and now they're all working twenty hours a day, trying to get the Legion of Merit. So everybody else has to work as hard as they do."

"Any way you can get back to the field?"

The captain hesitated, then smiled. "No. I'm not trying, either."

"No?"

The captain looked embarrassed. "You get used to it back here," he said. "Three square meals a day, sheets and a cot

every night. There's even some round-eyes. I'm just waiting
for my tour to finish and then get back to the States. You'd
feel the same, believe me."

The lieutenant didn't say anything. "You would," the
captain said.

He told the lieutenant he had more work to do, but that he
would see the lieutenant that night, at the officers club. "No
way I'm going to work tonight." He grinned.

The officers club was in a small wooden building that jutted
out from the hill. The lieutenant remembered it from the first
time he had been there, when he had just arrived in country.
The sun was still out when he got there now, but inside it was
air-conditioned. Slot machines lined the side wall. The lieutenant was the only customer.

He sat at the bar and nodded at the Vietnamese barmaid.
She was the same one who had been there before. What a
difference since then! The lieutenant smiled as he remembered how uncertain he had felt, the strong longing he had
had to be somewhere else. Now he felt free from having to do
or to worry about anything—a feeling, he thought, that all
soldiers must have when they get away from the field.

The only decision he had to make was what to drink. He
decided on a beer, to start with—an American beer. The
lieutenant hadn't had a beer in more than a month. It was so
cold it hurt his throat, but he drank it quickly and ordered
another, as well as a pack of cigarettes—Marlboros, which
were hard to get in the field.

Four more officers entered, three majors and a lieutenant
colonel, and sat at the bar. All wore clean, pressed utilities
and shined boots. They ordered drinks and immediately
started playing a dice game, as though it was something they
did every day at this time. The lieutenant felt proud that his
utilities were faded and dirty, that his boots had lost all their
blackness, and that the gold bars on his collar were tarnished
and scratched.

He spoke to the barmaid in Vietnamese. He told her he
remembered her from before.

"I remember you too," she said.

The lieutenant was surprised. He knew a lot of officers
went through here.

"But you look different now," she said.

The lieutenant took a drag on his cigarette. "What do you mean?"

She studied him a moment, then said, *"Ong xau."*

Xau? The lieutenant looked puzzled. *Xau* was the word he had learned for "ugly." Maybe it had another meaning, he thought. Or was it the mustache he had grown in fhe field?

"I've lost a lot of weight," he said in English. That's what war will do to you, he felt like saying. She wasn't so good looking herself.

The lieutenant drank another beer. The club became crowded and several officers whom the lieutenant had known from training came in. It was the first time he had seen any of them in Vietnam. They bought each other drinks and talked about what they had been up to.

Where are you at? Up north. Been up by the Z? Yeah, Con Thien. Know what it's like, was at the Washout. Any operations? Medea. No kidding; I heard that was bad. Yeah, lost half our company. Jesus. I was on Green Whirlwind. Oh, yeah? I heard that was bad, too. Hey, did you hear about Riley getting it? Yeah, saw his name in the *Navy Times*. That's too bad. Gordon bought the farm too. No! Yeah, didn't you hear? Two days before he was going to meet his wife on R & R; stepped on a mine and blew himself away. Jesus, that's too bad. Yeah. God damn, you heard about Titus, didn't you? I heard he got zapped, that's all. Christ, he had just got here, hadn't even got his platoon yet; went on patrol with another platoon to break himself in and insisted on taking point. Sniper got him between the eyes. Is that right? Man, that was really stupid. I guess that's the way Titus was, though—gung ho as hell. He was married, wasn't he? Hey, I heard Manny got wounded and is back in the States. No, it wasn't that bad; he went to Cam Ranh and is back in the field now. That's good, I heard he got hit real bad. Yeah, rumors have a way of starting over here. I've run into at least two guys that've looked at me and said, "Oh, I heard you were dead."

The lieutenant spotted Turkle.

"Hey, Toilet!"

Turkle turned around. "Hey, good to see you, man!" He had a big smile on his face. "Haven't been called that in a long time—I knew it was you."

"How are you doing, Toilet? I heard you got hit."

"Yeah, the bastards got me. Stood up once when I wasn't supposed to—just wanted to see what was going on." He laughed.

The lieutenant laughed too. "You haven't changed at all, have you, Toilet?"

"Why should I? Is there a war going on or something?"

The lieutenant laughed again. It did feel good, he thought, seeing Turkle, whom he had known in college as well as in training. The lieutenant had never really been friends with Turkle, but now that they were both in Vietnam there seemed to be a bond between them.

"Good to see you, Toilet," the lieutenant said, slapping him on the back. "What are you doing here, anyway?"

"Hospital visit," Turkle said. "Actually, I think my captain was getting a little tired of me." He laughed. "Doesn't think I'm serious enough, or something. How about you? You stationed back here?"

The lieutenant shook his head. "Still in the field." He told Turkle about the marine who had gone UA.

"Don't blame him," Turkle said.

"When are you going back?"

Turkle grinned. "Who knows? I'm in no hurry. How about you?"

The lieutenant shrugged. "Three, four days maybe."

"Great! Let's get drunk tonight."

"Right, let's get drunk."

The lieutenant bought a round. He had a lot of money on him and felt like spending it. That was part of being in war, he thought, money wasn't something one cared about.

He saw Captain Black.

"Hey, Skipper!"

Captain Black came over and the lieutenant introduced him to Turkle. "This is my old captain," the lieutenant said. "We were in the field together." Then to the captain, "This is Toilet Turkle."

"*Toilet?*"

The lieutenant laughed. "He was always called Toilet in college."

Turkle laughed. "Don't ask me why."

The lieutenant bought another round.

"Are you still in the field, Captain?" Turkle said.

"Sure he is," the lieutenant said. "He carries an M-one pencil—right, Skipper?" He laughed.

They drank some more and the club became less crowded. The captain said it was time for a movie to begin downstairs. He said there was a movie every night.

"War movie, Skipper?" The lieutenant laughed.

Turkle suggested they all go to the Stone Elephant in Da Nang.

"I thought Da Nang was off limits," the lieutenant said.

"It is," the captain said, "except for the Stone Elephant. It's about the only place that isn't."

"Great," the lieutenant said, "let's go."

The captain said they could get a navy taxi. Turkle went to call it and the captain told the lieutenant he didn't have to wear his pistol if he didn't want to.

The lieutenant hesitated. "Hell no, I don't want to wear it," he said, and went to the hooch where he was staying across from the officers club and put his cartridge belt under his cot.

He came back and the three of them got into the taxi, a pickup truck with a covered back, and rode down the hill toward the city. The lieutenant smelled the night air and gazed out the back of the truck.

"Hey—look at all those lights! I had forgot what it looks like—having lights on at night. You're right, Skipper—it's great back here. No weapons, no blackout."

"Yeah," Turkle said, raising his voice, "all we need now are some women—some round-eyed women!"

"Right," the lieutenant said, "some round-eyes!" They all raised their fists.

The Stone Elephant was crowded. In the cocktail lounge navy officers in light khaki uniforms stood and sat at the bar and around cocktail tables against the back wall. There were women too—American women, they looked like. The room was dimly lit.

The lieutenant swore. "Man," he said, "look at this place! It's like being back in the States. I don't believe it!"

The captain suggested they sit in the dining room, and the three of them walked past tables filled with navy officers. Here and there were marines in pressed utilities. The lieutenant was conscious of being the only one there who looked as though he had come from the field.

The waitress here was Vietnamese too, but prettier than the one at the officers club, and she wore an *ao dai,* the long Vietnamese dress with flaps in the front and back. She asked each of them very politely in English what they wanted to drink.

"Martinis!" Turkle shouted. "Let's all have martinis!"

"Right!"

They rolled the dice to see who would pay.

"Watch out, Lieutenant," the captain said, "I feel hot tonight."

"Right, Skipper."

The lieutenant lost.

"Your round, Lieutenant," the captain said, "you're loser."

The waitress came back with their drinks and suddenly the captain grabbed the front flap of her *ao dai,* stuck his face in it, and made loud nose-blowing sounds. She started slightly, and then the captain brought his face up grinning. Turkle laughed loudly. The lieutenant smiled.

They ordered another round of drinks while the waitress was still there and rolled the dice again. The captain leaned across the table and pointed his finger at the lieutenant. "I'm going to beat you again," he said. He wore a look of exaggerated intentness and there was a slight slur in his voice.

"That's what you think, Skipper."

"I mean it, Lieutenant: you're loser tonight."

Turkle laughed. The lieutenant lost.

"I told you, Lieutenant: you're loser tonight." The captain pointed his finger again.

"I admit you're better, Skipper," the lieutenant said, "you get all the practice." The lieutenant forced a laugh but the captain kept staring at him.

They rolled the dice again. The lieutenant tried to keep smiling. What was wrong with the captain? he wondered. What did it matter who lost? He just wanted to have a good time. The captain must be drunk, he decided, that was all.

This time Turkle lost. He laughed—he seemed to be laughing at everything now—and paid for another round. By this time they had a backlog of drinks and decided not to roll again for a while.

A girl stood in the doorway, as if looking for someone. Then she walked into the room, past several tables full of navy officers, and sat down by herself.

"Hey, Lieutenant," the captain said, "how about doing a recon on that round-eye—before the Navy gets to her."

"What?"

"Go on. Go over there. Don't be afraid."

"Wait a second," Turkle said, "are you seeing right? She's a dog."

"So what?" the captain said. "She's a round-eye."

Turkle laughed. "You're right—so what?"

"Somebody's going to get her," the captain said, "she's not going to last long. Go on, Lieutenant. Get over there."

"I've got it!" It was Turkle, shouting. "Let's roll for it!"

The lieutenant got up from his chair and walked toward the girl. "Excuse me," he said, bowing and introducing himself. "My companions and I would like to buy you a drink. Would you care to join us?" He tried hard not to slur. She got up and he led her past the navy officers and back to the table.

The lieutenant introduced the captain and Turkle.

"Toilet?" she said.

Turkle laughed. The waitress appeared and the captain did his nose-blowing trick again.

She said she was a nurse from somewhere in the States with some kind of civilian job somewhere in Da Nang. The lieutenant had a hard time following the conversation. He had a hard time seeing her clearly too, but he decided that Turkle was right, she wasn't very good looking. Something about her chin.

The lieutenant noticed that the tables around them were empty and he realized it was closing time. But he didn't want to leave, he wanted to keep the night going. Turkle and the nurse were next to him, talking. The lieutenant stood and went to the bar in the next room. The captain was there and so was their waitress. She was emptying a trayful of glasses.

"Ask her how much she costs," the captain said. "You can speak to her."

"She can speak English, Skipper."

"She says she doesn't understand. Go on, ask her how much she costs."

The waitress kept on removing glasses from the tray. She acted as if the captain and the lieutenant weren't there.

"Why do you want to know?"

"I want to know. I know she's got a price—they all do. Go on, ask her."

The lieutenant asked her.

"Khong hieu," she said.

"She says she doesn't understand, Skipper."

"She understands. Go on, ask her again." The captain staggered. He thrust out his hand and leaned against a wall.

The waitress left with an empty tray. Other waitresses went back and forth, cleaning up. Except for a few giggles, they ignored the captain and the lieutenant.

"Come on, Skipper," the lieutenant said, "we'd better go." He went outside and the captain followed.

Turkle was there; he said he had just called a taxi.

"What happened to the girl?"

"She's coming," Turkle said. "She invited us all to her apartment for drinks. She says she has a roommate."

"Isn't that off limits?" the lieutenant said.

Turkle looked at the captain, then laughed. "So what?"

The captain said, "Don't worry, I won't tell anyone."

"Aren't you coming too, Captain?"

"Negative. Don't want to upset the odds. Besides, I'm a married man."

Turkle laughed.

"Now don't blow it, Lieutenant," the captain said. "This is your big chance."

The taxi came and the lieutenant, Turkle, and the girl got in.

They got out of the taxi, walked up a few steps, and went through a door.

"Wow, a real house!" the lieutenant said.

In the living room, a girl with short blondish hair was sitting on a couch. She got up, and the first girl introduced the lieutenant and Turkle to her.

"Nice to meet you," the roommate said. She had an English accent.

The lieutenant grinned. "Well, 'ello, ducky," he said. Turkle laughed. The roommate sat back on the couch. The other girl asked the lieutenant and Turkle what they wanted to drink. Turkle said Scotch and the lieutenant bourbon.

There was a stereo set in the apartment and Turkle put on a

rock record, loud. The lieutenant sat on the couch, and Turkle and the first girl danced.

The lieutenant tried to remember the name of the roommate but couldn't. She was good looking, he decided, at least better looking than the one with Turkle. But it was hard to tell. He seemed to be having trouble seeing her face as a whole. He looked around. It was a nice apartment, he thought. The living room was big, with another couch and several chairs and a table. It was like being back in the States.

He turned to the roommate. "Are you English?"

She glanced at him. "Yes."

"I had a friend who's English—in college."

"Oh?"

"Are you a nurse too?"

"Yes."

"How'd you end up over here?"

"I volunteered," she said. She turned to him. "You Americans aren't the only ones over here."

"Oh . . . I mean—I knew that."

The girl turned back to watch the dancers and the lieutenant did too. Turkle seemed to feel quite natural dancing in his jungle utilities and combat boots. He threw his arms around wildly and jumped up and down. The lieutenant wondered whether he should ask the roommate to dance. He remembered what Andrew, his English friend in college, had told him about English girls: at first they're cold but they get very warm. When Andrew called girls "ducky" they'd always laugh.

"This is really a nice apartment," the lieutenant said. "I mean, I've never been in Da Nang before. I didn't know there were apartments like this. It must be nice living here." He smiled.

She turned to him again. "It isn't nice at all."

"Oh? Why do you say that?"

"Why do you think? There's a war going on. I have to see it every day, the people who are mutilated by it. I can't stand it. In fact, I'm breaking my contract and going home."

The lieutenant took another sip of his bourbon. What did she think—that he didn't know? Couldn't she see how he was dressed?

"I know," he said. He felt his voice get serious. He started to tell her about marines getting wounded and killed.

But she interrupted. "What difference does it make whether they wear a uniform or not?"

A slow song was playing now. Turkle and the other nurse were dancing very close. The lieutenant watched Turkle's hand move up and down her back. Turkle had always had a lot of girlfriends in college, the lieutenant remembered. He tried to think of something else to say. Why wouldn't she drop the subject and have a good time? Didn't she know he had to go back to the field soon? There was no breaking contracts for him. Didn't she want to know anything about him?

He got up, went to the kitchen, and poured himself another drink. There was a door at one side of the kitchen. He opened it and went outside.

He found himself standing on a sort of porch facing a courtyard. He breathed deeply. The night air felt bracing on his face and in his lungs. He decided he liked it out here better than inside with Turkle and the others; it was too much like being back in college. He looked around. To his right was another porch beyond which was a lit-up room. He decided to move closer and get a better look. He peered in the window and saw that it was a kitchen. Two young Vietnamese women were sitting at a table, talking. Another was standing by the wall doing something. Why were they up so late? he wondered.

He knocked on the door and one of the girls opened it.

"Chao co," he said, and walked in. He stood in the middle of the kitchen, bowed, and said chao co to each of the others. Then he announced, in Vietnamese, his rank and that he was a United States marine. He smiled and sat down at the table.

The three women continued talking. The one who was standing was ironing, the lieutenant could see. He listened to what they were saying, but he couldn't understand any of it.

Maybe they were prostitutes, he thought. Yes, maybe he would get laid after all. He had money on him. Two of them were pretty, he decided, but the one who was ironing looked like a horse.

He started to talk. He wanted to tell them about all the places he had been in their country, about all the VC and NVA he had fought, but he found he couldn't remember the words he thought he knew. Then he tried to ask them how much they cost, but he couldn't remember how to say that either.

The one who had been ironing left the room. The other two, at the table, kept talking, ignoring him completely. Or were they talking about him? Maybe they were VC. After all, that was why the city was off limits: once in a while the VC would kill a sailor or a marine. And officers were very good game. The lieutenant wished he had worn his pistol.

"*Co* VC, *phai khong?*"

Both women giggled.

The lieutenant looked around the room. There was a picture of Christ on the wall by the ironing board. So, they were Catholics. Just like being back in the States. He decided there was no adventure to be found here after all. He got up, bowed, said goodbye, and left.

Back in the nurses' apartment the three others were eating scrambled eggs and bacon and drinking tomato juice. The lieutenant joined them. When they finished, they went back to the living room. Turkle and the first nurse sat on a couch, close together. The lieutenant sat on the other couch with the roommate.

The lieutenant woke. He lay very still. He felt that if he moved, even a little bit, he would vomit. He kept his eyes closed and tried to pretend he'd never again have to open them. Where was he?

He heard someone moving; then there was the sound of running water. Outside a car went by.

He opened his eyes. A telephone was next to the bed, a French telephone; he had seen ones like it in movies. Where *was* he? Then he remembered the French had been in Vietnam too.

French. English. Ducky. The lieutenant looked around. His face got red. She didn't like the war, he thought. Well—so what? Who did? What had he said?

His clothes were on the floor next to the bed. He got up and began to put them on, then sat on the edge of the bed. He felt dizzy. He closed his eyes and told himself he was going to be all right. He finished dressing. For a moment he was afraid he had lost his pistol, but then he remembered. He looked down at where he had slept. It was a double bed; both pillows looked as though they had been slept on.

The roommate was in the kitchen, at the sink.

"Good morning," the lieutenant said.

"Good afternoon."

The lieutenant cleared his throat. The taste in his mouth was terrible. "Is, uh, Turkle still here?"

"Oh, no, he left hours ago."

"Oh?" He saw she was washing lettuce.

"Are you all right?"

The lieutenant smiled. "I guess so."

"Would you like something to eat? I'm having some friends over for lunch." She started tearing the lettuce leaves into small pieces.

"Friends?"

"Yes. They work in the refugee program."

"Oh." The lieutenant felt with his hand on his hip and then remembered again about his pistol. "No, uh, thanks," he said. "I guess I'd better be going, too. I have to get back."

"Oh?" She stared at him, with her head a little to the side. Her short hair was brushed back and she looked a little plain, the lieutenant thought.

Suddenly he felt his face redden. "Yes—I mean, I think I should. Thank you very much—I mean, for letting me stay." He thought he sounded English himself.

"That's all right," she said. "Would you like me to call a taxi?"

"Oh—yes. Thank you."

He waited in the front yard, crouched behind a low stone wall, looking out for MP's. It was a quiet, residential, tree-lined street. The houses were big and they all had front porches and lawns.

He smelled something. It was himself. At the same time he remembered the three Vietnamese from the night before. He told himself he had better take a shower.

A car stopped in front and a young man in a short-sleeved madras shirt got out, then a young woman wearing a skirt. They looked like college students, the lieutenant thought. They walked past the lieutenant and went up to the door. The roommate appeared, smiled, and the three of them spoke briefly. At one point the couple turned and looked toward the lieutenant, still crouching behind the wall. Then they went inside. The lieutenant pictured the three of them talking about their jobs and about how bad the war was, eating salad.

A gray navy pickup truck came by and the lieutenant jumped out from his hiding place and got in the back. He stayed down low, still on the lookout for MP's as they drove through the city and back to division headquarters.

That evening, after a shower and a nap, the lieutenant went to the officers club.

It was Sunday, and downstairs on the outside patio the charcoal grills were set up for the weekly steak cookout. The lieutenant still felt a little sick, but he picked out a steak anyway and put it on the grill. It was a T-bone.

He took the steak off the grill when it was still very rare. Just then Captain Black walked up to him, grinning.

"Well, how did it go?"

"What do you mean, Skipper?"

"Come on. You know what I mean. How was the room-mate?"

The lieutenant shrugged. "Not bad. She's English."

"Better than the other one?"

"I thought so."

"How did Turkle do with her?"

"I don't know, Skipper. He was gone when I got up this morning."

"Oh? So you spent the night?" The captain's grin got wider.

The lieutenant nodded.

"Well, how did you do?"

The lieutenant laughed, embarrassedly. "What do you want to know for, Skipper?"

"I want to know. I'm stationed here. I'll run into those girls again."

"Don't waste your time." The lieutenant started for the stairs, but the captain blocked his way.

"First, tell me. Did you get laid or not?" He stopped smiling.

The lieutenant glanced toward the stairs. "I'm going up, Skipper."

The captain shook his head. "First, tell me. Did you get laid?"

The lieutenant looked at the captain's face. He was frowning. The lieutenant could smell the steak on his plate; now he felt really hungry.

He forced a smile. "You know, Skipper, I was so drunk that I can't remember. That's the truth." He started to step around him.

The captain moved quickly and blocked his way again. "I mean it," the captain said. He leaned close to the lieutenant's face. "I want you to tell me."

The lieutenant stared at the captain's dark shining eyes. "All right, Captain, I'll tell you." He breathed deeply. "I didn't."

The captain grinned. "Ha! I figured you didn't." Then he stepped aside and went over to the grill.

The lieutenant made his way upstairs. On a table were sliced tomatoes, potato salad, coleslaw, pickles, and sliced onions. The lieutenant took some of each and got himself a beer.

He felt better when he had finished and went downstairs and put another steak on the grill. Off to the side, he saw the captain talking to a major. When his steak was cooked he went back upstairs.

It was dark now and the club was crowded once again, noisy with the sound of voices. The lieutenant looked for Turkle but couldn't find him. It was just as well, he thought. He wasn't in the mood for Turkle's constant laughter. He got another beer.

A lieutenant came up to him and held out his hand.

"Remember me?"

"Of course—how are you?" They shook hands. It was someone else from training, someone who had just been starting when the lieutenant was finishing.

"Good to see you," the lieutenant said. "When did you get over?"

The other lieutenant looked sheepish. "This morning," he said. "This is my first day."

The lieutenant grinned. "No kidding. Come on, let me buy you a drink." "

They sat at a table in the corner.

"How does it feel?" the lieutenant said. "I remember how you used to talk about how much you wanted to get over here."

The new lieutenant looked around. He seemed uncomfortable. His hair was cut short, the way they wore it in training; his utilities were clean. "To tell you the truth," he said,

"I'm a little frightened. I guess maybe I'm not as gung ho as I thought I was. Actually, I'm pretty scared. You know the first thing I saw when I got off the plane this morning?"

"What?"

"Caskets. Stacks of them. Waiting for shipment out."

The lieutenant nodded. He stared intently at the other. "I know," he said, "that was the first thing I saw too."

"Really?"

The lieutenant nodded again. "I was scared too. But listen—don't worry, you get used to it over here, believe me. You'll be all right."

"Really?"

"Really," the lieutenant said. "You'd be surprised at what you get used to."

The new lieutenant asked questions, and the lieutenant answered them, telling him what it was like in the field. Ambushes and patrols, firefights and operations; friendly villages and contested ones, VC and NVA and defectors; *punji* pits, mines, making trails with machetes; the heat and the cold, thirst and mud; C rations, rats, leeches; squad leaders, platoon sergeants, gunnies and tops; captains and colonels; indifference and enthusiasm; rewards and frustrations, write-ups and medals.

The lieutenant finished his beer and looked around. There were fewer people in the club now. The movie had begun.

"Well," he said, "I think I'm going to sack. I'm tired." He got up.

The new lieutenant stood up, too. "Listen," he said, "I really appreciate this—I mean, the way you've talked to me. I appreciate it a lot. I feel better now, I really do. Thank you."

They shook hands.

"When are you going back to your company?" the new lieutenant asked.

The lieutenant thought for a moment. Then he said, "Tomorrow."

"Really? You have to get back already?"

"No, not really. But I'm going to."

He went outside. The air was a little cool now and the stars were out; he could see his way on the narrow boardwalk. He thought about what he had to do the next day: go by the brig and pick up Foster, then try to get a flight at the airfield. He thought about how much he had looked forward to the cookout; maybe he should have eaten another steak, he thought. At least he had bought the first sergeant his bottle.

11: Cooks and Bakers

i.

The lieutenant looked at his watch again. Just after seven. How long had they been waiting? It had been dark when they first boarded the trucks. He felt uneasy now with the light; he wished it were still dark. Already he could see marines moving about on the base, going to and from chow and to their various offices. It was strange, the lieutenant thought, to be waiting to go into battle, while those other marines went through their daily routines.

At least, he thought, the sun wasn't out. For some reason he felt that sunlight would have made the waiting worse. Why did they have to wait so long?

The way the marines with him were talking, it sounded as if they were on a training mission. They were laughing and joking, bragging and bantering. They sounded so young, the lieutenant thought, as if they were too young to realize, even now, that what they were doing was real.

"How many you think we'll get, Lieutenant?"

It was the new corpsman. He seemed to be doing more talking than anyone.

"I don't know, Doc," the lieutenant said. He tried to think of the corpsman's name but couldn't.

"Corpsmen are allowed to kill gooks, aren't they, Lieutenant?" He looked at the lieutenant and grinned.

"Sure, Doc." The lieutenant dragged on his cigarette and turned away. Why wouldn't he smile? Didn't he want his men to be enthusiastic? No, not in the corpsman's way, not like a high school athlete bragging about the points he was going to score in the big game. Besides, the corpsman was being too familiar.

"How about that?" the corpsman was saying. "Soon as I get over here the gooks have their big offensive." He grinned again and looked around at the other men in the truck. He had a soft growth of black hair on his upper lip; he probably didn't need to shave yet.

Another marine said, "That's right, Doc, you waste 'em." Another laughed. So did the corpsman.

A message came over the radio. The marines grew quiet and looked at Chapel, who was sitting next to the lieutenant.

"Lieutenant Bradley says we're waiting for a tank, sir," Chapel reported. "It's supposed to lead the way. As soon as it gets here, we'll pull out. Should be just a few more minutes."

Immediately the talking resumed. A tank, the voices said, that was good. Yes, the lieutenant thought, it was good. As long as they had to go up by truck, in daylight, it was a good thing that a tank would lead the way.

"You figure we'll have to shoot our way into the city, Lieutenant?" It was the new corpsman again.

"I don't know, Doc. I hope not."

One of the marines shouted, above the rest, "Hey, Peaches —how many gooks you gonna waste?"

There was more laughter. Peaches smiled and his face turned red. He looked even younger than the corpsman. His helmet seemed big on him, as if he were a child who had put on his father's old helmet for play.

"I'll get some, you'll see," Peaches said. There was more laughter.

No, not even like a training mission, the lieutenant thought. More like a school outing. He wished they'd be quiet, that they would act as he thought men going to battle should act.

Someone said, "How about you, Foster? How many gooks you gonna kill?" There was an edge in this voice; not as much laughter followed.

Private Foster blew out a stream of cigarette smoke and said nothing. The lieutenant sensed defiance in him. Good, he thought, let Foster be defiant—let him show the others. The lieutenant turned to Gilbey, who hadn't said a word.

"How are you doing, Corporal Gilbey?"

"All right, sir," Gilbey said. His voice sounded flat.

But was Gilbey really all right? What had happened to all

his enthusiasm from the night before, when he had told the lieutenant about fighting house-to-house in Santo Domingo. He had said he was going to give a talk to the platoon on how it was done. That was the kind of talk the lieutenant would have liked.

Chapel, who was now standing, shouted: "Hello, Top!"

The lieutenant got to his feet. The first sergeant of the lieutenant's old company was standing by the side of the road, squinting up at the trucks.

"Hello, there, First Sergeant!"

The first sergeant looked toward the voice. "Oh, hello there, Lieutenant." His voice was squeaky. "What are you doing up there? I thought the colonel took you out of the field?"

The lieutenant nodded. "He did. But I'm going up to Hue." He spoke in a strong voice. "I've got the provisional platoon." For a moment he thought of calling them "cooks and bakers," but he knew they were listening.

"Oh? I didn't know that." The first sergeant sounded a little puzzled.

The lieutenant said, "What are you doing over here, Top? You going up, too?"

Corporal Henry and Peaches laughed.

"Yeah, why don't you come up with us, Top?" Peaches' voice sounded even squeakier than the first sergeant's. His helmet looked as if it were about to fall.

The first sergeant shook his head, as though he had taken the suggestion seriously. "Negative. Just came by to see if you had left yet. What're you waiting for, anyway?"

"Tank," the lieutenant said. "Going to lead the way."

The first sergeant nodded. "Tank. That's good." Suddenly he stiffened. "Henry!"

"Yes, Top?"

"You take care of Peaches, you hear?"

"I will, Top."

"Peaches!"

"Yes, Top."

"You keep your head down."

Laughter.

"Don't worry about me, Top."

"I'm worried about the record books. I need you two back

here." He stood there, squinting up at the marines. Then, in his squeaky voice, he said, "Well, guess I'd better be going. Don't want to miss breakfast."

"So long, Top," the lieutenant said.

The first sergeant walked away and stopped at the next truck. The lieutenant could see the gunny standing in the truck, chewing his gum and talking to the first sergeant. Then the first sergeant headed back toward the main part of the base. The lieutenant watched until he was out of sight. He sat down and looked at his watch again. Close to eight o'clock. He knew what would happen at eight; he hoped they'd be gone by then.

The talk now in the truck was about enemy weapons. There had been radio reports about the many weapons captured since the offensive began.

"I'm gonna get an AK-forty-seven," the new corpsman said. Another marine said he wanted a pistol, something he could take home with him.

The lieutenant had heard those reports, too. With Lieutenant Dobson, sitting on their cots in their plywood hooch, listening to the Armed Forces Network on the radio Dobson had bought at the PX. He had also bought a camera and stereo equipment, to send back to the States. The broadcasts told of the enemy suddenly invading province capitals throughout the country at the beginning of Tet, the lunar New Year; of the Army, Marines, and ARVN driving them out, inflicting heavy casualties and capturing great numbers of weapons. The announcers' delivery was polished and fast. In between the reports a disc jockey played rock music.

Dobson had talked with impatience about being left out just when the enemy had finally come out in the open to fight. "What are we here for, anyway?" Like many marines, Dobson had been away from his company when the offensive began. The company had gone out on a three-day patrol, leaving Dobson's platoon behind for a rest at Phu Bai, this big marine base that was the battalion's new home. When the enemy took over the roads, the company had been stranded on a hilltop ten kilometers west of the base.

The lieutenant had said little as he listened with Dobson to the radio. He felt remote from the excitement now that he was no longer in the field. A week before the colonel had told him he was to join the battalion staff. "But sir," the lieutenant had said, "I want to stay with my company." The colonel said no, the lieutenant had spent enough time in the field. And so he had waited in the battalion area for his assignment, eating three hot meals a day and drinking at the Phu Bai officers club every night. The days were warm and sunny, as the monsoon seemed to be coming to an end; the dirt roads on the base became dusty.

Then the enemy's Tet Offensive began, but it seemed to the lieutenant that the war for him was over—without his ever really experiencing it. Once in the evening a rocket hit near the O-club, sending everyone running for the trenches outside, but the lieutenant had stayed at the bar. He considered going to the PX and buying a radio and camera too.

Then came the news that the enemy had invaded the city of Hue, ten miles to the north, and taken over most of it, including the ancient Citadel, the jail, the hospital, and the university. The MACV compound in the southern, modern sector of the city remained the only part still under American and South Vietnamese control. The colonel of the lieutenant's battalion received orders to establish contact with the compound and then drive the enemy out of Hue. He went up by truck, taking two companies with him.

Dobson spent most of his time after that in the operations shack waiting for reports. The colonel and his men had had to shoot their way into the city. After reaching the MACV compound, they had tried to cross the Perfume River in order to take the Citadel, but they ran into heavy resistance; there were a lot more enemy than Intelligence had said. They withdrew to the compound. The operations officer was KIA; one of the company commanders was badly wounded, so was the padre. From the compound they started to clear the neighborhood around them, house to house.

The day after the colonel's group left for Hue, Dobson came back to the hooch and told the lieutenant he had bad news. His face was serious, his forehead wrinkled.

"What's that?"

"They just got a report. About Cao Tri."

"Oh?"

Dobson lowered his head. "KIA. Apparently the VC or NVA got him when he was home on leave. The Army found his body."

The lieutenant put down the book he had been reading and stared blankly down at the floor.

"I'm sorry," Dobson said. "I knew you were close."

The lieutenant could feel Dobson's eyes on him. "It's all right," he said. "I kind of figured it was going to happen."

The next morning Dobson got the word: his platoon was to go to Hue and help the colonel. Dobson's tone became eager as he readied his men for battle. That afternoon the lieutenant found out that a provisional platoon was to go up too. "Cooks and bakers," the battalion XO in the operations shack called them, a mixture of clerk-typists, supply workers, mail clerks, and stranded combat marines returning from R & R or the hospital who couldn't get back to their own companies.

The lieutenant walked to the staging area and looked at the platoon. It was dusk. The gunny from the lieutenant's old company was shouting, trying to get a supply report. The squad leaders were also from his old company: Gilbey, Douglas, Yates. Good ones, the lieutenant knew. Chapel was off to one side with a radio. Corporal Henry and Peaches were there, and Baylor, the supply sergeant, and Richman, Chapel's best friend.

"What's going on here, Gunny?"

The gunny turned and saluted. "Sir," he said. Then he smiled in a clownish way. The mustache he was trying to grow looked like a smudge of dirt. "They made me platoon commander—of the provisional platoon." He shrugged and grinned. "I guess they didn't have anybody else."

"Oh? You all recovered from your dysentery?"

The gunny shrugged again. "Doctor says so."

Marines were shouting out what supplies they needed. The gunny hollered for everybody to shut up, but moments later the babbling resumed.

The lieutenant stood there a while longer. Then he strode to battalion headquarters. He opened the door to the plywood operations shack and went to see the battalion XO.

"Sir. I'm taking over that provisional platoon. I'm going up to Hue."

Bald Eagle glanced up from a map. He looked distracted.

"I'm going to do it, sir," the lieutenant said. "They need a lieutenant. And I know a lot of those men."

Before the major could reply, the lieutenant turned and left
the shack. He smiled to himself at the look on Bald Eagle's
face.

"Gunny!"

"Yes, sir."

"You're the platoon sergeant now. I've just been appointed
head of this platoon."

"Aye, aye, sir!" The lieutenant thought he heard relief in
the gunny's voice.

The lieutenant was standing to one side, letting the gunny
and the squad leaders conduct their business, when Private
Foster came up, saluted, and asked to have a word with him.

"What is it, Foster?"

Foster was standing close to the lieutenant and his pale blue
eyes fixed on the lieutenant's face. "I want to join your
platoon, Lieutenant. I want to go up there and fight." His
voice was a scratchy whisper.

"But you're up for court-martial, Foster."

"I know, but I'm asking you to let me go with you,
Lieutenant. I want to make up for what I've done."

The lieutenant decided. "All right, Foster," he said, feeling
a thrill that Private Foster, the company shitbird, would speak
to him like this. "Report to Corporal Gilbey."

"Aye, aye, sir. Thank you, sir." Foster saluted, held his
eyes for a moment longer, then turned away.

Later that evening, after the platoon's supply was completed, the lieutenant saw Dobson in their hooch. Dobson
was in a good humor. He told the lieutenant several anec-
dotes about the men in his platoon getting themselves ready
to go to Hue. The lieutenant told him what he had done.

"You *volunteered?*" Dobson said, frowning. "Why did you
do that?" It wasn't the reaction the lieutenant had expected.

He hesitated. "Like you said, what are we here for,
anyway?"

"Yeah, I know. . . . But I don't know if I'd *volunteer.*"
Then he lay down on his cot and went to sleep. The lieutenant
lay on his, thinking.

Eight o'clock. The lieutenant held his breath. Maybe they
were too far away to hear it, he thought. But his watch was a
minute fast.

Then it happened, suddenly. The sound was simply there.

"Sir, do we stand or not?" It was Chapel. Everyone in the truck looked at the lieutenant.

"Negative." Why should they? This wasn't training.

A message came over the radio.

"Sir, Lieutenant Bradley says to stand for colors."

The lieutenant saw the marines in the truck behind them get to their feet and he and his men got up too.

Standing, hearing the music and seeing the neatly ordered rows of one-story buildings in the distance, the lieutenant remembered his thoughts of the night before when he had lain on his cot, unable to sleep, and fantasied how it was going to be the next day. Bloody and vicious, he would lead his platoon from house to house, killing enemy after enemy, some with his bayonet. Wounded—at least twice, but not so badly as to be stopped—he would remain silent and give no orders, while his men would follow in awe: could this man be human? He himself would wonder the same thing.

But now, in the daylight, among the young marines, listening to the distant, tinny anthem and looking at the rows of buildings, the lieutenant found the night's thoughts stale and embarrassing.

The tank arrived and the trucks began to move. They left the base and headed north on the highway toward Hue. They passed ruined houses. Villagers looked up without expression. Small children in dirty clothes held out their hands. Some of the marines stood in the trucks with their rifles ready, while the rest remained seated.

Where would the ambush come from, the lieutenant wondered—if there was to be one? To the left were high, round, dark hills, but they were miles away. Close by to the left were lowlands, and along the road, houses. Near one group of houses, like a relic from a previous war, stood a broken-down tank. To the right were rice paddies.

Then there were different buildings—three and four stories high, right next to one another. The city, the lieutenant thought. Suddenly there was firing—from up ahead to the right. Everyone in the lieutenant's truck got down low. The truck began to move faster, very fast, faster than the lieutenant thought a truck like that could travel. Next to him a marine he didn't know raised his rifle over his head and fired on fully automatic. On the other side, a big fat marine with a machine gun stood up, flopped on top of the cab, and fired at the buildings to his right, holding his machine gun like a rifle. The lieutenant didn't know him either. It occurred to him that the wooden boards on the side of the truck he was crouching behind were not much protection, but he remained crouched.

There were cries of *"Hold your fire! Hold your fire!"* The truck slowed. Ahead the lieutenant saw a big yellow gas station sign. SHELL.

"This is it," Chapel said. "Hue."

The lieutenant called out, "Anyone hit?"

There was silence. Then Gilbey said, "Negative, sir."

Chapel reported, "Negative on the other squads, sir, everyone's all right."

Off to the left the lieutenant saw someone he knew — Captain O'Gara from Alpha Company, standing in front of a large house. He was waving. The lieutenant waved back. Now he saw the colonel, who was much shorter, next to O'Gara. He didn't wave, he simply stood there. Then he turned and went inside the house.

A little farther up the street the trucks turned right and then left through an opening in a building. They stopped in the middle of a large courtyard. Surrounding them on all sides was a four-story building with balconies and iron railings. On the balconies Vietnamese soldiers wearing gas masks stared down.

"Must be the MACV compound," Chapel said.

The lieutenant and the other marines jumped down off the truck. Firing could be heard from outside the compound. The lieutenant could tell that it was close. He looked around and then up at the Vietnamese. In their black masks their faces looked like those of ants.

Gas masks? What for? Gas. Yes, the lieutenant thought he could smell it now. Who was using gas? What were his men going to do for masks? The lieutenant realized he didn't even have a handkerchief. What was all that firing about? And what were those ARVN doing up there, anyway, just staring down, with their faces hidden? Why were they so calm?

Because they didn't have to fight, he thought. They were probably office workers stationed at the compound. No, it was the marines who had to fight. What did he think? That he had come up here just for the ride? He was going to have to go out on the street, out where the firing was, out where there was an enemy who would try to kill him. That was right: the NVA were in buildings and had weapons. And they weren't going to go away; they were going to shoot at him.

It occurred to the lieutenant that he might piss in his pants. No, he told himself, he wouldn't do that, that would look bad. He imagined how it would look, the dark, spreading stain. His men would see it. He decided to have a cigarette, walk around a little.

"Smoke, Chapel?"

"No thank you, sir."

Of course. Chapel didn't smoke. The lieutenant knew that. He just forgot for a moment. Or maybe he thought Chapel would want one now. Maybe Chapel was scared, too. Was he? Could Chapel tell how scared he was?

"What do you think, Chapel?" The lieutenant tried to smile. God, he thought, it must be a sick-looking smile. But he'd be all right. As long as he didn't piss in his pants. No, he wasn't going to do that.

"I can think of some places I'd rather be," Chapel said.

The lieutenant smiled. A better smile, he could tell.

Then he heard someone say his name. It was Lieutenant Bradley, standing next to a truck, a map spread out on the hood. The lieutenant went over to him.

Dobson walked up to them. His shoulders were hunched up and his mouth hung open.

"Tom," the lieutenant said, "how's it going?" He smiled.

Dobson nodded. He looked serious. "What's up, Brad?" he said. "What do we do now?"

Bradley looked up from the map. "Here's the setup," he said. "Before we join the colonel we've got to do a little rescue mission for MACV."

The lieutenant and Dobson nodded. Bradley sounded all right, the lieutenant thought. It was good to have Bradley here. The lieutenant didn't know Bradley well, but he liked him. Bradley was older, a mustang. He was the battalion personnel officer—a kind of cook-and-baker himself. But now the lieutenant saw him as a leader. His jaw was square, his face looked strong. He had a tall, lean body and was gray around his temples.

A three-man intelligence team, Bradley explained, had wandered out an hour ago assuming the area they were headed toward was secure. It wasn't, and they had been taken under fire and trapped over by the stadium. No one knew whether they were still alive.

"Stadium?" Dobson and the lieutenant said it together.

"Yeah," Bradley said, "for athletics. Here, look on the map."

The lieutenant and Dobson looked. It was a city map, with the emblem of another gas station on it. ESSO. The lieutenant stared at the familiar emblem; it seemed a source of comfort. Bradley pointed out their present location, the compound. Down the street was an oval, the stadium. The lieutenant concentrated on the map.

"Two of them are supposed to be here," Bradley said, pointing with a pencil to a spot on the side of the stadium away from the compound. "The third is in the open, in front of the stadium; he's been wounded."

Bradley moved the pencil again. "It looks like there's a nest of NVA holed up here." There was a small rectangle at the end of the street, just past the stadium. "They're supposed to have rockets and automatic weapons. One platoon'll go in to get the guy out, and the other will go in back to find the other two. There'll be a tank in support." He asked the two lieutenants how many men they had in their platoons.

"Thirty-three," the lieutenant said. Dobson said forty-two.

"You'll go in front of the stadium," Bradley told Dobson. "I figure we'll need more men there." Dobson nodded. His eyes were open wide, looking up at Bradley.

Bradley said, "I don't know, that's still not enough." He said to the lieutenant, "You'd better lend him one of your squads."

The lieutenant thought for a moment. Which one to send?

"Take Corporal Yates' squad," he said. "It's my smallest, but he's a good squad leader."

Dobson nodded.

"How about gas, Brad?" the lieutenant said. "Is anyone using gas? My men don't have masks."

Bradley shook his head. "That's only a little leftover tear gas."

Dobson's platoon moved out first, behind the tank, then the lieutenant's platoon. The lieutenant was on the sidewalk, his men on both sides of the street using the trees that lined the street for cover. Up ahead there was firing. The lieutenant felt all right now, rushing from tree to tree, pausing, rushing forward again, looking back and ahead, making sure his men were moving too.

The lieutenant smelled something and suddenly felt sick to his stomach. On the other side of a tree he saw a body, an NVA. The face was discolored; part of it was black.

The marine ahead of him moved to the next tree and the lieutenant moved too. He took a deep breath and the sickness passed. So, he thought, that was what it smelled like. What would his men have thought if he had thrown up? But it was only the smell that had made him feel sick, he thought.

They got to the stadium, to a street that went off to the right. The firing was heavy. There was a blast from the tank. Next to him, behind a tree, Chapel was shouting into his radio, telling the squad leaders to keep their men moving. Chapel was good, the lieutenant thought, he knew when to shout.

The lieutenant peered around from behind a tree. There was a house at the end of the street, then he saw a flash in the window. He jerked his head back and something hit the front of the tree. He looked at Chapel.

"I saw that, Lieutenant," Chapel said. "Be careful."

The lieutenant rushed to his right and jumped into a ditch next to the stadium wall. He and his men began to go around the outside of the stadium in the ditch.

"Get down, Lieutenant!" Chapel shouted.

But there was no one shooting at them here, was there? With all the noise it was hard to tell.

They were now behind the stadium. There was a field, and beyond that another street with houses. Were there more NVA? The lieutenant stood up and looked.

"Get *down*, sir!"

But he didn't want to get down. He turned and looked at his men, crouching and hiding in the ditch. He wanted to remain upright, to know each moment that he wasn't getting hit.

Gilbey passed by him, crouched low in the ditch. He was yelling at his men, keeping them moving, fire team by fire team. The lieutenant got down and started moving again.

He came to an opening in the wall and through it he could see a playing field and stands. It all looked so normal. Of course, he told himself, what did he expect? It was a stadium.

Gilbey came back. "Can't see them, sir—they must've got killed. I think we should go back. If we keep going, we'll be right by the house where the gooks are. I think we should go back."

A few strands of Gilbey's long wavy hair came down over his forehead, giving him a kind of wild look. Was there panic in Gilbey's voice? the lieutenant wondered.

"All right," the lieutenant said suddenly, "let's get out of here."

But then Chapel said, "Sir, Lieutenant Bradley says we should go all the way around the stadium. There's a squad that's trapped in front on the other side. He wants us to put fire on the house where the gooks are."

"Tell him Roger." The lieutenant turned to Gilbey. "All right, Corporal Gilbey, keep your men moving."

Gilbey stared hard. He hesitated a moment, then moved off.

They found the two men from the intelligence team in another ditch that ran along the street on the far side of the stadium.

"Good to see you, Lieutenant," one of them said. He was a captain and he sounded as if he hadn't been worried at all.

Another message came over the radio. The trapped squad was disengaged, the lieutenant's platoon was to go back the way it came. Everyone was going back to the compound.

A body lay on its back, just inside the compound. Bradley was standing over it, looking down. The lieutenant stopped.

"He the one from in front of the stadium?"

Bradley nodded. "Looks like he's been dead awhile."

The lieutenant agreed. He thought the body had been dead a long time; it had a grayish look. Then he realized that the man had had gray hair. There was a several days' growth of whitish beard.

"Anybody know him?" Bradley asked no one in particular. Marines were still coming into the compound from the street. A few of them stopped and looked.

"Check his dog tag," one of them said.

Nobody moved. Suddenly Bradley knelt down. He hesitated a second, then quickly opened the dead man's shirt and pulled out his dog tag. There were curly gray hairs all over his chest.

Bradley read the name aloud. "Yeah," he said, "I thought I knew him." He sounded as though he were talking to someone in particular. "Not very well. We were stationed together once. Okinawa." He paused. "Good marine. Too bad." He put the dog tag back in its place.

Bradley stood up. "Your squad got shot up pretty bad, Jim," he said. "I don't know the names, you'd better check. I'm sorry. It was nobody's fault—they just got caught in the open."

"Oh, no!" The lieutenant went to find the gunny.

"Gunny, who got hit from first squad?"

The gunny recited five names. One of them was Yates, the squad leader; another was Baylor, the supply sergeant. And Richman.

"Any KIA?"

The gunny shook his head. "But Richman's hurt pretty bad, sir. They're all in the aid station already."

"Where's the aid station?"

"I don't know, sir."

The lieutenant turned around. "Chapel! Did you hear about the first squad—about Richman?"

Chapel nodded. "Yes, sir." His usually ruddy face was pale. "I've tried to get into the aid station, but they're keeping everybody out, they say it's too crowded already." He spoke a little fast.

"What happened to Richman?"

"Rocket—ricocheted off the stadium wall. About tore his shoulder off, I heard."

"Is he going to be all right?"

Chapel shook his head. "Might lose an arm."

"I'll go over and see him. Where is the aid station?"

Chapel shook his head again. "It's right across the street, sir, but they won't let you in, believe me. They'll probably medevac him out pretty quick anyway. They've got choppers going out all the time."

The lieutenant stared at Chapel. "I'm sorry," he said.

"Yes, sir, so am I. It's a damn shame; he only had a month and a half to go."

"I'm sorry, Chapel, I really am."

"Yes, sir. But at least he's getting out of it. I figure they'll probably ship him right back to the States."

"Really?" The lieutenant looked in the direction Chapel had pointed, across the street from the compound.

He went back to Bradley and asked what he should do next.

"Take your platoon and report to the colonel," Bradley said. "You're no longer under me." He said that Dobson had already gone over to the battalion CP, in the building from where Captain O'Gara and the colonel had waved.

"How about you, Brad?"

"I'll do the same." He shrugged. "Whatever they want me to do."

The lieutenant sat with his platoon on the front lawn of the CP building. It was a big house, with a wide front porch and a high stone wall around the yard. On the porch, a marine from headquarters told the lieutenant to keep his platoon spread out, there were snipers in the neighborhood. He pointed to a window upstairs and said their side had snipers too. The lieutenant asked him what the building had been and the marine said some kind of private school.

Gilbey crawled, on his hands and knees, over to where the lieutenant was, next to the porch.

"What do you think we'll be doing, sir?"

"I don't know, Corporal Gilbey." The lieutenant took out his cigarettes and gave one to Gilbey. "You did a good job," he said, "going around the stadium—the way you handled your men."

"Thank you, sir." Gilbey looked around at the buildings beyond the wall, then moved a little closer to the lieutenant. "What I mean to say is, sir . . . I mean . . . if there's any kind of choice, when you talk to the colonel . . . I mean, I sure would rather we stayed out of the fighting. If there was something else we could do. I mean, a lot of these men aren't really trained for combat, they don't have the experience. What I mean is, sir. I don't think we should fight."

"I don't think there's going to be much choice," the lieutenant said. "What's wrong, Gilbey? Yesterday you were talking about how you wanted to come up here."

"I know, sir." Gilbey lowered his voice. "But I've been thinking about it. I've been over here almost twelve months, sir. I've seen my share of action; more, maybe. I was at Santo Domingo, too. I've got a wife and kid back home, sir." He stared at the lieutenant.

The lieutenant tried to think of something to say. He said: "How old are you, Corporal Gilbey?"

"Twenty-one, sir."

The lieutenant nodded. He felt certain that Gilbey's wife would be pretty.

A marine came out onto the porch and told the lieutenant the colonel was ready to see him.

There was a large front room full of desks and chairs. Most of the desks were upside down and there was plaster all over the floor. The colonel's office was in a small room off to the left. On one wall was a blackboard. The colonel sat alone at a bare table, staring directly ahead. He was wearing a helmet and flak jacket—a new flak jacket, the lieutenant noticed, still clean, and brighter green than his own. A pipe stuck out of one of the pockets.

"Hello, sir." The lieutenant was glad to see the colonel. But why? He didn't know the colonel very well; he had been with the battalion for only a month. The lieutenant wasn't even sure whether he liked him or not. With his short graying hair, pipe, and mild way of explaining things, he seemed to the lieutenant more like a college professor than a marine officer.

He lifted his head. "What are you doing here?" There was a look of annoyance on his face. "I thought I took you out of the field."

The lieutenant straightened. "I came up this morning, sir, with the provisional platoon. I'm the platoon commander." The words *cooks and bakers* went through his mind. He told the colonel about going around the stadium and rescuing the two men from Intelligence. "One of my squads got shot up pretty bad, sir. I've really only got two squads left now."

The colonel looked over at the blackboard.

"How has it been going up here, sir?"

"Slow," the colonel said, then he cleared his throat. "Very slow."

The lieutenant spoke softly. "I heard . . . about the casualties, sir. I'm sorry. Is the padre going to be all right?"

The colonel moved his head. "I don't know. He was trying to pull one of the wounded back. He shouldn't have." He frowned slightly.

The lieutenant said, "I just want to say, sir, my men and

I—we're here to help. Even though it's only a provisional platoon."

The colonel seemed not to hear the lieutenant. He cleared his throat and nodded toward the next room. "Captain O'Gara, our new S-three, will tell you what to do."

"Aye, aye, sir." The lieutenant hesitated, then went through the doorway.

Captain O'Gara shook the lieutenant's hand. "Welcome to Hue," he said. He smiled wryly. He had a three-day growth of beard. On a plastic-covered map with grease-pencil markings he showed the lieutenant the buildings they had taken since they had broken out of the MACV compound and started fighting house-to-house two days before.

"It's slow work," the captain said. "And that's just what it's like—work. An eight-to-five job. Seems like both sides have the same quitting time; we must be in the same union." He smiled faintly again. "It's weird. You're in one building, perfectly safe; but the building next door, or the street, or yard . . ." He shook his head.

Then he told the lieutenant to take his platoon and report to the new commander of Alpha Company, who was in a building near the backyard of the school.

The company commander, a first lieutenant, told the lieutenant to look—quickly—out the window. "But watch out—they can see you!" he shouted in the lieutenant's ear. There was firing from close by, and some of it was heavy.

The lieutenant looked. Across a yard at the side of their building he saw a church. The company commander yanked him back from the window. At the back of the yard to the left were two marines trapped in a hut, he said. They had tried to rush a building behind the hut too soon. Both were wounded; they had a radio. The enemy had a sandbagged automatic-weapons position in the building in back of the hut and no one could get to the two without coming under close-range fire. A tank couldn't be used for fear of hitting the marines.

"I want you to take the church," he said. If the lieutenant's platoon could do that, they could provide covering fire from a different angle for the trapped marines.

The lieutenant looked out the window again. The company commander again yanked him back.

"Watch out! You're in their range."

The lieutenant nodded. "Are they in the church?"

"Don't know. Maybe. Nobody's been over there yet."

He told the lieutenant how to get across the open area, how the other platoons had been doing it—wait for the covering fire and run across two at a time. He said to go into the church the same way, two at a time, the first man tossing in a grenade and the second firing. The company commander made it sound routine, but the lieutenant's heart was pounding.

The lieutenant went downstairs and outside to the front of the building where his platoon was waiting out of sight of the enemy. He briefed his two squad leaders and the gunny.

He looked from Gilbey to Douglas. Gilbey had done this kind of thing before, the lieutenant knew. Santo Domingo. But Gilbey had a wife and a kid. But that couldn't matter.

"All right, Sergeant Douglas," the lieutenant said, "your squad will lead out. Send them over two at a time." That was right, he thought, Gilbey had led out around the stadium.

"Are there gooks in the church?" Douglas said.

"Don't know."

Douglas nodded.

The lieutenant told Chapel to radio the company commander that they were ready. The first two marines waited by the corner of the building until the covering firing increased. Then Douglas yelled and the two marines ran.

They made it across the yard. Then Douglas and his radioman went. The four of them crouched behind an iron fence in front of the church. The lieutenant could hear Douglas yelling at the first two marines to get over the fence. Then he started to push them.

The two marines made it over. One of them opened the door to the church and threw in a grenade. They waited for the explosion, then both went in with their rifles at their hips. One came back and shouted to Douglas.

A message came over the radio.

"Looks empty so far," Chapel said.

The lieutenant and Chapel rushed across the yard and climbed the fence. The rest of the platoon followed.

The lieutenant stood by the door and stared at the crucifix above the altar. It was the biggest he had ever seen.

"Chapel, radio Six, tell him we're in the church."

"Aye, aye, sir."

The lieutenant looked around. Along the left wall, toward the front of the church, was a door.

"Sergeant Douglas—get some fire going out that door!"

"Aye, aye, sir."

Was there another room?

"Gunny—take a couple of men, see what's behind the altar. See if there's any stairs or anything."

"Aye, aye, sir."

The lieutenant looked at the crucifix. The Christ figure had a narrow, pointed mustache and smooth, shiny, light-colored skin; it looked as if it were made out of plastic.

"Lieutenant, Six says to put more fire out that door in back."

"Right, Chapel. Douglas—get more fire going out that door!"

"But Lieutenant, we're wide open there."

"Then put some benches or something in front of it—make a position!"

"Aye, aye, sir."

"Chapel, tell Six there's only one opening to fire from and it's in a bad position—they can fire in on us. Ask him if we should blow open some holes of our own with demo."

"Aye, aye, sir. Those men in the hut are in bad shape, sir. I think one of them is dying. The other is crying like hell. You can hear them over the radio."

"I know, Chapel. Douglas—get more fire out!"

The men put a pew on its side in front of the door. A machine gunner—the big one the lieutenant had seen in the truck—was beside it. He stuck his machine gun out the door, fired a burst, then pulled it back. Off to the right, beside the crucifix, the gunny was on one knee, watching, chewing gum.

"You find any stairs, Gunny?"

"No, sir. Looks like there's a folding ladder that comes down from the ceiling, but it's pulled up."

The lieutenant looked up. There was a flat wooden ceiling about twenty feet high. He saw a hole.

"Chapel, you think anyone's up there?"

"Maybe, sir, I've been watching that hole. I don't like it at all—*LOOK OUT!*"

There was a quick movement in the hole, then an explosion near the lieutenant's head. He was off his feet, then on his knees. Had he somersaulted? There was ringing in his ears.

"LOOK OUT!"

Another blast, this one not as close. A marine next to the lieutenant stared dumbly down at him, his face covered with blood. Quickly the lieutenant touched his own face: no blood. He recognized the marine.

"Henry—you all right?"

"I . . . I . . ."

"You're all right!"

Loudly, without thought or hesitation, the lieutenant ordered his men to shoot at the ceiling.

He didn't expect what happened next. Like an explosion, the sound of his men's firing came all at once, and it kept coming. It boomed from wall to wall, from floor to ceiling. A pinkish glow seemed to pulsate with the sound, to dominate it. Were the walls pink? Or was pink the color of their fire? The lieutenant was still on his knees, turned toward a wall, away from his men. He felt trapped, as if to move would be dangerous. But then, for a moment, he relaxed and welcomed the light and sound.

The platoon ceased fire. The lieutenant got up. A message came over the radio: they were to leave the church and go back to the building where the company commander was. The two marines in the hut had been reached and brought back.

"Gilbey, Douglas—get your men outside! Make sure you've got everybody!"

They assembled in front, between the church and the iron fence. The marines, shouting, were pushing each other around in the narrow space. The lieutenant was in the middle. He felt safe, protected, borne by them. It was beginning to get dark.

They moved back across the open space the same way they had come, two at a time. Each pair of marines waited until the covering fire began. Suddenly the lieutenant wanted to run, as if it were some school kids' dare. Then he and Chapel ran to the other side.

The lieutenant watched while the rest of his men made their way across. A few feet away, at the corner of the building, the big machine gunner from Douglas' squad stepped out in the open and fired a long burst toward the rear of the yard, by the hut. His machine gun was at his hip, the ammo belt dangling like a decoration. The other marines fired for only a second. Then the machine gunner stepped back, threw himself against the house, and checked the breach of his gun. The lieutenant saw a gold earring in the machine gunner's left ear.

"*Corpsman!*"

The lieutenant looked. A marine from his platoon—one of the last to run across—had been hit in the hand.

"You all right?" The lieutenant said it even as he saw that the man wasn't. The hand was a mass of blood and bits of white bone; it didn't look like a hand at all. The marine was hopping with pain.

"Oh, *Jesus,*" he said, "*do* something, Doc, give me a *needle!* It hurts, man, it hurts bad. Oh, man—can't fire no more. No more! *Gettin' out*—gettin' out! I'll take it, man—I'll *take* it!"

The lieutenant watched as the marine and Corporal Henry and one of the platoon's corpsmen walked away, down the street to the aid station.

The company commander came out of the building. He told the lieutenant to take his platoon back to the battalion CP and find out where he was supposed to spend the night. That was it, he said, no more fighting that day.

The lieutenant walked around the backyard of the head-quarters building with Gilbey and Douglas, assigning positions to each of their squads. The lieutenant told them to dig in in case of a mortar attack—just as they would out in the field. He told them to tell their men to watch out for snipers too.

"You hear anything about air support, sir?" Gilbey said.

The lieutenant said he hadn't.

"I wish they'd bomb the hell out of this place—that would drive the gooks out." He swore. "They don't need us. Why don't they call in air?"

The lieutenant finished assigning positions and walked back to the school. The men were busy digging holes. Some were eating C rations. There was a lot of talk about getting air support and naval gunfire, of bombing the enemy out of the city.

Someone came up to him. "Lieutenant, I've got to talk to you."

It was the new corpsman. The lieutenant tried to remember his name but couldn't.

"What is it, Doc?"

Suddenly the corpsman shouted. "What was it for, Lieutenant? What was it for?"

Now, through the darkness between them, the lieutenant could see the corpsman's face more clearly. His lower lip was quivering.

The lieutenant spoke firmly. "What is it, Doc?"

"It was so *stupid!*" The words rushed out. "God! They were just laying there—dying! One of them *died!* What did he die for? For a *building?*" He swore—a string of obscenities. The lieutenant thought he could see spittle on the edge of the corpsman's mouth. It occurred to him that he should have known this might happen, after the way the corpsman had bragged on the truck.

"Hold on, Doc. Take it easy." The lieutenant almost shouted it.

"Take it *easy?*" The corpsman moved a little closer to the lieutenant. "What do you mean, *take it easy?* I *heard* them, Lieutenant—I heard them on the radio. I *heard* them—how can I take it easy after that? And what did they get hit for, at the stadium? For a dead body? I want to get *out* of here, Lieutenant. This isn't right."

"We all want to get out, Doc." The lieutenant said it without thinking.

The corpsman seemed a bit stunned. "Do you? Do you really?"

The lieutenant hesitated. He thought of the others in the platoon behind him. He knew that some of them could hear.

"I don't believe you," the corpsman said. "You don't care." He sounded like a little boy.

Now the lieutenant's voice was louder and it sounded cold to him. He talked of how he *did* care, about all of them. How they all had to do their job, whatever it might be—bringing back one of their dead or taking a building. How it wasn't easy, but how they couldn't quit, because if they did they'd be dead.

When he finished the corpsman turned his head away. "I know," he said, "you just want me to shut up."

"I want you to do your job," the lieutenant said, "just like everybody else." He stared at him. The corpsman seemed to be trying to make up his mind about something. He was frowning. "Look, Doc," the lieutenant said, "I'll come by and see you later, all right?"

The corpsman shrugged. "I don't care." Then he went back to his position.

The lieutenant, the gunny, and Chapel ate a C ration dinner in the lieutenant's headquarters, a little room off the back porch of the school. Chapel said that some of the marines in the colonel's CP had whiskey. A liquor store, just down the street, had been broken into.

After dinner the lieutenant went to a meeting in the operations room. The colonel was there, along with Captain O'Gara, the two company commanders, and Lieutenant Bradley. The lieutenant nodded at Bradley and sat down. Captain O'Gara indicated on the map the buildings they had cleared out so far and where they would probably be fighting the next day. He said there was little word on the fighting north of the river, around the Citadel.

The colonel sat to the side of the map, staring in front of him. He held his pipe in his hands on his lap. When the S-3 finished, the colonel cleared his throat. Everyone in the room was quiet.

"There has been talk—rumors—about our getting air support." He cleared his throat again and frowned. It seemed an effort for him to speak. "I don't think it does the men any good to expect what will not be coming." He looked above the seated officers, as if at a picture on the back wall. "The decision has been made. There will be no close air support. There will be no naval gunfire."

He looked down at his pipe and shuffled his feet. He looked up. "It is not our mission to destroy the city of Hue," he continued. "Our mission is to destroy as many of the enemy as we can, and keep our own casualties to a minimum. It is not an easy mission, I know. But I also know that the enemy would consider it a victory if we destroyed Hue. He doesn't care; we have to." He looked around the room and nodded to the S-3.

After the meeting the lieutenant inspected his platoon's positions. Some of the holes were too shallow and he made the marines dig them deeper. When Gilbey asked about air support again, the lieutenant told him what the colonel had said.

The lieutenant stopped by the new corpsman.

"How are you doing, Doc?"

He was sitting on the ground. His helmet was off and he had his medical kit open in front of him. His hair was dark and curly.

"I'll be all right," he said. His voice sounded dull and sullen. "Don't worry about me."

For a moment the lieutenant thought about patting him on the head. Then he walked away.

A high-pitched voice called his name. The lieutenant moved closer and saw a shock of blond hair.

"Peaches," he said, "how are you doing?" He smiled.

"Oh, all right, sir. I was just wondering—have you heard anything about Corporal Henry?"

The lieutenant shook his head. "I'm sure he's going to be all right. The doc said the wounds were superficial. . . . Good thing they were only concussion grenades—we were all pretty lucky."

Peaches nodded. "Thank you, Lieutenant."

The lieutenant kneeled down. "Are you all right?"

"I guess so," Peaches said. There was sadness in his voice. "It just seems kind of strange without him. We've been together about eight months, now—in the company office."

The lieutenant was silent. Then he got up. "If I hear anything more about Henry, I'll let you know, Peaches."

"Thank you, sir."

Back in the lieutenant's CP Chapel set up the radio watch. He, the lieutenant, and the gunny would share it. The lieutenant took the first watch; he wasn't sleepy.

He sat by the radio, in the dark, going over the day's events. How scared he had been!—when they had first arrived, when he had thought he might piss in his pants. He had never felt fear like that before—as a force that suddenly took him over, completely. Yet behind the stadium he hadn't been afraid at all—he had stood up, as though daring the enemy to shoot him. He smiled as he remembered what the intelligence captain had said when he went up to him in the ditch: "I've got some intelligence for you, Lieutenant. There's enemy around here." That was the way to do it, the lieutenant thought: make fun of danger. He smiled again as he thought of himself in the church, when he had ordered his men to shoot at the ceiling. Had he really said that?—*Fill the sky with lead!* Yes, he had. How many gooks had been up there? Would he ever know?

The lieutenant thought he hadn't done so badly after all. Of course, he wasn't in the real war yet—that would come tomorrow, he felt sure, when his men would go from house to house, fighting. The lieutenant felt ready for it.

ii.

The next morning was overcast and cool again. The lieutenant, Chapel, and the gunny had a C ration breakfast. Gilbey came to the door.

"Yes, Corporal Gilbey?"

"I've got a problem, sir."

"What is it?"

"Foster."

"What about him?"

"He says he won't fight any more."

The lieutenant stared at Gilbey. Gilbey looked and sounded blank.

"What do you mean, he won't fight any more?"

"He told me he won't go out with the squad, sir."

"Oh? And what did you tell him?"

Gilbey shrugged. "I told him he had to. But he says he doesn't. Because he's up for court-martial."

There was no strength in Gilbey's voice, the lieutenant thought; it was resigned. But Gilbey could be forceful. He had a reputation as one of the best squad leaders in his company. He even had the look of a good squad leader: tall, broad shoulders, a rugged-looking face.

Gilbey gestured with his head. "He wants to see you, sir."

Now the lieutenant could see Foster standing just outside the door. The lieutenant remembered a leadership class he once had had in officers training—a movie in which a young lieutenant is confronted by a marine who refuses to fight.

"All right, Corporal Gilbey, send him in."

"Yes, sir. Can I go back to my squad, sir?"

"Yes."

"Thank you, sir."

Gilbey went out the door and Foster came in. The gunny and Chapel both stood up, excused themselves, and left.

"What is it, Private Foster?"

Foster shook his head. "Uh-uh. I'm sorry, Lieutenant, but I'm not going out there. And you can't make me, neither. I'm up for court-martial." His voice was a raspy whisper. His pale blue eyes, next to his light brown skin, looked unnatural, like a genetic defect.

"What's the matter with you, Foster? You *asked* to come up here—remember? What happened to all that talk about how you were going to make up for your past?"

Foster shook his head. His eyes stayed on the lieutenant. "Uh-uh. That was yesterday. I'm not going out there. And you can't make me. I'm up for court-martial." Foster seemed to get strength from repeating himself.

"Come on, Foster! You're a member of this platoon. You've got a job to do, just like everyone else. You're not going to turn chicken now."

Foster shook his head. Somehow his eyes made him appear vulnerable and the lieutenant had to force himself to stare into them. "I don't care what you say, Lieutenant. I'm not going out there. And you can't make me. I'm up for court-martial. I'll stay here and help out in the CP."

"Damn you, Foster!" His damn simpleminded confidence, the lieutenant thought, like a snotty school kid with a note from Mommy. What kind of war was this, anyway, if someone could just quit?

But what could the lieutenant do? Go to the colonel? He imagined the colonel looking at him, saying nothing, turning away. He tried to remember how the training movie had ended, what the instructor had said. But hadn't the real mistake been his own—for letting Foster join the platoon in the first place? For believing Foster?

"Get out of here, Foster. I don't want to look at you any more. You're a shitbird, that's all, and you always will be. I'm going to do everything I can to make sure you pay for this."

Foster bowed his head, as if in gratitude, and slowly backed out of the room, keeping his eyes on the lieutenant for as long as he could.

The lieutenant received word to report to the operations room. The company commander of Alpha was there, and he briefed the lieutenant on the plan for the day. More house-to-house fighting. The lieutenant's platoon would be the backup again, but they would probably be called into action early.

The company commander asked whether the lieutenant had any questions. He hesitated, then said no.

"Moving out in fifteen minutes."

"Roger." The lieutenant tried to make his voice sound determined. But why did he have to try?

He called a meeting of the gunny, Gilbey, and Douglas and told them the plan. Douglas and the gunny looked at the lieutenant's map as if they found it interesting. The gunny was chewing gum. Gilbey stared at the lieutenant; he seemed to want to speak.

"Any questions?"

Gilbey had a question. "You think there's a chance the gooks might have pulled out, Lieutenant—like, during the night?"

"No," the lieutenant said. His voice was cold. He realized it was the same question he had wanted to ask the company commander.

A messenger came in. The lieutenant was to report to the S-3 immediately.

In five minutes the lieutenant came back.

"You can forget everything I just told you," he said. "We're not going with Alpha. MACV just found out about a National Police compound that's been holding out against the NVA the whole time. They want us to check it out and then run a sweep though the neighborhood. It's supposed to be deserted."

"God damn, Lieutenant, that sounds much better." It was Gilbey. How was he going to lead his men if he was thinking like that?

"It sure does," the gunny said. He was grinning and his jaws moved up and down.

"Nobody's sure," the lieutenant said. "There might be something over there. So let's not do any relaxing."

They walked past the MACV compound and then turned east on the main street that ran parallel to the river. The platoon was in a double column, as if ready for combat, but Vietnamese in civilian clothes swarmed around them as they moved down the street.

"Now I see why they call this the modern part of the city," Chapel said.

They passed tall, white, new-looking buildings. It was like

some futuristic setting out of a science-fiction novel, the lieutenant thought, in which people from the past had to fight in a city of the future. Farther on, the street became residential and there were no more civilians.

At the end of the street was a large building surrounded by a five-foot wall. A door in the wall opened and a dozen Vietnamese dressed in utilities rushed out. They were smiling, laughing, and talking rapidly. The lieutenant and his men went through the gate and into a courtyard.

The lieutenant spoke in Vietnamese, trying to find out who was in charge, and immediately they all gathered around him. One of them said that he—a captain in the National Police—was the leader, but his men kept interrupting. They were all trying to tell the same story at once. They had been surrounded by the NVA; the NVA had threatened to kill them all if they didn't surrender; they had held out; they were glad, now that the marines were in Hue. This was the first time they had opened their gate in five days, they said.

Suddenly there was firing from the direction of the river. The Vietnamese, shouting, jumped and fired over the wall. Some of the marines also fired.

"What is it?" the lieutenant asked Chapel.

They went to the wall and looked. In the middle of the river a South Vietnamese gunboat was shooting tracer rounds at a house on the far bank.

"I see 'em," Chapel said. "Looks like NVA." He was pointing across the river.

The lieutenant saw a movement in a yard of the house, then he saw a door opening and closing. It must have been two hundred meters away. The gunboat rocked back and forth on the water as it shot off its rounds.

Suddenly the gunny shouted. "I got one, I got one!" He looked around, beaming.

"You sure, Gunny?"

"Yes, sir," the gunny said. "I saw him go down and he didn't get up. That's one thing I am, Lieutenant—a good shot."

"All right, Gunny. Let's not waste all our ammo."

The gunny shouted at the marines to watch their ammunition. The gunboat stopped firing, swung around, and sped away up river. The firing stopped.

Chapel sent a report to headquarters, and then the platoon

left the compound. The neighborhood they were to search was across the street.

"I've seen worse places to live," Chapel said.

The lieutenant agreed. It seemed like a nice neighborhood. Small wooden houses, tended lawns, shrubbery and trees. It was almost like where he had grown up, except the houses here were smaller, closer together.

"Door's locked, Lieutenant. Should we break in?"

It was Gilbey, standing by one of the houses. Chapel said that Douglas' squad asked the same thing. Apparently all the houses were locked.

The lieutenant went up to the door. It was wooden, painted red, with no knob. He gave it a push but it didn't move. He looked at the windows; they were boarded up.

"Might be snipers hiding inside," Gilbey said. "They wait for us to go by, then take a few shots." He pointed his rifle at the door. "We could break in easy."

The lieutenant imagined the noise of firing, the door in splinters, the explosions of grenades, Gilbey smashing down more doors.

"Negative," he said. "The colonel said we're not here to destroy the city. Just have your men check around the houses. Go in only if they're open and make sure they watch their rear."

Chapel, who had wandered ahead, called back to the lieutenant; "Sir, there's gooks up here—I mean people, civilians. Houseful of 'em, looks like."

The lieutenant climbed a fence and found Chapel.

Chapel put his hand to his mouth and lowered his voice. "Damn—she's about the prettiest thing I've seen since I've been here."

The lieutenant looked and saw a girl standing in a doorway. She had black hair and wore a bright red sweater and a black, Western-style skirt.

"*Chao co,*" the lieutenant said, and smiled. Chapel was right, he thought. She was the prettiest Vietnamese girl he had ever seen. She must be a college student, he thought. She looked as though she were dressed for a football game. The curve of her red wool sweater reminded him of someone he knew.

"Is there going to be more fighting?" She said it in English.

"What?" the lieutenant said. "I mean, I don't know." He

noticed that she was trembling a little, and he stopped smiling. Behind her inside the house he could see more people—an old woman, some children, a baby. There was low, excited talking.

"What are you doing here?"

"What are *we* doing here? We live here. What are *you* doing here?"

"We're looking for the enemy—VC and NVA. Have you seen any?"

She shook her head. "We just want to stay here. We don't want to leave."

"All right, I'm not telling you to leave."

"But we don't have any food. We're hungry."

"I think there's food at the university. I heard they're handing it out there."

"But we don't want to leave. This is our home. We want to stay. Is there going to be more fighting?"

"I don't know. If they come back there will be."

"That's what they say too."

The lieutenant tried to see past her better. It was dark inside the house. She moved a little, blocking his view.

"We just want to stay," she said, again. "We don't care about any war. But we have no food."

"All right," he said, "I'll see what I can do."

He told Chapel to pass the word for extra C rations. In a couple of minutes they had twenty cans.

"I'll have some men bring them into the house," the lieutenant said.

"No," the girl said. "Just leave them there."

The platoon moved on.

They rounded a corner and suddenly the lieutenant saw the stadium, not far away.

"Looks like this is the house where those NVA were holed up yesterday," Chapel said.

The door to the house was open. One of its walls had a hole in it. In front, on the street, was a dead NVA.

"Check out the house," the lieutenant said to his men. "See if there's any weapons!"

There were empty ammo boxes stacked against the front windows and scattered around the floor. On the floor and walls were big blotches of bright red.

"No weapons, Lieutenant. Nothing."

"All right, Chapel, call the CP and make a report. Tell them about the body. Ask them what they want us to do next."

The lieutenant looked out of a window, trying to see whether he could find the tree he had been behind when the bullet had hit it.

They set up for the night by a warehouse on the river. Next to it was a large loading area enclosed by a wall. The lieutenant had his men blow holes in the wall with demolition to make their firing positions. He had a machine gun position set up on the sidewalk by the entrance. Just inside the entrance was a small office and he made his headquarters there.

In the evening the lieutenant walked around the area with the gunny and inspected the positions. All the men asked the same questions: "What next, Lieutenant? . . . How's the fighting going, sir? . . . How long are we gonna be here?" The lieutenant said he didn't know.

They walked outside to inspect the machine gun position. It was getting dark but there were still many civilians about. Two came up to him and asked for food. The lieutenant shook his head and told them to go to the university.

The machine gunner with the golden earring sat behind a tree next to his gun, eating from a C ration can. A Vietnamese came up to him and held out his hand and pointed to his stomach. The machine gunner kept eating. The Vietnamese stood for a while and then walked away.

The lieutenant and the gunny went back to the little office. Chapel was sitting at the desk. A candle burned on top of it.

"Chapel, where'd that candle come from?"

He smiled. "From some gook out on the street, sir."

"How'd you do that?"

"It was easy. You can talk pretty well with your hands—especially if you've got a couple of C-rats." He laughed. "I got candles to last a month."

The lieutenant looked around the office.

"It's safe, Lieutenant," Chapel said, "there's no windows and the door faces out to the courtyard."

The three of them opened C ration cans for dinner. The

lieutenant said, "Chapel, do you know that machine gunner —the one in Douglas' squad—the big one, he wears an earring?"

Chapel shook his head with authority. "No, sir, not personally. But I've heard of him. He's from Bravo. Kind of a legend, from what I hear."

"Oh?"

Chapel nodded. "Yes, sir. Name's Mad Dog. That's what everyone calls him—or just Dog. He's on his second extension—been over here three years, almost. He's turned down promotions a few times. He just wants to be a machine gunner, he says. Likes to kill." Then Chapel told about another machine gunner he had known who was like that, a former motorcycle gang member who had become a mercenary because he thought the Marine Corps was getting too soft.

The gunny, who had been quiet, said, "Personally, today was my kind of fighting." He smiled.

"How's that, Gunny?"

"Shooting over the wall by the river—that's my style. Long-distance warfare." He laughed. "I used to be on the marksmanship team," he said. "I can still shoot pretty well." He took a mouthful of beef and potatoes. Still chewing, he said, "You know something?"

"What's that, Gunny?"

"I've got a feeling. I think that tomorrow is going to be just like today: I think we're going to luck out again. And I don't mind saying, I wouldn't mind that at all."

"Oh?" the lieutenant said. "Why do you say that?"

The gunny smiled and his head bobbed up and down. "Because I've always been lucky. I've been in the Corps almost twenty years and I've always pulled good duty."

"I thought we were here to fight a war, Gunny."

"Yes, sir," the gunny said. He stopped smiling. "When we have to."

After dinner the gunny took several small containers out of his pack and took different-colored pills out of each.

"For my dysentery," he said, as if answering a question. "Four different pills, three different times a day, four different amounts. You need to be a genius to keep track." He laughed.

They made up the radio watch. Chapel took the first turn.

The lieutenant went out and took another walk around the area, then returned to the office.

The gunny was sitting on the floor, his back against a wall, reading a letter. Chapel was at the desk, by the candle and radio, reading a book.

"Mail call, Gunny?"

The gunny smiled. "It's an old one, sir. I'm pretending I just got it." He laughed. After a few minutes he folded the letter, put it in his pack, and lay down.

The lieutenant sat on the floor against a wall and smoked a cigarette.

Chapel looked up from his book.

"Sir?" His voice was low.

"What is it?"

Chapel looked at the gunny, who was now snoring softly, then back at the lieutenant. "I just wanted to say something, sir."

"Sure. What is it?"

"I've made a decision."

The lieutenant stared at him.

"Remember how I used to talk about going to OCS— becoming an officer, making a career out of the Marine Corps?"

The lieutenant nodded.

"Well, I've decided."

"Oh?"

"Yes, sir. I'm getting out—I mean, if I ever get out of here." He rapped his knuckles lightly on the desk. "I've decided to go back to school and study agriculture. I'm going to be a farmer."

They stared at each other. Then Chapel said, "Yes, sir, I just thought I'd tell you. I mean, that's how it is with me. I think about something for a while, and then suddenly I decide. Telling somebody kind of makes it official. Doesn't matter who it is." Chapel picked up his book again.

The lieutenant lit another cigarette. He looked across the narrow room. The gunny was sleeping on his side, one of his hands under his head. His helmet, pack, and rifle were neatly arranged in a corner. Yes, the gunny was probably right, the lieutenant thought: he would keep staying out of it until he retired, and then he'd stay out of whatever else there was to stay out of. The lieutenant pictured the gunny as older, proudly taking his daily medicine, his different-colored pills. He'd have his marksmanship trophies in the den.

The lieutenant looked at Chapel's book. It was a family saga, a best-seller. The lieutenant found himself wishing he had brought his book, too. He could be reading it, now that he couldn't sleep, now that they had candles. He remembered what he had thought at Phu Bai, that this time he wouldn't need a book. But what had happened? Was it the gunny's luck that was keeping them out of the fighting? Or was it that he, too—like the gunny—was "lucky"?

Chapel's lips were moving slightly. His cheeks were a bit pudgy. How did Chapel stay heavy on the food they ate? How could he keep reading—didn't he want to talk some more? The lieutenant realized that he wanted to talk with Chapel— the way that Richman used to. Was it because of Richman that Chapel had made his decision? He imagined him and Chapel staying up late, forgetting their difference in rank, talking about the times they had had together. Maybe they'd get a bottle of booze—from the looted liquor store—get quietly drunk and talk about why they joined the Corps. They could talk about their hometowns too, about their old girlfriends. He looked at the gunny again. How could he always sleep so easily?

The lieutenant checked his watch. He thought he'd better get some sleep.

Later, he woke. Had he heard a shot?

"What's that?"

The gunny was at the desk. "I don't know, sir. Sounded like a shot."

Chapel was sitting up too. It was quiet. For a moment the lieutenant wondered whether they had all had the same dream.

"Chapel, check with the squads, find out if everyone's okay; find out if anyone knows what that was."

Chapel got on the radio. Then he said, "Negative, sir. Everyone's okay, nobody knows where it came from. They say it sounded about a block away."

The three of them sat for a while longer, listening. Then Chapel and the lieutenant lay down again.

Suddenly the lieutenant remembered his dream—the one he'd been having when the shot had woke him. He had been

back in college. But there was a war going on. On the grounds
outside the classroom there was fighting and killing. The
lieutenant kept telling his professor that he wasn't going to
quit. No, he kept saying, I won't quit. I'll fight. The professor
was the colonel. He didn't say anything, but just kept staring
at the lieutenant. The lieutenant could sense the colonel knew
something about him, something the lieutenant was hiding. I
won't quit, he kept saying, I'll fight.

iii.

The next morning was overcast, cooler, and a little raw. It
seemed that the monsoon wasn't over after all. Chapel called
the battalion CP to ask for instructions, and the answer was to
wait. There was a report that an NVA company had been
caught in the open the night before while crossing a street. A
platoon from Alpha Company had opened fire, killing
seventy-three.

At ten o'clock a jeep pulled up outside the entrance to the
platoon's area. Out stepped a tall, thin, middle aged man
with long arms and eyeglasses, carrying a small canvas bag.
He looked out of place in his jungle utilities.

It was the regimental chaplain. "Good morning, sir," the
lieutenant said and introduced himself. He told the chaplain
they had met once before, but the chaplain frowned and
seemed not to remember.

"I just came by for a couple of minutes, Lieutenant," he
said. "I'd like to hold a service. Communion. It's Sunday."

"Yes, sir. Protestant, right?"

The chaplain nodded. The lieutenant told the gunny to pass
the word that there'd be a communion service in five minutes
for anyone who wished to attend.

The chaplain decided to hold it behind the warehouse, by
the river. The lieutenant waited by a corner of the building
and watched. Seven marines attended; Gilbey was one of
them. They took their helmets off and the chaplain, who now
had a silver cross around his neck, read in a low voice from a
small Bible. The marines bowed their heads and the chaplain
prayed. Then, out of the bag he carried, he gave them each a
small wafer and sip of wine. Behind them, a gunboat was

shooting tracer rounds toward the opposite bank. The lieutenant turned and went back to the office.

A little after noon a message came over the radio. The lieutenant was to take his platoon back to the battalion CP and receive instructions.

"Back to school?"

"Negative, sir," Chapel said. "They're in the church now."

This time the lieutenant walked into the church while his platoon waited in the yard next door.

Inside he stopped. On the right, toward the altar, Captain O'Gara, the company commander of Alpha, and Lieutenant Dobson were bent over a map. On the left the colonel sat in a pew by himself. Between them was the tall, shiny crucifix with the ribs sticking out, the cloth low on the hips. In the rear corner to the lieutenant's right, some marines stood and sat around a table. They were talking softly, laughing, smoking. One of them was Foster.

Foster saw the lieutenant, stopped talking, and stared at him. His light blue eyes seemed to probe the lieutenant for something he badly wanted.

"Hello, Lieutenant." His voice was like a whisper. "How's everyone doing?"

The lieutenant stared back. Then, as though he had to force himself, he turned away and walked down the aisle.

The colonel was wearing his helmet and new flak jacket. His pipe was in the flak jacket pocket and the jacket was zipped to the top, as if he was cold. Beside him on the pew lay three captured weapons. One was a machine gun; its barrel was mangled and its stock splintered. On the dark polished wood of the pew the weapons looked dirty and out of place.

"Hello, sir."

The colonel turned his head slowly and looked at the lieutenant. Then he turned it back again, facing straight ahead.

What was wrong with him? the lieutenant wondered. Why did he just sit there bundled up in his new jacket, his hands in his lap, like a little boy?

The lieutenant spoke again. "Sir."

The colonel nodded slightly.

"Sir. When we were in here"—the lieutenant had to think of when it was—"two days ago, I mean, my platoon . . ." *Cooks and bakers* went through his mind. "What I mean is—see that hole up there, in the ceiling?" The lieutenant pointed, but the colonel didn't move. "They were up there, sir—lobbing grenades down on us. I don't know how many, but we fired up there, the whole platoon. I'm sure we got them. What I mean is, they're probably still up there—KIA. With weapons. I think there's a folding ladder over there." The lieutenant pointed. "If you were to send someone up . . ." He glanced back at Foster.

The colonel said nothing. But he nodded his head slightly.

Captain O'Gara, the S-3, called the lieutenant over.

Outside the church the lieutenant saw Dobson and called to him.

"Tom. How's it going?"

Dobson turned around. His eyes were bloodshot and he had a dark stubble of beard that made the rest of his face look pale, almost sickly.

"Bad," he said, and shook his head. His voice sounded lifeless. "There's only two officers left in the company. I'm down to about half my platoon."

"Any KIA's?"

Dobson nodded. "Five." He said their names as though he expected the lieutenant to know them. "I was really close to them."

"I'm sorry," the lieutenant said. "How about the gooks—you been getting a lot?"

"Yeah." Dobson lifted his face a little. "Jesus, I don't see how the gooks take it—how they hang in there. We've really been blasting them."

"It must be tough—the fighting, I mean."

"Yeah," Dobson said. Then he frowned. "You've really got to kick ass to keep these guys going. Sometimes when I move out I wonder if anyone's coming with me. But you've just got to kick ass." He paused, thinking, then smiled a little. Energy returned to his face. "Remember what it was like in training—house-to-house fighting? Man, this is so *different*. I mean, you use that stuff too, but this is like another world. You think you've been fighting for hours and it's only been a few minutes—and you've gained maybe a few feet." He shook his head; he looked puzzled. "The fighting is so close. You step out at the wrong time and you're gone. It's like you never know what's going to happen the next moment. Like Bradley, he—"

"Bradley? What happened to Bradley?"

"You didn't know?"

The lieutenant shook his head. He felt hollow.

"Yesterday afternoon," Dobson said. "He took over one of the platoons. Anyway, there was this wall they had to go over and Bradley went first. NVA machine gunner on the other side, about twenty feet away. Killed instantly."

The lieutenant swore softly under his breath.

"I'm sorry," Dobson said. "I guess you knew him pretty well, huh?" His mouth hung open. For a moment the lieutenant thought he looked like a dog.

"No, not really," the lieutenant said. Suddenly he remembered Bradley bending over the body just inside the compound, needing to know who it was. "Not that well," the lieutenant said. "But I liked him. He was a good man."

Dobson nodded. "Yeah."

Then the lieutenant said, as though he needed to explain: "We had it pretty easy, didn't run into a thing yesterday."

"Oh?" Dobson showed no interest. "Well, I guess I'd better get back to my platoon. We're leading out." He looked at his watch. "Ten minutes."

"Say," the lieutenant said, "what's with the colonel, anyway?"

"What do you mean?"

"I mean . . . He seems a little out of it. Is he okay?"

Dobson shrugged. "I don't think he's been getting much sleep."

"Oh."

"Well, good luck," Dobson said.

"Yeah, good luck."

The lieutenant went back to his platoon. He called over the gunny, Gilbey, and Douglas. At the edge of the yard by the street they all knelt around the lieutenant's map.

"All right," the lieutenant said, "here's what we're going to do." He felt a new determination. They were going to be back in the fighting now; he knew what he had to do. On the map he showed them the buildings the S-3 had told him they were going to attack.

"We'll be last in the column. There'll be a tank going with us, leading the way. The enemy is known to have sandbagged, automatic-weapons positions and probably rockets. When we get near the first objective, the tank will prep it, and then the company commander will issue further orders."

He looked at Douglas and then Gilbey. "Corporal Gilbey, your squad will lead out. I'll be up front, right behind the first fire team. Gunny, you'll be back with Douglas' squad. Any questions?"

Douglas kept looking at the map, as if he could find out more from it. The gunny chewed hard on his gum.

But Gilbey had something to say, didn't he? The lieutenant was sure he was going to speak. Gilbey opened his mouth, just a little. His eyes were open wide.

"Any questions?"

Gilbey stared a moment longer, then got up and went to his squad.

Slowly they moved down either side of the street in a double column. It seemed to be a nice street, the lieutenant thought, tree-lined, the houses with porches and lawns. He could see the tank up ahead. It squatted in the middle of the street like a huge green cockroach.

The column stopped. There was a commotion in back, by Douglas' squad. Chapel was on the radio.

"They've found a couple of gooks, sir."

"What? Who are they? Any weapons?"

"Negative, sir. They don't know who they are; they were hiding in some shed. They're in uniform, though. Douglas wants to know what he should do."

The lieutenant looked ahead. No one was moving.

"Come on, let's go back and take a look."

Marines crowded the side of the street. The lieutenant pushed his way through. The machine gunner known as Mad Dog stood in front of a shed, his gun pointing down at two Vietnamese. His sleeves were rolled up, showing thick forearms covered with curly blond hairs.

"What is it?"

Mad Dog kept staring down. He seemed not to have heard the lieutenant. One of the Vietnamese looked like a teenager. Both were crying.

The machine gunner swore. "Go on, cry," he said. "You're gonna die."

"Wait! Don't shoot!"

The machine gunner turned his head toward the lieutenant. His jaw muscles were tensed, his nostrils flared.

The lieutenant spoke to the two in Vietnamese.

"Nam Viet Quon Doi," the older one said, and repeated it. He pointed to the patch on the other one's shoulder, then pointed to his mouth and spoke again.

"He says they're ARVN," the lieutenant said, to no one in particular. "He says they've been hiding from the NVA. They didn't know who was out here. They haven't eaten in three days."

"He's lying," the machine gunner said. The younger Vietnamese cried louder.

The lieutenant tried to figure out what to do. He imagined the marines around him were all on Mad Dog's side. He didn't want to hear any more crying.

"Douglas, have a man take them back to the church. Give them to the Three, tell him they claim they're ARVN—he can tie them up till he finds out for sure. But tell him they say they haven't eaten in three days."

The lieutenant thought his voice sounded weak. He turned and saw the machine gunner back in his place in the column, his machine gun at his hip, his weight on one leg, as if bored.

The lieutenant and Chapel went back to their places. The column moved again, then stopped. Then it started again.

The lieutenant heard a whistling noise.

"Uh-oh," Chapel said.

There were four *crack*s in rapid succession. Fifty meters ahead four small gray clouds rose up from the street.

Word came down the column: "Incoming!"

"Be ready to take cover!" the lieutenant shouted. He turned to Chapel, but he was already running across the street.

"Chapel, where the hell are you going?"

Chapel turned. "To that building, sir. I just heard 'em drop some more down the tubes. Hell, I'm getting out of here."

The lieutenant watched Chapel, his radio on his back, run

toward the building. His plump body seemed to hobble more than run. Several thoughts seemed to fill the lieutenant's mind at once. How could Chapel hear that?—his ears weren't *that* good. How did he manage to stay so heavy, anyway, on the food they ate? And why was he leaving the lieutenant alone?

The lieutenant shouted at his men to take cover.

Ringing. A loud ringing, much louder than in the church. Pressing. A hard pressing—*very* hard. Ringing and pressing in the lieutenant's ear. And something else, he realized: spinning. He was spinning around and he couldn't stop. Ringing, pressing, and spinning. He couldn't stop any of it. He couldn't walk, raise his head, look around. He couldn't be his normal self. He wanted to shake his head and be the way he had been before, but he knew he couldn't. He knew he had been hit.

Hit! *You bastard,* he told himself. *You stupid bastard. You never thought this would happen, that you could be reduced to this. Now you know. You're just like all the rest, a target for them to hit. And it can't be undone. You're hit. And you're going to die. Fool.*

The lieutenant felt weak. He sank to his knees. He realized he hadn't been spinning at all, it had just seemed that way. He had been standing in the same spot the whole time. Time? How long had it been? Just a few seconds, he realized . . . but all those thoughts!

He felt weaker. He was lying on the ground now, on his stomach. He felt weaker still. It occurred to him that he wouldn't be conscious for long.

He had a thought. How peaceful this was, how simple! Everything had come to this and it seemed all right. At least he was getting the chance to experience it. The lieutenant thought himself lucky. Bradley had died right away. He felt that now he knew what he had come up here for: not to fight, but for this. All he wanted now was to tell everyone he knew—his parents, the friends he grew up with, his teachers in college, the girlfriend he lost—how easy this was, how there was nothing to fear.

But how could he tell anyone? Wasn't that the meaning of this—that he wouldn't be able to? He felt great sadness, far greater than he had ever known before. For the first time he had something to say, something that mattered, but now he was unable to say it.

He was aware of blackness entering his mind. Just then he happened to see, out of the corner of an eye, a stream of red. He moved his hand and pressed his fingers against his ear.

There were shouts of *Corpsman up, Corpsman up!,* and swearing and crying. Hysterical crying. The lieutenant had heard these sounds before and knew what they meant. They were from men who were dying—or who thought they were dying. How strange, the lieutenant thought, that everything could change so suddenly. Were they really the same men who had been standing quietly on the street a few moments before ready to do battle?

He realized that no one knew he had been hit. Then he thought that that was all right—let the others get the attention. He would just lie there. Maybe sleep. It was hard to stay awake, he felt so weak. It was hard just to breathe. Was there something in his throat? It was hard, too, to keep his fingers pressed against his ear. Had he ever felt this tired? No, he decided. He just wanted to sleep. If he lived, then he'd wake; if he didn't, he'd never know. It seemed simple.

For no reason that he was aware of, the lieutenant raised an arm.

Someone knelt beside him.

"Lieutenant? Are you all right? Oh, my God. Oh, my God!"

It was the gunny. The gunny started to shout, but the lieutenant put his arm around his neck and pulled his head down to his lips, as though he wanted to kiss him.

In the gunny's ear the lieutenant whispered about his own ear, about how he had stopped the blood with his fingers. *"Get someone to press it, Gunny,"* he whispered, *"going to pass out soon. Can't press it any more. Too weak."* He felt the thick muscles in the gunny's neck and the rough whiskers on his lips. For a moment he wanted to keep the gunny down there, just to feel him.

"Don't worry, Lieutenant, I'll take care of it, don't worry!" The gunny was whispering, too, but his whisper was panicky and hurried.

The gunny raised his head and shouted orders. He was bellowing, as if forcing all the authority he could into his voice. The lieutenant thought he understood. His own voice, he knew, had sounded like that. *Worry?* he thought. No, it was the gunny who had to worry now. The gunny was in charge.

"We'll have you out of here in a second, Lieutenant." The lieutenant felt the gunny put a bandage around his head and then there was someone pressing in his ear. It was a black marine—the lieutenant could tell by the arm; a thin, muscular, hairless arm. Was it Douglas? The lieutenant whispered as loud as he could, *"Don't stop pressing."*

"Don't worry, Lieutenant," the marine said, "I'll stay with you." No, it wasn't Douglas. But the lieutenant liked the voice anyway. One of the cooks and bakers, he thought.

Then he was being carried, and next he was inside a building, on the floor. A stone floor; it felt cold. A voice said, "Where else does it hurt?" Then somebody was stripping off his clothes. The lieutenant could hear the sound the bayonet made as it ripped down his shirt and trousers. Then he felt the cool air on his body. He felt like a baby.

"Turn him over," a voice said, "see if there's any more wounds." Other voices said, "You're going to be all right, Lieutenant, you're going to be all right." But did they know? No: he could tell by the way they were saying it. But he didn't mind their saying it. Who were they? he wondered. He didn't know any of their voices. Where was Chapel?

He heard a voice from farther away. Swear words, and then, "It's Peaches." Another voice said, "KIA?" There was no reply.

Another voice said, "Who is it? Face is all messed up." "Check his dog tag." Then, "It's Gilbey," and more swearing. *Gilbey,* the lieutenant thought, *he was a good marine. Didn't really know him that well, though.*

The lieutenant saw an arm lying next to him. He couldn't see the end of it, just the forearm and fingers. He whispered. *"Whose arm is that?"*

There was a short laugh, and someone said, "That's yours, Lieutenant. Don't worry, it's all right."

The lieutenant reached over with the arm he could move and picked the other one up. It didn't *feel* like his arm. There was no feeling in it at all. He thought: *I don't care, only to live. Please.*

He heard the sound of mortars and became frightened. No, he thought, no more incoming, no more confusion. But a voice said, "Hear that, Lieutenant? That's ours. They'll knock out those gooks."

Soon he was being carried on a stretcher. It was hard to breathe. In panic, the lieutenant tried to say something. But he couldn't. He felt he was choking. He threw up. Now he could breathe. He thought about his panic and it seemed to him there was something good about it. The vomit seemed good, too; it felt warm against his face. He smiled. He was lying in his own vomit, naked, and he liked it.

He was in the back of a moving truck. It stopped. Then he was being carried again. Suddenly the lieutenant realized where he was. He smiled again. He was put on a table. A doctor looked down at him, shined a flashlight in his face. The doctor was Vietnamese.

"Chao ong," the lieutenant whispered. It seemed important to show the doctor he could speak his language.

But the doctor didn't reply; he just turned his head. "Get an American doctor," he said in English.

A voice said, "Check his dog tag. What's his religion?"

He felt a hand on his chest and someone said, "Get the chaplain."

Then the chaplain was looking down at him, frowning. The lieutenant whispered, *"I saw you this morning, remember?"*

The chaplain seemed not to hear him.

One of them was killed, the lieutenant wanted to say, *from the service. Gilbey. Remember him? I made him lead out. It was his turn.* But the lieutenant couldn't even whisper.

An American doctor came and the chaplain stood aside.

A voice said, "Last chopper's about to go out—better get him on it."

He was in the back of a truck again, next to another wounded. The truck moved. It stopped. The lieutenant could hear and feel the rush of helicopter rotors.

A voice next to him said, "It's all right, Lieutenant. We're going to be all right."

The lieutenant saw who it was: the new corpsman; his chest was wrapped in bandages.

"I'm going to be all right," the corpsman said. He was grinning. He looked young, the lieutenant thought, like a high school kid.

"You're going to be all right, too," the corpsman said. "Honest. I know. You're going to be all right—we both are."

The lieutenant tried to speak but couldn't.

"Isn't that great?" the corpsman said. "We're getting out of here—both of us! We're going home, Lieutenant, back to the States."

The lieutenant tried to think. Was what the corpsman was saying true? How did *he* know? And was it right that the corpsman should be so happy?

The lieutenant decided he didn't know—that he didn't have to know, not right now. But he wanted to do something. He couldn't speak but he could move one of his arms, and he did. He reached over and put his hand on top of the corpsman's head. He rubbed the corpsman's curly black hair and smiled.

CONGO

The National Bestseller by

MICHAEL CRICHTON

Author of THE ANDROMEDA STRAIN

"Darkest Africa. Strangling vines. Rain forest. Pygmies. Clouds of mosquitoes. Rampaging hippos. Roaring gorillas. Killer natives. Gorges. Rapids. Erupting volcanoes. An abandoned city full of diamonds, lost in the jungle. Maybe a new animal species, a weird cross between man and ape, but unheard of in 20th-century anthropology. Zaire. Congo. Michael Crichton's newest thriller. And of course: technology, which is what it's all about today, isn't it? Zoom!"
The Boston Globe

"A gem of a thriller!"
Playboy

"Oh, is this ever a good one!"
Detroit News

"The master of very tall tales plunges into the heart of darkness. . . . A dazzling example of how to combine science and adventure writing."
People

"What entertainment! . . . Crichton has created in Amy a 'talking gorilla' of enough charm to enshrine her in pop culture as firmly as R2D2."
Saturday Review

Available wherever paperbacks are sold, or directly from the publisher. Include 50¢ per copy for postage and handling; allow 6-8 weeks for delivery. Avon Books, Mail Order Dept., 224 West 57th St., N.Y., N.Y. 10019.

AVON Paperback

56176 • $2.95
Congo 10-81

The National Bestseller by
GARY JENNINGS

"A blockbuster historical novel. . . . From the start of
this epic, the reader is caught up in the sweep and
grandeur, the richness and humanity of this fictive
unfolding of life in Mexico before the Spanish
conquest. . . . Anyone who lusts for adventure, or that
book you can't put down, will glory in AZTEC!"

The Los Angeles Times

"A dazzling and hypnotic historical novel. . . . AZTEC has
everything that makes a story appealing . . . both
ecstasy and appalling tragedy . . . sex . . . violence . . .
and the story is filled with revenge. . . . Mr. Jennings
is an absolutely marvelous yarnspinner. . . .
A book to get lost in!"

The New York Times

"Sumptuously detailed. . . . AZTEC falls into the same
genre of historical novel as SHOGUN."

Chicago Tribune

"Unforgettable images. . . . Jennings is a master at
graphic description. . . . The book is so vivid that this
reviewer had the novel experience of dreaming of the
Aztec world, in technicolor, for several nights in
a row . . . so real that the tragedy of the
Spanish conquest is truly felt."

Chicago Sun Times

AVON Paperback   **55889 . . . $3.95**